The Three-Body Problem
A Cambridge Mystery

The Three-Body Problem
A Cambridge Mystery

CATHERINE SHAW

This edition published in Great Britain in 2004 by
Allison & Busby Limited
Bon Marche Centre
241-251 Ferndale Road
London SW9 8BJ
http://www.allisonandbusby.com

A catalogue record for this book is available from
the British Library.

10 9 8 7 6 5 4 3 2 1

ISBN 0 7490 8347 6

Printed and bound in Great Britain by
Bookmarque Ltd, Croydon, Surrey

My dearest sister,

This morning, for the first time, I felt a breath of springtime in the air. I opened the window and the soft breeze pushed the curtain inwards and brushed my cheek, carrying a hint, a suggestion of warmth within its coolness, instead of the chilly sting I've become used to over these winter weeks. I do like the dark evenings, the flickering firelight, the tea and crumpets and books, but I do so detest the cold, bleak mornings, and not being able to walk about outside without being bundled like a traveller to the Poles, and crimped to the bones against the cold even so. If the warm breeze has reached you before me, as is probable, you might even be seeing the first crocuses and daffodils poke up their green shoots, joining the carpet of white snowdrops and blue scylla under the great chestnut tree. If I close my eyes, I can see it exactly as though we still shared our little bedroom and peeped out of the diamond-shaped window panes early on the winter mornings, hoping for snow. I know, darling, that you will write to me when you have the strength, and in the meantime, the endless memories speak to me with your voice.

Beautiful memories, darling Dora — it seems strange, sometimes, even to me, that with so much happiness and delight, I so longed to leave it all. I felt like the baby robins in the nest (have the robins come back to the beech tree this year?); they used to be so delightful and delighted, and yet the day inevitably came when some unseen force drove them to spread their fluttering wings. I felt the nameless call very early, and dreamed in confused silence, until the day when Mrs. Squires so suddenly seemed to understand, and offered me to become her assistant in her little school here in Cambridge. On that day, only on that day, I understood the source of my dissatisfaction. Now I know that finally you understand me, and why I need to be far away from home, although I love you all so dearly.

The little girls will be here in one hour; soon I shall leave off writing in order to get some work ready for them. I have come so far in just a year and a half! Why, I can still remember when the only thing I was fit for was teaching the smallest ones to read — and even then, I had to struggle to find the patience! Mrs. Squires made me read dozens of books, instructed me endlessly in Latin and arithmetic, and questioned and scolded me for months before she allowed me to teach anything else. How frightened I would have been if I had known that at the end of just one year, she would be so lucky as to inherit an unexpected windfall, and give it all up, leaving her school to me alone! But it has turned out wonderfully. Not a single family has removed their daughter since September, and two more little girls have even joined the school. The schoolroom is quite overcrowded with the twelve of them now; perhaps I should suggest that after the age of thirteen they be sent elsewhere for a higher level of instruction. And yet, poor things, there is nowhere for them to go, and not many families care to hire governesses or tutors for their daughters. And they do so enjoy themselves here, and are getting on so well. Indeed, the oldest ones are my especial pets and I would be heartbroken to bid them farewell, though I myself am having to study ever harder in order to find things to teach them and keep them interested. I shall just have to find another idea. Sometimes I imagine you could be here with me, darling, taking care of the littlest ones. But I do not believe you would desire it, would you, even if it were possible? Cambridge is not a big town — you can walk from one end to the other with ease, and then out into the fields and countryside — yet it does not really feel spacious, and then living in rooms is so different from living in a house. I am dearly proud of my rooms — a room of my own, and a small sitting room, and the schoolroom, all mine! Not really mine, of course, since the things belong to my landlady, and Mrs. Squires arranged them, but they are lovely —

and they do contain my very own few things, my drawing of you, and most of all the freedom to do what I like within them. I am never bored for a single moment, between studying and preparing lessons for the girls, and writing letters, within doors, and walking and shopping and exploring, out of doors, being greeted kindly by the members of the different families who live nearby. I am so glad I was not able to accept Mrs. Fitzwilliam's offer to do for me and provide meals, as she does for the lodgers who reside on the upper floors, but the small fee I receive from the little girls really would not have sufficed — and now I find myself joyful and busy in making my modest purchases, preparing tea things on a spirit lamp, and even in the dusting and mending which I learned so well and disliked so deeply at home. I do believe that people looked askance at me, when Mrs. Squires first took her departure, and I chose to remain here, alone and independent, but the wary looks have since disappeared, to be happily replaced by friendly smiles.

There, I really must close this letter — I have prepared a most wonderful lesson this afternoon, about magnets. I have obtained quite a strong magnet, and with it we sweep metal dust this way and that upon the table into feathery shapes. And then the needle — it is so remarkable! If you have a magnet by you, dear, try this magical experience: take an ordinary threaded needle, and while holding the end of the thread firmly in the fingers of one hand, bring the magnet to the needle so that it holds, then draw it slowly, slowly upwards. The needle will rise with the magnet, until the thread is taut, and then continue to rise until it is standing erect, touching the magnet only with its very point. And then — this is the miracle — if you draw the magnet, ever so slowly, ever so gently, the tiniest distance in the world away from the needle, the needle will not fall, but remain erect and quivering in the air, straining upwards as though with human desire. Let the magnet abandon the needle by a single hair's breadth further, and needle and thread will collapse in despair.

Yours tenderly, until my next letter

Vanessa

Cambridge, Tuesday, February 14th, 1888

My dearest twin,

I am sitting at my little writing table, looking out of the front window onto the street, and observing the most interesting scene. Several gentlemen are collected in a tightly knit group, and one of them has just rushed into this very house, apparently to summon someone. They are clearly gentlemen from the University, clad in their black gowns; it is quite rare to see them grouped so upon the streets. One of them is knocking at the landlady's rooms, across the hall from mine; yes, she is sending him upstairs, dear me I cannot resist opening the window a crack wider. Here is the gentleman back down again together with a gentleman from upstairs, yes indeed, it is one whom I have had occasion to lay eyes on very briefly once or twice, just passing through the entrance hall. I did not know he was from the University as well. Naturally, how should I have known? Indeed, I know very little about any of the people who live upstairs; Mrs. Fitzwilliam keeps a close watch on all comings and goings, so that it is inconceivable to hold even the slightest conversation in the hallway. I know only that the lodger just above me often paces over my head in the night time. I mentioned it to Mrs. Fitzwilliam laughingly once, but did not ask her to mention it to the pacer, as in the end I found myself becoming oddly used to the regular, gently creaking sound. I also hear occasional clinks and bumps, but have never yet heard the sound of a voice until — why, until just now! Yes, I do believe our visitor cannot have gone higher than the first floor, he was so quick. Perhaps my nocturnal pacer is this very gentleman who just went out. Heavens, they are telling him the news, whatever it may be —

and how excited and distressed they appear to be! and what exclamations of "shocking — impossible!" they pour forth! Off they go, in a body, black gowns floating, like a group of crows.

Well, I shall probably never learn the meaning of all the commotion, any more than I shall penetrate within the mysterious walls where these gentlemen scholars spend so much of their time. What can be hidden there? I know that it can be no more than rooms within and gardens without — some of the gardens can easily be glimpsed even from the street, through the stone gateways of the Colleges. Yet in my imagination, they seem so filled with mystery and magic. How strange it must be to go to University, so that one not only studies but actually resides, completely and wholly, in a world of constant thought and contemplation. Why, all the usual activities of walking, eating and laughing must be imbued with the philosophical and scientific ideas, and the words of the ancient languages must be mingled daily with the modern. If only we had a brother who could share some of its secrets with us! I do long sometimes to study better, differently; to be guided by a teacher as well as by books, and to share my difficulties with other students who know the same ones, just as the little girls in my class do, when they bend their curly heads over their desks together, sharing the same book. Oh, well, I suppose I should not even bother to indulge in such idle thoughts.

The girls are gone for today; I shall make tea, and save the anecdotes and mishaps of these last few days for my next letter.

Yours tenderly, until next time

Vanessa

Cambridge, Monday, February 20th, 1888

My dearest Dora,

Thank you so much, darling, for the few words you added to Mamma's letter. I was so sorry to read about how tired you have been. Mamma says it is not really any particular illness, but merely fatigue. I do so hope that the springtime will bring you health and happiness. If you are having a warm spell as we are, you should sit in the garden at least a little bit each day. I feel in haste to return home for a visit, but it will not be possible before the Easter holidays. I do hope, I do expect to find you entirely recovered by then. In the meantime, until you feel well enough to write me a true, long letter, I do not suppose I shall hear a single word about the interesting Mr. Edwards, as Mamma would not mention his existence for the world. Dear Dora, if you have even so much as glimpsed him lately, do please just put an exclamation mark in next time you send me a word — then I feel I shall understand more. And if you read some bits of this letter aloud later on, please leave out that last sentence!

I hesitated a moment about putting in this newspaper clipping from the *Cambridge Evening News*, a newspaper only recently established here. It dates from the 15th, and it does seem a bit unsuitable for an invalid, but then — I know you want to know what happened, just as much as I want to tell it to you. You couldn't possibly guess it! I do believe I have found out the mystery concerning my upstairs neighbour, whose name I now know to be Mr. Weatherburn. The very day after I wrote to you, I saw this alarming headline right on the front page of the evening newspaper, announcing the shocking discovery which you may read for yourself.

Mathematician Mysteriously Slain

Dr. Geoffrey Akers, a Fellow in Pure Mathematics of St. John's College, aged 37, was found dead in his rooms today, struck down by a violent blow to the head with the poker taken from his own fireplace. Still clad in his overcoat and scarf, his hat hung upon a nail near the door, he appeared to have barely stepped into the rooms when the fatal blow fell. The body was discovered this afternoon by a student, Mr. Rayburn, who, having waited in vain for his tutor to appear at their scheduled meeting, walked to his rooms in the college to check if he had forgotten about the appointment. "He frequently forgot meetings or lost track of the time," Mr. Rayburn said. The unfortunate young man, having arrived at his destination and knocked in vain, tried the door as a mere gesture before turning away, and found that it opened at once.

Thereupon he saw the body of his tutor stretched lifeless upon the floor, and after taking only the briefest moment to ascertain the situation, he dashed off immediately to call for a doctor and a policeman.

The doctor being the first to arrive upon the scene, examined the body and was immediately able to absolve the student from all blame, as the Fellow had been deceased for between twelve and sixteen hours, which is to say that the fatal blow was struck between nine o'clock last night and one o'clock this morning. Having alerted the police, Mr. Rayburn then hastened to let his colleagues know of the dreadful event, and it soon emerged that the unfortunate victim had dined last night with another mathematician, Mr. Weatherburn, a Fellow at Trinity College, who must have been the last person to see him alive.

The question of whether Mr. Akers had any particular enemies who might have wished him ill elicited a peculiar reaction from the tightly knit group of his erstwhile colleagues. After an awkward silence, a voice spoke up: "There's not many that Akers hadn't offended or quarrelled with, when you think of it." "Yes indeed, Weatherburn's one of the few that would still talk to him," added another. "If they want to find out who did it," put in a third voice in calm and level-headed tones, "it doesn't seem that motive is going to be a very useful angle of attack."

Mrs. Wiggins, the bedder who did the deceased's rooms, could not but agree. "A very nasty gentleman, 'e was," she informed us after due negotiations had been concluded. "I shan't miss 'im. And 'is rooms, very dirty they was sometimes, at least not so much dirty as dusty and messy, and 'im grumbling whenever anything was moved. 'Ow one could do one's job properly is beyond me, when a man's that way."

Fortunately, our police force have experience and intelligence behind them, and we feel certain that the mystery will soon be entirely cleared up.

Dora dear, the newspaper doesn't say so, but isn't it dreadful to think that someone really did strike down that poor man, no matter how horrid he might have been, and that very person is hiding it inside himself right this very minute, and smiling and talking and probably even telling people how he never disliked poor Mr. Akers so very much, though everyone else did. Perhaps they really do ought to be looking for the only person who didn't hate him. Oh no — that would bring them to my poor neighbour, Mr. Weatherburn, then, wouldn't it? Oh, he did look so upset the evening of the article, when he came home. He was brought back to the house by policemen; I didn't notice it myself, as I was making toast (I really should not live quite so much on toast), but I heard Mrs. Fitzwilliam's voice in the hall, and she talked ever so much more than usual, and she sounded Most Displeased, and the words Police and My House were very frequently to be heard. I felt sure she must be scolding poor Mr. Weatherburn for something which really was not his fault, and already he paces at night, the poor man, and I so wanted to come to his aid, but I couldn't think of any reason, so I just suddenly opened my door and said "Mrs. Fitzwilliam, I am so very sorry to disturb you, but I – I —" and I was just feeling quite foolish when the toasting fork, which I had balanced with care, fell over and crashed into the fire, sending up a shower of sparks and a fearful smell of burned toast. Mrs. Fitzwilliam said "The carpet!" and rushed into the room, and Mr. Weatherburn looked at me and then turned away quietly

16

up the stairs. Mrs. Fitzwilliam swept up the ashes, a little angrily, but then she said "such goings on!" and I saw that she wanted more to talk about it than she wanted to be cross with me. But as she never gossips, in fact almost never speaks, she could only say "such goings on, and a respectable house!" I tutted and sympathized, for she is immensely proud of her stately home on the Chesterton Road, although she does have to let nearly all of it. I told her that surely nothing so very dreadful could be associated with her house, and she asked what it was I had wanted of her, and I said it had quite gone out of my head, and she said how were the girls doing and I said lovely. I could see a great struggle in her, because she truly believes that respectability has a great deal to do with not telling anything, in which she is perhaps not entirely mistaken, but dismay and indignation, perhaps even some excitement were boiling up in her too. In the end, though, she simply bid me good evening — it was a great triumph of discretion over curiosity! Hmph, if I have another opportunity to do so, I shall offer her of cup a tea, and try to break the ice. I do think it is all so interesting — at least, well, not *interesting*, not about poor Mr. Akers ... but, well, a little of the rudeness of real life has irrupted into this quiet household. Whatever will come of it, I wonder?

Your very loving sister

Vanessa

Cambridge, Tuesday, February 28th, 1888

Dearest Dora,

Oh dear. No exclamation mark. Do you know — tiredness and sadness are not so different as one might think. One feeling might be so easily mistaken for the other. It's strange how little one knows about one's own feelings really. Do you know that I felt quite a new one, the day before yesterday? Here I was, all alone in the evening as usual, quietly making — no, not toast, for once, but soup over the spirit lamp, and I felt quite an odd feeling inside me. At first I thought I might be hungry, but then I had such a very incongruous thought — I thought of stepping across the hall and visiting Mrs. Fitzwilliam! — and it suddenly came to me that I felt lonely. I looked at my books and did not feel like taking any of them up. It would be nice to have a companion, someone sharing the rooms, as I used to with Mrs. Squires. We did have such nice conversations, often. But then, I love to be alone, and no hint of loneliness ever crept into my life at all, until today. It is beautiful to meet someone's gaze, sometimes, with understanding, however briefly, but it can also unsettle sweet habits. At least, I know that you and I understand each other and always will — with or without words, as only twins can — about this and everything else.

Then yesterday morning, I found that the best antidote to unusual feelings of lassitude was activity, as I had absolutely no time to indulge in them from the moment I arose, and ended by quite forgetting them. Indeed, I had promised the oldest group a surprise in their arithmetic class today, as yesterday they not only complained quite bitterly about the boredom of the sums I had set them, but worked them correctly one and all, so that they clearly have nothing further to learn in that domain, and senseless repetition would engender only loathing, it seems to me.

I racked my brains and looked in my books in vain. Finally, I decided that the best solution would be to search if I could not find a better book, so I donned my wraps and ventured out into the cold, to a bookshop where I often go, to ask advice of the knowledgeable bookseller. "Why, don't you read *The Monthly Packet*, Miss?" he enquired of me in astonishment, when I had laid my difficulties before him. "There's a mathematician, Mr. Lewis Carroll, used to publish puzzles for young people there; a better way to teach reasoning while

18

enjoying oneself can scarce exist." He dug out a large pile of old and dusty copies for me, and I carried them home forthwith and turned the pages until I found the puzzles he spoke of.

I had never seen *The Monthly Packet* before. Dear me, it is very edifying — perhaps a little too edifying at times, so many morals are concealed within its pages, which are essentially addressed to young ladies. But the puzzles, when I found them, turned out to be most delightful; there is a whole story in sections called *A Tangled Tale*, and each section contains a puzzle. Some of them seem so difficult I can't even begin to think how to solve them myself yet. After having read through them at length, I decided to begin at the beginning, and copied out the first "Knot" in the Tangle from the April 1880 number. When the girls arrived, I sent my darling advanced class — consisting of Emily, aged thirteen, and Rose, eleven — into my sitting room with the paper, with instructions not to come out until they had solved it between them. They disappeared with a flutter of frocks and ribbons, and I set regular sums to the middle group and began counting dried peas with the little ones, who are still learning that if Violet has four peas and Mary takes three of them, then when Violet opens her mouth in an O of protest to wail that it is not fair, because she has only one pea left, this means that she has solved the subtraction correctly and has earned a kiss, much to her surprise.

The first knot is so entertaining, that I am sending it to you bodily; as the author says, if you have a headache, it will distract you from it, and if you do not, it will give you one.

A Tangled Tale, by Mr. Lewis Carroll
Knot One: Excelsior
Goblin, lead them up and down

The ruddy glow of sunset was already fading into the sombre shad-

ows of night, when two travellers might have been observed swiftly — at a pace of six miles in the hour — descending the rugged side of a mountain; the younger bounding from crag to crag with the agility of a fawn, while his companion, whose aged limbs seemed ill at ease in the heavy chain armour habitually worn by tourists in that district, toiled on painfully at his side.

As is always the case under such circumstances, the younger knight was the first to break the silence.

"A goodly pace, I trow!" he exclaimed. "We sped not thus in the ascent!"

"Goodly, indeed!" the other echoed with a groan. "We clomb it but at three miles in the hour."

"And on the dead level our pace is — ?" the younger suggested; for he was weak in statistics, and left all such details to his aged companion.

"Four miles in the hour," the other wearily replied. "Not an ounce more," he added, with that love of metaphor so common in old age, "and not a farthing less!"

"'Twas three hours past high noon when we left our hostelry," the young man said, musingly. "We shall scarce be back by supper-time. Perchance mine host will roundly deny us all food!"

"He will chide our tardy return," was the grave reply, "and such a rebuke will be meet."

"A brave conceit!" cried the other with a merry laugh. "And should we bid him bring us yet another course, I trow his answer will be tart!"

"We shall but get our desserts," sighed the elder knight, who had never seen a joke in his life, and was somewhat displeased at his companion's untimely levity. "'Twill be nine of the clock," he added in an undertone, "by the time we regain our hostelry. Full many a mile shall we have plodded this day!"

"How many? How many?" cried the eager youth, ever athirst for knowledge.

The old man was silent.

"Tell me," he answered, after a moment's thought, "what time it was when we stood together on yonder peak. Not exact to the minute!" he added hastily, reading a protest in the young man's face. "An thy guess be within one poor half-hour of the mark, 'tis all I ask of thy mother's son! Then will I tell thee, true to the last inch, how far we shall have trudged betwixt three and nine of the clock."

A groan was the young man's only reply; while his convulsed features and the deep wrinkles that chased each other across his manly brow, revealed the abyss of arithmetical agony into which one chance question had plunged him.

It doesn't seem clear, somehow, when you first read the story, where the problem lies. I wondered what the girls would make of it, and left the sitting room door open a little, to hear their discussions. At first there was silence, as each one read through the problem separately.

"I can't make head or tail of it," I heard Rose's adorable voice complaining.

Although there is only a year or two between them, Rose seems much younger than Emily; a dimpled child still, with a long fall of honey coloured hair held back from her face by a wide pink ribbon. "Whatever does it mean?" she went on, rather crossly. "What is 'clomb'? what is 'trow'?"

"'Clomb' means 'climbed', you silly," said the ever reasonable Emily. "And 'trow' means ... well, it doesn't mean anything really. Don't pay any attention to it."

"But I don't see what one is to do," continued Rose.

"Oh really, the men are walking from three to nine o'clock, and we want to know how far they went, and when they got to the top of the hill," said her friend.

"But what do they do after they walk to the top of the hill?" Rose's voice became more and more plaintive.

"Why, they come down and back again!"

"How silly! Whatever for?"

"They took a walk, for goodness' sake! Now Rose, we have to find out how long they walked, seeing that they went three miles an hour climbing, four miles an hour on level ground and six miles an hour descending."

There was a moment's silence.

"Oh," said Rose, "well, if they walked for one hour before climbing the hill, and then climbed up for two hours and down for one hour ... why then ... no, it doesn't make sense."

"Yes, it does," Emily helped her. "If they walked on level ground for one hour, and came back on it for one hour, then ... they had four hours to go up and down hill and so ... they spent twice as much time climbing as descending. That means that they must have spent two thirds of the time going up, and one third coming down. Two thirds of the four hours makes ... makes two thirds of two hundred and forty minutes, oh bother, I hate doing this; one third eighty, that's one hour and twenty minutes, oh do help me Rose! Two thirds makes one hundred and sixty, that's two hours and forty minutes. So they took two hours and forty minutes to go up, and one hour and twenty to come down. Then that means they reached the top at six forty."

"All right," said Rose with some pleasure. "Then we're done. But it's a silly problem. Why does it say 'within half-an-hour'? "

"Oh, you *are* a goose! Don't you remember that we started by guessing they walked one hour on the level? Why, we don't know that — we don't know how much they ... OH — I see — I don't think it matters! That must be the answer. Let's suppose the hill began at the very door. Come now, tell me how much time they spent going up and how much coming down."

"That's easy; they climbed for four hours and came down for two," said Rose, "so they got to the top at seven."

Emily scrutinized the puzzle once again. "And what if they did the other thing — spent the whole time on level ground?"

"And what about the hill?"

"Perhaps the hill was small — so small they could jump right over it in one second!"

"Oh, that's silly," said Rose, "they wouldn't be panting so."

"Well, perhaps they're easily tired. Anyway, they'd get to

the top at six o'clock, of course, so whatever happens, they must get there between six and seven. The answer's six thirty!"

"I don't think I understood it really," Rose was beginning, looking doubtful and tripping over the ample petticoats she always wore, but Emily seized her arm and pulled her triumphantly back to the schoolroom, where she stood in front of me, her pre-Raphaelite face framed in the sheath of dark hair which fell over her shoulders, earnest and all unaware of her loveliness, and recounted her solution to the problem with pride.

This triumph of teaching had a surprising consequence. Today, when five o'clock arrived and the girls were putting on their wraps and looking out of the window to see who came to fetch them, I saw to my surprise that Emily's mother had accompanied her governess. I have only met her once before, in September, when Mrs. Squires left and Emily's mother, Mrs. Burke-Jones, came to tell me that Emily was very fond of the day-school and wished to continue on with me. She was very kind then. Today, she told me with a smile that Emily had quite astonished her uncle Mr. Morrison, Mrs. Burke-Jones' brother, last night at table, by setting him yesterday's puzzle and then explaining her solution to him! It turns out that Mrs. Burke-Jones' brother is a mathematician, and personally acquainted with Mr. Lewis Carroll, the author of the puzzles (who goes under another name in real life, where he is an Oxford Don, it seems). He told his sister (somewhat to her surprised dismay, I seem to guess) that Emily had inherited his own delight in mathematics, and that she could consider, if it continued, going on with her studies as long as she liked, even to University. Yes — Mrs. Burke-Jones informed me that there is a college for ladies, right here at the University of Cambridge — two of them, in fact! Of course, the ladies may not take degrees, but they may study and have tutors and follow the classes and even pass the examinations — good heavens! Emily jumped with joy at the prospect, while her mother looked doubtful and said, "Fortunately, she is only thirteen, there is plenty of time to think about this."

At any rate — this is the most exciting thing — Mrs. Burke-Jones has invited me to a dinner party next Saturday, of ten people at her house! It is the first such invitation I have received since living in Cambridge, though I have been to tea a few times with the governesses of some of the girls. The famous brother will be present, as he expressed a wish to meet the teacher who provides such delightful lessons to his niece, and various other friends and colleagues of the family. I know nothing as yet about Mr. Burke-Jones, but shall surely find out more on Saturday. I did learn that Emily has a brother of eleven, and that the two children will have dinner in the nursery, but will be allowed to come down and greet the guests. I shall write to you afterwards with every detail!

Good night, my dearest twin

Vanessa

Cambridge, Sunday, March 4th, 1888

Dearest Dora,

Last night was the great event! I never imagined myself in the midst of such a lively group — and nearly all mathematicians. There were six mathematicians altogether, four bachelors and two married gentlemen with their wives. Most surprisingly of all — one of them was neither more nor less than my Mr. Weatherburn from upstairs! We were equally surprised to see each other there.

But let me tell you everything in order.

I arrived punctually in front of Mrs. Burke-Jones' lovely house. The windows were all lit up festively, and it looked very tempting; light spilled out onto the walk, and the air was so bright and crisp you could see your breath spiralling away. Some people had already arrived. As I waited, feeling too shy to ring, a carriage drew up and an elderly couple alighted. Their driver came around to open for them, and guided them up the walk to where Mrs. Burke-Jones' kindly maid was standing at the open door. I meekly followed up behind them, all nervous, but she welcomed me just as kindly as she did them, and led us into the drawing room, where she announced "Professor and Mrs. Cayley and Miss Duncan". I know now that the gentlemen is Professor Arthur Cayley, a very senior and much respected professor at the University, with an important Chair whose name escapes me. The others treated him almost like a king. Inside the drawing room, I was all prepared to be quite paralysed, not knowing anybody, but immediately Mrs. Burke-Jones took me under her wing, and introduced me to a young lady of about my own age or even younger, but very much more at ease than myself, called Miss Chisholm, and two further gentlemen called Mr. Wentworth and Mr. Morrison. Following my arrival, there appeared yet another bachelor, Mr. Young, then a married couple, Mr. and Mrs. Beddoes, and finally, last of all, Mr. Weatherburn, who greeted everyone warmly, as he clearly knows them all well, and then looked extremely surprised as he was brought round and introduced to me. I noticed that he is afflicted with a slight stammer when shy.

"Dear me, b-but we are already very nearly acquainted!" he exclaimed in surprise, levelling his brown eyes upon me with the same intentness I had noted in them, the other day, in the hall.

"How so?" said Mrs. Burke-Jones, surprised.

"Why, my rooms are in the same house as Miss D-Duncan's," he explained, and added that he knew I held a class there each afternoon, but had had no idea that "Morrison's niece" was one of the fortunate pupils.

Mrs. Burke-Jones was as nice as could possibly be.

"Oh, Miss Duncan does wonders," she cried effusively,

"Emily does so love her lessons, and the mathematical parts more than anything!"

Whence a short discussion with Mr. Weatherburn about my interests and methods, in which I showed myself to be woefully ignorant, alas, and was deeply grateful to have heard tell of Mr. Lewis Carroll at all, for it was certainly the only thing he mentioned that was the least bit familiar to me!

I floundered on, my dear Dora, blushing greatly, and felt most relieved when Mr. Weatherburn moved away from the subject of mathematics to other topics. The guests soon gathered into one or two larger groups, and the conversation, seemingly quite naturally, turned to the death of their poor colleague, Mr. Akers. As the newspaper article I sent you hinted, nobody seemed to like him at all. They did make some attempt to speak of him more or less with the respect due to the deceased, but even so, I suspect a certain dose of snideness lay behind some of the remarks. Mr. Beddoes in particular seemed to sneer subtly behind his apparent admiration, when he spoke of his colleague's work. But his remarks elicited only knowing smiles from his colleagues, although they freely discussed the character of the poor defunct gentleman. "He was quite insufferable," appeared to reflect the general opinion; Miss Chisholm even put in that "a sarcastic smile was part of his permanent apparel." Mr. Weatherburn did not say anything at all, as the others traded remarks and observations, and for some little time the question of the nature of his death was politely avoided, but suddenly someone could not resist any more, and directly put the question which must have been tickling all of them from the beginning, to judge by myself!

"Well, Weatherburn, you dined with him on the fatal evening, so what did you actually talk about, eh?"

"Yes, uh, well," said Mr. Weatherburn, whose speech is slow and careful, perhaps because of the stammer, "he seemed to want to talk about an absolutely remarkable idea he had conceived lately. He was quite excited, I recall."

"A remarkable idea? What kind of idea?" came a chorus of excited cries from the throats of all the mathematicians present.

"Apparently he had been working on the n-body problem. He didn't want to get into details, however. The closest I got was when he pulled a piece of paper from his breast pocket and scribbled the solution down onto it, to show me, saying that it provided a complete and incredibly original solution to the differential equations of the n-body problem. But he shoved the paper away, naturally, before I could really inspect it closely. He told me that he had already written a rough manuscript of his proof of convergence of the series. Indeed, I quite believe he asked me to dine mainly from a need to vent his irrepressible feelings of triumph. He seemed particularly concerned with the possible reaction of Professor C-C-Crawford."

"Ah yes, I'm not surprised. I believe Crawford's been working on the n-body problem in secret for several months now, ever since it was set as the main problem of the Birthday Competition organised by King Oscar of Sweden, though he won't admit it," remarked Mr. Wentworth.

"Except for making elliptical allusions to it after he's had a few glasses!" added Mr. Morrison.

"Well, Crawford certainly has been working hard lately," remarked Mr. Young. "My word, he's been almost invisible for over a week now, shut in his rooms working from morning till night. Normally, he wouldn't miss an evening at Mrs. Burke-Jones' for the world."

"Crawford's been saying he's working on the n-body problem — really?" cried Mr. Beddoes, looking aghast. "But that's – that's quite impossible! Utterly impossible. Ha!" There was a moment's pause, and then he added in a different tone, somewhat aggressively, "It's far too difficult for a mathematician like Crawford. Why, the man has ideas, but no rigour! How can he hope to compare with a genius like young Poincaré in France?"

"Does anyone know what became of the paper Mr. Akers had in his breast pocket — the one he showed Mr. Weatherburn at table?" enquired Miss Chisholm suddenly.

It was exactly the question I had been longing to put, but I really didn't dare insert even a word into a conversation about things I knew nothing of. I must say that my heart warmed to her because of her forthrightness. I noticed that every time she spoke, Mr. Wentworth, Mr. Morrison and Mr. Young all looked at her with favour.

Upon her remark, everyone looked at each other, and there was a moment's silence. Nobody appeared to know the answer to this very interesting question.

"Yes, it's worth finding out about that, isn't it," said Mr. Weatherburn slowly.

Then dinner was announced, and we all went in, arm in arm; Mr. Cayley took in Mrs. Beddoes and Mr. Beddoes took in Mrs. Cayley. Mr. Morrison took in his sister, and Mr. Wentworth took in Miss Forsyth, who is Emily's governess, and was asked by Mrs. Burke-Jones to join the dinner in order to even out the numbers. She teaches Emily all the things I know nothing of (alas): music, embroidery, French and German. Mr. Young took in Miss Chisholm, and you can see for yourself who was left.

The dinner was delightful, in a lovely room, not very large but spacious and attractive. Mrs. Burke-Jones' house must be very nearly as large as Mrs. Fitzwilliam's, and it is all for herself and her family, and her servants! Her brother, Mr. Morrison, lives there too, as I learned afterwards. During dinner we talked about all kinds of things; that is, the others talked, and I listened a great deal, and exchanged only a very few words with my left-hand neighbour, as I did not seem to be able to do more without blushing uncomfortably. Things were somewhat easier with my right-hand neighbour, Mr. Beddoes, who became quite agreeable as the dishes succeeded each other, and barked out kind remarks in my direction, such as "So you teach, do you?" and "Whereabouts are you from, my dear?" before becoming reabsorbed in his plate and glass. The others spoke of general things, politics, India, Queen Victoria, and various other topics, to all of which I listened eagerly, feeling sadly ignorant because of my sheltered life. Dear me, to think that I dare to teach anyone anything, when I know so little! Between the stammering awkwardness on my left and the sharpness on right, and my own feelings of ignorance, I was a little nervous the whole time and unable to appreciate the details of the meal itself, although it did seem very different from either toast or soup.

After dinner, the six ladies retired to the drawing room, actually only five of us, because Miss Forsyth returned upstairs to the children. The conversation was most interesting — Mrs. Burke-Jones appears to have lost her husband some years ago — at least she did not say so, but seemed sad for a moment, and said that six years ago she had asked her brother to occupy the upstairs apartments, as she felt uncomfortable alone with children and servants in such a large house. He, naturally, was only too happy to oblige, and be spoiled and pampered. (She really did say this, with nothing like the respect due to a promising young Research Fellow of the University!) I believe he is her younger brother. She told me that Emily also has a younger brother, Edmund, who is to Emily just as Mr. Morrison is to her. Edmund is sent to a very good boarding school, which strains the family fortunes rather, I gathered, though Mrs. Burke-Jones only sighed and said it was not always easy. She added that Edmund is very fragile, and that she feels she must have him home occasionally on weekends, although the school does not approve. He did make a brief appearance later with his sister, and it was like seeing a frail white rose next to a blooming pink one. Mrs. Cayley asked him if he enjoyed his school and was looking forward to going back next day. I think it was a mistake. Already pale, he became paler and cast his eyes about, until Emily stepped forward and relieved the situation by stating categorically, "Naturally he likes home better."

The most amazing thing I learned, however, in the course of our postprandial conversation, was that Miss Chisholm is a student at the University! She studies mathematics at Girton College, of those two colleges I learned about from Mrs. Burke-Jones, where ladies may enroll. Mr. Young is her tutor there. She says that in England, ladies may only study for the degree called the Tripos, but they may not attempt to write doctoral dissertations. It is, however, possible although rare for a lady to write one in Germany, and she would like to travel there after having passed her examinations here. When she talks about it, she sounds like the way I felt when I first thought of coming here: eager, but almost frightened. I do hope I will have a chance to meet her again.

I digested all these facts and allowed my mind to dream and roam, this afternoon, during a lengthy ramble, taking advantage of the lovely weather on the one day that I am not required to spend all the afternoon indoors. Although most often, I love to wander out of the town into the fields, or take the direction of Grantchester, today my legs carried me straight towards the University: down the Chesterton Road past Jesus Green, left on Magdalene Street and then into St. John's Street; why, it is almost as good as reading one's Bible! I could not resist taking a particularly good look at St. John's, where poor Mr. Akers was a Fellow. I remained there for a moment, gazing upon the imposing red facade, above whose main gateway, flanked by octagonal towers decorated with white brickwork upon the red, a set of ancient arched windows is topped by medieval crenelations over which one half expects to see the tip of an arrow pointing, ready to shoot.

I passed the less imposing although similarly styled gateway leading to Trinity College, somewhat distracted by recalling that it was not only the College whose walls once were home to Isaac Newton, but that they also constituted the daily place of work of my neighbour Mr. Weatherburn. Turning into Trinity Lane, I passed the more modest Colleges there as in a dream, and turned to walk along the Cam, between the green fields dotted with daffodils and crocuses, upon which gave the back parts of Trinity and St. John's with their tempting and mysterious ramparts and bridges with nostalgic names. Cambridge is a beautiful place, Dora, not least because its fields and buildings are all steeped and burnished with meaning from the past. No, decidedly, I have no regrets about coming here.

My very best love until next time,

Vanessa

Cambridge, Monday, March 12th, 1888

My dearest sister,

I have made great friends with Emily since the dinner party. She would like to see a new Knot every day, but I am restricting her to a single Knot each week; they require successively more and more reflection, and she has promised on her honour not to seek help from her uncle. I am to go to tea at her house at least once a week, from now on, she says! I must say that such outings hold great pleasure for me, as a change from my own rooms, and Emily is a delightful girl, not in the least bit infantile, and possessed of a sharp, inquiring mind.

Today was our very first tea date; we had it in the nursery together with Miss Forsyth, whose first name is Annabel, though I must not use it because Emily may not. We took it in turns to tell Emily about our early childhood, and asked her a great many questions about hers, for Miss Forsyth has been with her only six years. Before Miss Forsyth, she had a French governess, who cared for both herself and her brother, and she told us how happy the family had been all together, and talked at length about her father. There was something sweet and strange about the way she spoke of him, almost as though she did not know, or feel, that he was dead, but thought of him as being somewhere far away, but thinking and caring about her and waiting to see her again some day.

We asked her how it had happened that her governess had left, but she answered rather oddly, that she really did not know what had become of her, with a curious undefinable tone in her voice. It seems as though she is holding back some secret, or perhaps has simply heard tell of things she could not understand, and keeps them in her little heart, waiting for the future to bring wisdom. She told us that the decision had been taken at that time to find a school for her brother, and that he cried terribly and begged not to leave home. Although poor Emily was only seven years old at the time, she understood that after the changes that had been so suddenly wrought within the family, little Edmund would scarcely be able to endure an even greater one, whereas their mother seemed to think that a fatherless life at home would be unbearable for him. The children were compelled to submit, naturally, but Emily's mutinous little face told us how right she still believed herself to be. After what seemed a great effort to remain discreet and ladylike, under the gentle pressure of my questions, she suddenly burst out in a passion and told me how her brother hated school with all his heart, and longed only to return home, that he was vexed and tormented there day and night by the other boys, all of whom undergo brutal treatment by the masters. "Oh, Edmund says they beat them horribly," she cried heartrendingly, "he says they have to go into the headmaster's office, all white and trembling and then those outside hear the most awful screams. Edmund says it's near as bad or worse when it's somebody else as when it's himself. I'm so happy, so happy I don't have to go to boarding school! If only he could just stay at home with us, and go to your school, Miss Duncan!"

Could such awful things really be true, Dora? I so often envied boys their luck, free to travel, to leave home, to go to school and later explore the whole world. But perhaps—in fact quite probably, I am learning, having had no brothers, I understood nothing of the masculine realities, and keep only an ideal image within me. Poor Edmund! I would be only too happy to include one pale little boy in my group of blooming girls, if only it could be allowed, but I expect it is perfectly unthinkable. I tried greatly to cheer up Emily in all kinds of ways, and distracted her so well with foolish stories that in a few moments she was shouting with laughter instead of near tears.

And who should come into the nursery just at that very moment, as we were finishing our tea, but Mr. Morrison! He sat down on a low stool, stretching his legs out in front of him, and said we seemed to be having a far better time than the grownups at proper tea down below, and that he'd be dashed if he didn't prefer to stay with us. Emily played the fool, teasing him in all kinds of ways and saying he would do nothing of the kind, until he laid a bet with her that he would not only come along next time she had a tea party, but bring his friends. Dear me—I do hope he was merely joking.

"I would be so grateful," I asked him, "if you would tell me something about the Birthday Competition I heard mentioned the other evening. Was it not a celebration of some king's birthday? What king could possibly wish to celebrate his birthday with mathematics?"

"Why, by all means," he answered eagerly. "Our benefactor is King Oscar II of Sweden, of the Bernadotte family. He studied mathematics in depth while at the University of Uppsala, and has a great fondness for the subject, as well as a close friendship with Sweden's leading mathematician, Gösta Mittag-Leffler. The Birthday Competition was his own suggestion, and I believe that rather than using mathematics to celebrate his own anniversary, he entertains the hope that the illustrious date, surely to be accompanied by pomp and festivities of all sorts, may shed some glory onto at least one member of the horde of unknown but devoted researchers scattered all about Europe, and illuminate the one and only Swedish mathematical journal. Furthermore, in posing a specific problem as the subject of the competition papers, he hopes to motivate such work as may possibly produce a solution."

"And is it possible to tell me what the subject of the competition is?"

"Why, I have a couple of volumes of *Acta Mathematica* in my room below," he said, "the announcement of the competition appeared there some two or three years ago, and I may well have it." And ignoring my remonstrances and expostulations that he not disturb himself, he sped away to investigate, and soon came back with the volume in hand, to show me a page so unintelligible to me, that he might not have taken the trouble! To begin with, not only the announcement of the competition, but the entire volume, is written partly in French and partly in German, without a single English word between its two covers. The volume begins with the announcement of the competition, written in columns with the left-hand one German and the right-hand one in French— it looks rather as though French were a briefer language than German, with great gaps between the French paragraphs, so as to make them begin at the same levels as the corresponding German ones. I could not understand much of it, although many of the French words such as "anniversaire" and "mathématiques" certainly do appear familiar. But Mr. Morrison sat himself at Emily's school desk, and taking her quill in hand and drawing a bit of paper towards him, began to translate it for me, transferring his gaze from the page to his writing to my face, and interspersing his translation with all manner of interesting remarks and explanations, so that I could not be bored for a single moment, although the text is not only quite long but almost impossible to comprehend without the aid of friendly explanations!

HIS MAJESTY Oscar II, desirous of giving a fresh proof of the interest SHE—no, I mean *HE*, but in French it is always 'she', as for some peculiar reason His Majesty becomes Her

Majesty—Mr. Morrison explains that Majesty is feminine—
and that the possessive agrees with the object rather than the
subject in French—oh dear—*feels in the advancement of the
mathematical sciences, an interest SHE*—I mean HE, these capital letters make it seem rather Biblical somehow, but they are
really that way in the original—*has already shown by encourag-
ing the publication of the journal Acta Mathematica, which lies
under HIS august protection, has resolved, upon the 21st of
January 1889, the sixtieth anniversary of HIS birth, to offer a prize
for an important discovery in the domain of higher analytical mathematics. This prize will consist of a golden medal, carrying the
image of HIS MAJESTY and having a value of one thousand francs,
as well as a sum of two thousand five hundred golden Crowns (1
crown = about 1 franc and 40 centimes).*

"Must all mathematicians, then," I enquired, "necessarily
be familiar with the French and German languages?" Emily
had crept near us and was listening with interest as her uncle
translated.

"Oh," he responded with a slight blush, "not to speak, so
to speak. We merely need to read the languages, and even
then, only to read mathematics in the languages. It is far easier than trying to read a novel; why, at worst, we need only
look as far as the next formula, which is written in a kind of
international language, equally intelligible to everybody."
And he showed me a formula on the first page of the article
following the announcement of the competition, which said
something to the effect that $x\,dx + y\,dy = 0$ has for general
integral $y = \sqrt{c^2 - x^2}$. My goodness.

*HIS MAJESTY has deigned to confer the care of realising HIS
intentions to a commission of three members: Mr. CARL WEIER-
STRASS in Berlin, Mr. CHARLES HERMITE in Paris, and the
Chief Editor of this Journal, Mr. GÖSTA MITTAG-LEFFLER in
Stockholm.*

"Weierstrass is really the most venerable and famous of
German mathematicians of today," Mr. Morrison told us, "the

father of them all, in some way, something like Professor Cayley here in Cambridge, who should have been on the commission, they say, had an Englishman been included at all. Do you know, Miss Duncan, that Mr. Weierstrass is quite famous for having produced not only mathematical 'sons', but also a 'daughter'? Yes, the famous Sonya Kovalevskaya was his student, she who two years ago won the Bordin Prize from the French Academy of Sciences with a paper so impressive that they doubled the prize money to recompense it as it deserved. She now holds an extraordinary professorship in Stockholm, is an editor of the very journal I am holding in my hands, and advises Mittag-Leffler, I believe, on the organisation of the Birthday Competition."

I was amazed. Germany and Sweden appear to be countries with wonderful ideas about ladies who wish to study, and England appears to lag far behind (particularly if one judges by the ideas expressed in *The Monthly Packet*, which greatly stress the value of obedience and docility). I wonder if I shall ever have the good fortune to visit such a country.

The work of the commissioners was the object of a report considered by HIS MAJESTY, and here are their conclusions, of which SHE—I mean HE—has approved:

Taking into consideration the questions which, for different reasons, both occupy analysts and whose solutions would be of the greatest interest for the progress of science, the commission respectfully proposes to HIS MAJESTY to attribute the prize to the best memoir on one of the following subjects.

1. Given a system of an arbitrary number of material points which mutually attract each other according to NEWTON's laws, we propose, under the hypothesis that no two points ever collide, to represent the coordinates of each point in the form of a series in a variable expressed in known functions of time, and which converge uniformly for every real value of the variable.

"What on earth does all that mean?" asked Emily curiously.

"Well, let me show you," said her uncle, warming to his task of explanation. He cast about her schoolroom, and moving to the shelves where various toys were gathered, took up a ball and a box of marbles and sat with them upon the floor.

"Now," he told her, "you know what gravity is, don't you? You know that objects fall to the floor because they are attracted by the gravitational force of the earth, which is very large compared to themselves."

"Well," she observed guardedly, "I know that an apple fell upon Newton's head."

He shouted with laughter. "Indeed, nobody can grow up in Cambridge without knowing that! And there is truth to it, you know, and to the notion that that event sparked the whole theory of gravity in his brilliant mind. Ah, he was our great genius, unequalled in the last hundred and fifty years. He understood that if you have a giant body, like the sun, for instance," and he set the ball upon the floor, "and a smaller body moving near it," he suited the action to the word with a marble, "it will enter the sphere of the sun's gravity and begin to orbit around and around, unable to escape the power of the sun."

"Why does it not fall to the sun, just as a marble falls to the earth?" asked Emily in surprise. "A marble does not orbit—how queer that would be, to see it flying around and around."

"Thanks to Newton and his Law, we know the answer to that; it is because the pull of gravity is exactly proportional to the inverse square of the distance between the bodies. But don't trouble your head with that—suffice it to say that thanks to this, we on Earth do not fall to the sun, nor does the moon fall upon us! At any rate, before Newton, Kepler determined the form of the orbit and found that it is an ellipse rather than a perfect circle, and will continue endlessly in the same manner. That is the two-body problem, with a large and a small body. Now, suppose you have the sun and two planets. That is a *three-body problem*, in the rather special case which really does occur in our solar system, where one is extremely large and two of them are relatively small. What do you think would happen?"

"Well, wouldn't the two planets just go on orbiting in ellipses around the sun, as they do in our solar system?" said Emily.

"You are almost correct! But not quite," cried her uncle, "because you imagine that each of your two little planets has a relation of gravity only with the sun, and acts exactly as though it were alone with the sun, and you forget the tiny influence of each planet upon the other! Small though they are, they pull about on each other and cause tiny distortions in the shape of the ellipses, and it becomes nearly impossible to find what the exact nature of the paths they trace will be as time goes on. You see—take this little planet going around this star. If the other planet wasn't there, it would go like this: round and round in a stable ellipse, for ever. But now add the other planet. What happens is that when the first planet goes once around the star, its ellipse is deformed a tiny bit by the influence of the gravity of the other planet, so that it doesn't quite, quite get back to where it started from. The difference is minuscule – if we were talking about the influence of the other planets in our solar system on the earth, why we make an ellipse around the sun once a year exactly, and the deformation is probably a matter of a few inches or so. Now, the planet will orbit around the star again, in an ellipse very similar to the old one, but not quite identical. And again, it won't come back exactly to its starting point. This will keep happening and happening, so that instead of getting one neatly drawn ellipse again and again, you get a spiral of ellipses, each one a little different from the previous one."

The marble in Mr. Morrison's hand began to move around the ball in a spiral which grew progressively more distorted and wild.

"And the question is," he continued eagerly, "what if, due

to the tiny deformations of the ellipses over time, they finally end up spiralling away like mad things, and perhaps even breaking loose altogether and hurtling off uncontrolled into space! It must happen eventually — even in our very own solar system! No, don't bother to look worried — the calculations show that it isn't going to happen for a very, very great many years. So you have plenty of time to study mathematics and learn about the n-body problem."

"So that is the influence the planets have on each other," I remarked thoughtfully. "It really seems to describe the way in which the relations between human beings come to distort the direct and pure relations between each individual and the Divine."

"It does, awfully!" he answered. "Well said. Now that you mention it, I seem to know rather a lot of people who are in the process of drifting away from their research—which I suppose could be considered the mathematician's relationship with the Divine—for reasons of jealousy and resentment, or such. Mathematicians do tend to go a little mad sometimes. Perhaps it's a result of all that concentration." He took up the journal, and continued his translation where he had left off.

This problem, whose solution would considerably extend our knowledge with respect to the system of the world—this odd expression is French for the solar system, with the sun and the planets—*appears to be solvable using the analytic methods we already have at our disposal; at least we may suppose this, since LEJEUNE-DIRICHLET communicated, shortly before his death, to a geometer amongst his friends, that he had discovered a method to integrate the differential equations of mechanics, and applying this method, he had succeeded in giving an absolutely rigorous proof of the stability of our planetary system. Unfortunately, we know nothing of this method, unless it is that the theory of infinitely small oscillations appears to have served as the starting point for his discovery. We may, however, assume almost with certainty that this method was not based on long and complicated computations, but on the development of one simple fundamental idea, which we may reasonably hope may be rediscovered by dint of deep and persevering work. In the case, however, where the proposed problem cannot be solved before the date of the competition, the prize could be attributed in recompense for work in which some other problem in mechanics was treated in the indicated manner and completely solved.*

"Ah, now here is an interesting thing," Mr. Morrison told us. "Dirichlet told a mysterious friend that he had solved a fundamental problem, and thereupon immediately died, nearly 30 years ago, leaving no clue as to his method. How thoughtless of him."

"Could we not identify the friend?" I began hopefully.

"Oh, actually, he has been identified; indeed, he has identified himself, and quite arrogantly at that. It is the German mathematician Kronecker, a great rival of Weierstrass. He claims that what Dirichlet told him is ill-represented in this paragraph. But for all that he says, he clearly has no idea or no clear memory of what Dirichlet's method might have been. He is more likely to be protesting out of anger that he was not included in the commission. Now come the three other problems set for the Competition, but they are less interesting."

2. Mr. FUCHS proved in several of his memoirs that there exist uniform functions of two variables, which are connected, by the way in which they are generated, to ultraelliptic functions, but are more general than these, and which could probably acquire great importance in analysis, if their theory were developed further.

We propose to obtain, in explicit form, the functions whose existence has been proved by Mr. FUCHS, in a sufficiently general case, so that one can recognise and study their most essential properties.

3. The study of functions defined by a sufficiently general differential equation of the first order whose first term is an integral and rational polynomial with respect to the variable, the function and its first derivative.

MM. Briot and Bouquet opened the way to such a study in their memoir on this subject (Journal de l'Ecole Polytechnique, cahier 36, pag. 133-198). The geometers familiar with the results discovered by these authors also know that their work is far from having exhausted the difficult and important subject which they were the first to investigate. It appears probable that new research undertaken in the same direction could lead to propositions of great interest to analysis.

4. We know what light was shed on the general theory of algebraic equations by the study of those special equations arising from the division of the circle into equal parts, and the division by an integer of the argument of the elliptic functions. The remarkable transcendental number obtained by expressing the module of the theory of elliptic functions by the quotient of the periods similarly leads to the modular equations, which have been the source of absolutely new notions, and to results of great importance such as the solution of the fifth degree equation. But this transcendental number is just the first term, the simplest special case of an infinite series of new functions which M. POINCARÉ has introduced to science under the name of Fuchsian functions, and applied with success to the integration of linear differential equations of arbitrary order. These functions, which play a role of manifest importance in Analysis, have not yet been considered from the point of view of algebra, as the transcendental associated to the theory of elliptic functions, of which they are the generalisation. We propose to fill this lacuna and to obtain new equations analogous to modular equations, by studying, even in just a special case, the formation and the properties of the algebraic relations relating two Fuchsian functions when they have a common group.

"For those in the know," Mr. Morrison told us, "this Henri Poincaré is considered sure to win the competition. He is a kind of genius, and all of his work is exactly round about the questions proposed above, all four of them, really; he might try his hand at whichever he pleases. He is much admired in Sweden, look—he has published two articles in this very volume. He was formerly a student of Hermite, the commissioner from Paris." And he turned some pages, and showed me the first mathematical article in the volume, written in French by this very H. Poincaré, and whose title was precisely "On a theorem of Mr. Fuchs", before concluding his translation of the announcement.

In the case where none of the memoirs presented for the competition on one of the proposed subjects would be found worthy of the prize, this can be attributed to a memoir submitted to the competition, which contains a complete solution of an important question of the theory of functions, which is not one of those proposed by the commission.

The memoirs submitted to the competition must be equipped with an epigraph and with the name and address of the author in a sealed envelope addressed to the Chief Editor of Acta Mathematica before the 1st of June 1888.

The memoir for which HIS MAJESTY will deign to attribute the prize, as well as that or those memoirs which the commission will consider worthy of an honorable mention, will be inserted into Acta Mathematica, and none of them must be published beforehand.

The memoirs may be redacted in whatever language the author wishes, but as the members of the commission belong to three different countries, the author must provide a French translation together with his original manuscript if the memoir is not already written in French. If no such translation is included, the author must accept that the commission has one made for its own use.

The Chief Editor.

"The 1st of June, why that is in just three months!" remarked Emily. "Are you submitting a memoir to the competition, Uncle Charles?"

"I? Why no, absolutely not," he exclaimed. "I know next to nothing about the questions posed here. There are not many people in England nowadays who would be capable of seriously solving them, although if there are any at all, they would be right here in Cambridge."

"Really? Do you know them? Are they doing it?" she asked.

"No one has actually declared that he is setting about it," he said thoughtfully. "But you know, that doesn't prove much, does it? After all, it's quite imaginable that a person might keep the whole thing silent, to avoid embarrassment in case of failure, and yet submit a secret manuscript nonetheless."

"And if someone were doing it secretly, who could it be?"

'Strike me pink if that isn't exactly what Akers was thinking of doing," he said suddenly. "Why yes, wasn't my friend Weatherburn telling us that Akers had said he had found a solution on the night before he died? The poor fellow, what hard luck for him—perhaps he was finally on the brink of the fame and recognition he always dreamed of."

"Did he, poor man? And why didn't he get it?"

"Oh, Akers was a good mathematician, he had a good, swift brain, but he lacked something which could have made him really great. He didn't have a fundamental grasp of the larger nature of things. It was as though you put him in front of a puzzle, Emily, and he would grasp two pieces and try to put them together, and if they didn't fit, he would try another and yet another, very quickly and with a sharp eye, so that eventually he would put quite a number together, and yet somehow he would have no idea of what the picture puzzle was actually showing. It's difficult to explain."

"But do you think he might have found a solution to the first problem anyway?"

"Why not? Perhaps it was there for anyone to see, and just needed a sudden, blinding vision to find it. Perhaps he found it by dint of 'deep and persevering work', or even by doing the kind of 'long and complicated calculations' he was not supposed to need! Unless he wrote something down, we shall never know now; why it's just as bad as Dirichlet."

"But he did write something," I observed. "He had a paper with a formula in his breast pocket, and he even told Mr. Weatherburn that he had written a rough manuscript!"

"Oh! Has anybody searched through the papers he left in his rooms?" Emily squeaked, jumping up and down eagerly.

"Oh yes, naturally, his notes and papers have been gone through carefully and inspected and organised, by the police, and also by mathematicians, I should think. Nobody appears to have found anything like a manuscript containing a complete solution to the n-body problem—if they had, we would certainly know about it by now."

"Perhaps he already sent it in?"

"Unlikely, if he told Weatherburn the day before his death that it was just a rough manuscript—and he would have had plenty of time before the 1st of June to better it."

"If only we had the breast-pocket paper he showed Mr. Weatherburn," I put in, "surely it would help!"

He looked at me musingly. "You are right, really, Miss Duncan. Imagine—what you are saying might actually turn out to be very important! The personal effects he had on him at his death are probably still in the Police Station, as his death is still being investigated. I wonder if they have found that paper; I wonder if anybody has been to ask. I shall go down to the station tomorrow and enquire about it myself."

"Oh, how *exciting*," cried Emily. "Imagine if you find it—then you could solve the problem and win the prize, and you could give the medal to Miss Duncan as a gift."

"Emily!" Mr. Morrison was quite shocked. "One doesn't *steal* other people's ideas."

"Really? Can ideas be stolen?" she responded in surprise.

"Oh yes, ideas are more valuable than property for a mathematician. He would far prefer to lose his money or belongings than his ideas."

"Well, but here it would be from a man who's dead!"

"You may steal from a man's memory, Emily," he

answered. He looked intensely serious, and I felt deeply impressed. I will not soon forget how he spoke.

For men like these, ideas seem greater, more real, more meaningful, more desirable, than all the treasures which have made men dream since the beginning of time. It is a moving thing.

I send a great many kisses to everyone,

Your loving

Vanessa

Cambridge, Tuesday, March 20th, 1888

Dear Dora,

The delight at receiving, finally, a long letter from you almost outweighed my feelings at your sad news. So Mr. Edwards is leaving for India. No wonder after he learned it, he hesitated for so long to come and see you. It must have been difficult for him to face the necessity of giving you news that he knew must grieve you. And thus, he himself is reluctant to go, and disappointed in himself for not having succeeded more brilliantly in his studies, thereby leaving only this option open to himself. Oh, Dora ... many ladies marry civil servants and join them in India. It is quite frequent, so you must not think that everything is necessarily over. But I understand that you could not even think of such a thing now, when you still know him so little. You would have needed a long courtship, as anyone would, and now you will have only letters. Surely you will soon be one of the most written-to creatures in the country! And you will have his leaves to look forward to. I dearly hope that you will find that knowing what happened, however sad, is far better than not knowing, and your taste for life will return with the springtime.

I was very much hoping, I must confess, to have some

exciting news to be able to continue my mathematical tale; I awaited the results of Mr. Morrison's visit to the police with great interest. But alas, Emily has told me that he returned empty-handed, as all of Mr. Akers' personal effects have already been transferred to his closest kin, who is a woman living somewhere on the Continent. The police showed Mr. Morrison a list, and it seems that not only was there a paper in his pockets, but even a great many bits of paper, all covered with mathematical scribbling, as well as the usual assortment of keys, coins, diary and so on. At any rate, it is all gone now.

Emily also showed me a newspaper clipping from a few days ago, which her uncle gave her; I had not seen it.

Death of Mathematician Remains Mysterious

The murder of Dr. Geoffrey Akers, Fellow of St. John's College in Pure Mathematics, remains unexplained. The police have but a single, seemingly inexplicable clue. Upon asking themselves whether the murderer may not have been a thief, they examined his rooms completely to see if anything had been taken. The investigation apparently proved inconclusive. The room showed signs of having been thoroughly searched; it was very disarranged, and the drawers were standing open, but nothing of value had disappeared. "'e probably made the mess himself, 'e did," said Mrs. Wiggins, the bedder. "It could 'ardly be messier than it already was. Nought but dirty papers and cigar ends. Mr. Akers had nothing of value in his rooms anyway, unless they wanted to steal his old clothes." It is conceivable that the murder could have been perpetrated by a disappointed thief, who had been hoping for better.

So, so! This may explain the absence of any manuscript solving the n-body problem. As for the famous bit of paper, either it has been sent off to his next of kin, or else he may have simply thrown it away ... or else ... the gruesome thought cannot be avoided ... perhaps the very selfsame person who struck

46

the dreadful blow then slipped his hand slily into the dead man's pocket, searching there ...

Oh, Dora, what am I saying? It sounds as though – instead of a mere thief – the murderer could be a *mathematician*, killing in order to *steal the idea*? That very idea which Mr. Morrison spoke of as being *more valuable than money or belongings?*

What a terrible train of thought! And yet, the more I consider it, the more I feel that it must be so. He was killed in his rooms at the University. Why should a stranger have made his way there? Oh dear. I wish I could speak to someone about this. Next Thursday I return to tea at Emily's. Perhaps Mr. Morrison will step upstairs. Dare I ask him what he thinks? But what if it should be *he*? No, this is ridiculous. I *must* stop!

I leave you quite nervously,

Vanessa

Cambridge, Wednesday, March 28th, 1888

Dearest Dora,

My mind continues filled with a confusion of mathematicians and murderers. On Monday, I returned to Mrs. Burke-Jones' house together with Emily and Miss Forsyth after the afternoon lessons were over. For several days, I had somehow succeeded in keeping these thoughts at bay, and concerning myself with my work, and long walks at dusk as the days become longer. I cannot tell you how lovely the town is when the darkness is just beginning to settle over it. Without erasing any the beauties of the medieval Colleges, it merely eliminates those little things which etch out the details of modern life; shop signs become illegible in the gloaming, and all fashions look the same. Of all the lovely Colleges, it is King's which seems the most beautiful to me at dusk. The College buildings themselves are hidden behind a screen of stonework lace, the upper border of which stands out black against the deepening sky. One can perceive the garden through the decorated arched openings; the screen is in fact purely unnecessary, a fairy-like folly. We walked past it on our way, and could almost imagine that it sheltered princesses, and knights in shining armour, rather than hordes of black-gowned students labouring over equations and dates ...

We arrived at the house at length, and no sooner had we settled ourselves to our charming tea, then who should appear, but Mr. Morrison, not alone, but *accompanied by Mr. Weatherburn!* My heart pounded in my ears and the blood rushed to my face, as it was borne in upon me with unmistakable clarity that the dreadful thought I had been avoiding with such concentration for the past three days was precisely this: *that he should be the murderer.* Oh, Dora—the paper, the fatal calculation ... nobody knew about it but Mr. Weatherburn!

Exactly as the thought rushed uncontrollably into my mind, I became calmer. Just as it was for you with Mr. Edwards, thinking it was more healthy than ever pushing the thought back. I remembered that Mr. Weatherburn himself had talked about the paper and Mr. Akers' discovery, in front of a whole gathering of guests. Whyever should he have done such a thing, if he had in fact stolen it? Surely he would have kept it buried in silence forever. I felt better, and was able to meet his eyes frankly, and took great relief in his kind and steady brown gaze. I felt rather foolish about my momentary confusion, which must have been visible to everybody, and which could easily be attributed to all kinds of ridiculous causes!

"Your mother is having several ladies to tea, my dear," said Mr. Morrison to his niece, "and I'm sure we should only get in their way, so if you don't mind, Weatherburn and I would be delighted to join you here."

"Oh, Uncle Charles, Uncle Charles, oh yes, please do!" cried Emily, jumping up and down with delight, and rushing to add cups and saucers to the tea table.

Never have I enjoyed tea more than I did yesterday. So friendly were the gentlemen, so gay was Emily, and so welcoming was Annabel, that I forgot I was a guest and began to feel entirely one of the family. So much so, that I even dared to take Mr. Morrison aside for a moment, while the others were engaged in some absurd game, and quietly ask him if there had been any progress at all on the case. Perhaps it was a mistake.

"Good heavens," he said startled, "are you still thinking about that sad story, Miss Duncan?"

"Oh, I am so very sorry," I began with dismay. "It was just because ... oh, I don't know how to say it — I thought that — oh dear, oh dear."

"Well, well, out with it!"

"It's that paper, Mr. Morrison, the one he wrote something on and put in his pocket that evening. I feel quite sure it must be important whether it was found or not."

"Well," he said rather uncertainly, "we can hardly know about that now. All his personal effects were sent away to his only surviving relative, his sister, who has been living in Belgium these last ten years. Do you really believe there could have been a great discovery written down upon that paper, Miss Duncan? After all, he claimed there was a manuscript, and nothing of importance was found in his rooms."

I perceived that he was still considering the paper as though its importance lay in its contents, whereas for myself, I desired to know whether it had been taken or not by the murderer, for to me, this would signify whether or not the murderer was actually a *mathematician*. As he did not catch my meaning, I tried to hint at it in a delicate manner.

"Goodness gracious," he exclaimed in reply, "Heavens alive! Why, you don't really think someone would have whacked poor old Akers on the head just to steal that little bit of paper, do you? You really suppose he might have been killed by one of his colleagues, for his idea? How you do go! Why, you'll be suspecting me next!"

"Oh no, certainly not you, or Mr. Weatherburn," I burst out, and although these last words were perfectly true, they had been false so very recently that I felt a deep blush creeping over every visible part of me.

"Well, well," he said hastily, "do not worry—the police will surely solve the mystery. They are very good at these things, you know."

"How can they?" I wondered. "They can't have considered the breast-pocket paper important, as they sent it away, assuming it was there at all, and they haven't any other clues, have they?"

"The police showed me the list of what he had upon him at his death; they seemed quite annoyed to have to get it out again, saying that some other 'amateur' had already been asking to see it. I wonder who that might have been. The list said he had keys, coins, handkerchief, his pocket diary, and all kinds of paper scraps," he answered with a shrug, running his hands through his own pockets; "exactly what I've got in mine. Well, almost," he added, pulling out two marbles, a whistle to make bird calls and a piece of pink quartz.

"Mr. Morrison, the murderer must be found," I said urgently. "Just think—the man who struck down poor Mr. Akers is freely walking the streets and smiling, at this very moment!"

The words struck me powerfully even as I said them. I suddenly realised, really realised, that it was true. I had known it before, of course, but I saw that some part of my brain had refused the knowledge—it had seemed to me that there was *someone*, but merely some unidentified and unidentifiable shadow, *not a real person*. It is a strangely reassuring state, if somewhat in the style of ostriches. It was clearly Mr. Morrison's.

'Smiling?" he said, half-jokingly. "More likely frowning

away, if you really think he pinched that paper and is trying to understand poor old Akers' scribbling. Why, if you're right, we really only need wait and see who submits an entry to the Birthday Competition, eh, Miss Duncan? Oh, I'm sorry—it is stupid to joke about it. Please forgive me. Yes, you are right to be so serious, and I am a fool. Please ignore me, you can't do anything better. Come along and let me pour you a cup of tea!"

It sounded kind and consoling, Dora dear, and I allowed myself to be led away, for what good can come of my brooding upon the murder? I do not want to develop a morbid streak. I tried to put it out of my mind, and the remainder of our tea-time passed very joyfully indeed. We played various parlour games, especially charades. At first Mr. Morrison told us a wonderful charade due to Mr. Lewis Carroll, with whom he is personally acquainted, as I told you. He wrote this one for a family of three little girls.

They both make a roaring, a roaring all night:
They both are a fisherman-father's delight:
They are both, when in fury, a terrible sight!

The First nurses tenderly three little hulls,
To the lullaby-music of shrill-screaming gulls,
And laughs when they dimple his face with their sculls.

The Second's a tidyish sort of a lad,
Who behaves pretty well to a man he calls "Dad",
And earns the remark, "Well, he isn't so bad!"

Of the two put together, oh, what shall I say?
'Tis a time when "to live" means the same as "to play":
When the busiest person does nothing all day.

When the grave College Don, full of love inexpressi-
Ble, puts it all by, and is forced to confess he
Can think but of Agnes and Evie and Jessie!

Naturally, we could not guess it at all at first, but upon Mr. Morrison's hinting and helping, we understood that the First is *Sea* and the Second *Son*, so that the whole turns out to be *Season*.

This inspired us to attempt our own creations. To make it simpler, we decided to use only the names of the people present. We wrote out our five names on pieces of paper, put them in a hat, mixed it, and each chose one; then we tried to compose charades about the names we had chosen. It was frightfully difficult, and the results are not so charming as Mr. Carroll's. We read them out nevertheless, and it was not always so easy to guess the answers! Here they are; see if you can discover the solutions.

This is Mr. Morrison's charade:

My first are birds on rooves which take not wing,
That we need not rely on serendipity
My next describes the majesty of a king,
In spite of its peculiar femininity!

My third a lovely colour, soft and buff
A perfect match for wraps of fur and sable,
The sweetest shade for collar, stole and muff.
My fourth is another word for to be able.

My whole before me sits, engaged in writing.
What poem is she weaving round a name?
Mayhap my own is just the one she's citing!
Her light verse surely will put mine to shame.

My goodness – I'm quite sure I was the only person who knew what he was referring to, with his "king's majesty"! Here is Emily's charade:

My first is unpredictable and wilful.
Because of it we put on hats and coats.

My second can be horribly painful,
It's also what Ulysses did to the boats.

My whole is someone in this room,
I'm sure you will easily guess whom.

"Who, dear, not whom," murmured Miss Forsyth.

Here is my own humble effort — it isn't quite accurate, was the general opinion! But I really could not do better.

My first is an appellation of style,
Which often, they say, is as good as a mile.
My second with "you" forms a phrase of great joy
To a child who's offered a gaily wrapped toy.
My third is a tool used for cutting the hay,
My whole is a person sweet, youthful and gay.

Miss Forsyth claimed that she could absolutely not divide the name she dealt with into syllables that made any sense in English, and had to resort to French, upon which everyone looked at each other with a shadow of dismay, even the two much-educated gentlemen.

Here is Miss Forsyth's charade, which I copied from her paper.

Ici présent s'avance un gentilhomme
Tiré par sa passion des lointains altiers.
Tel Phoebus, juché sur mon premier,
Il trébuche sur la comique grammaire,
Qui lui conte aussitôt avec son charme austère,
Que mon innocent second bel et bien s'appelle
Dans son bizarre jargon : article défini pluriel !

Ses coursiers trop fougueux jetés dans la carrière
De mon troisième avalent la dernière lettre.
Auraient-ils donc henni, ou bien serait-ce leur maître,

La journée terminée, le cavalier descend
Et s'attable devant un copieux dîner.
Ses chevaux se mettent à table également,
Des sacs de mon cinquième à leurs museaux accrochés.

Alas for the loveliness of her poetry, and her beautiful accent — not one of us was able to understand it, and instead of guessing, we began by compelling her to translate.

"What jolly French you speak and write," said Mr. Morrison, "how lucky for you."

"I spent six years of my youth in a convent in France," she explained, blushing slightly.

"I am sorry the charade is so difficult. I will do my best to explain it. Here is a gentleman drawn forth by his passion for the distant heights — that is a mathematician. Like Phoebus, he rides upon my first — it is a Roman chariot, *char*."

"It's Charles Morrison," shouted everybody.

"Of course," said Annabel with a smile. "He stumbles over the comical grammar, which immediately tells him, with its austere charm, that my second is known, in its bizarre jargon, as the plural definite article, *les*.

"His too eager stallions gallop forth and swallow the last letter of my third; it is *mors*, the bit; we say that horses galloping very fast "swallow the bit".

"Did they neigh, or was it their master, who, forgetting his deep reveries, tastes the sweet madness of my fourth; it is "laughed", *ri*.

"At the end of the day, the horseman descends, and seats himself in front of a copious dinner. His horses also set to eating, each with a bag of my fifth on its muzzle. It is bran, *son*."

We all felt that our efforts paled in comparison with the sophistication of hers!

Mr. Weatherburn's effort came last. He said he found it too

difficult to write a charade, and offered us the following double acrostic instead, in which not only the first letter of each line must be read vertically, but also the first letter of the last word of each line.

Ode to a perfect moment

Each precious moment of gravity or Jest,
Mingles the twinkling lights in Opalescence
In her dark eyes. Too soon, this charming Nest,
Like everything, will fade in Evanescence.
Yes, precious moments never Stay.

Brief is the moment — soon, with measured Tread,
Unconscious future will the present O'ertake.
Reality will realise hope or Dread,
Keen is the pain of the dreamer who must Awake.
Each time, today is Yesterday.

He wrote it for Emily, yet he looked much at me as he read it.

I feel more than unusually tired after such an eventful evening and such a long letter, and shall put out my candles and retire for the night.

Good night, my dearest twin

Your loving Vanessa

Cambridge, Wednesday, April 4th, 1888

My dearest sister,
How I wish I could have spent Easter Sunday with you, at home! I did not teach for two days after it, and spent the short holiday delightfully, rambling about in the fields and along the rivers. The great banks of daffodils have been in bloom for some time now, and the primroses and wild flowers of all kinds are making their appearance. The fields are emerald, and the hedgerows covered with a faint fuzz which will soon be a mass of tiny blooms. The weather is cool and damp, yet

carries such freshness within it that the call of springtime is irresistible.

Yesterday, on my way down the long field path to the village of Grantchester, where I had decided to take my tea outdoors, I met Mr. Weatherburn, bent on the same errand (if one may call it so). Grantchester is so lovely and dainty, with its thatched cottages, that one feels far away from any town, and I can almost imagine that I will soon see our own dear house appearing before me. We walked together, and talked at length, mostly about books, plays and poems. He knows a great deal of poetry, and we talked much about Shakespeare, Keats, and Tennyson. Arriving at Grantchester, we sat ourselves at a small table in the garden of the tea-room, and ordered tea and scones. They came delightfully accompanied with cream and jam, and apart from the kindly lady who brought the things out to us, we were quite alone there, for the weather is still too cool for most people, who preferred to take their tea within doors. The rest of the afternoon passed for me in a haze of delight — I do hope there was no impropriety in it. If there was, Mrs. Fitzwilliam will soon come to know of it, and scold me. I have now discovered that Mr. Weatherburn's Christian name is Arthur. He invited me to use it, but I really feel too timid to do so, though I will often think it.

We talked at great length about all sorts of things. He asked me many questions about my childhood, and I am afraid that I told him all about us, and the fields and flowers and how we used to jump on the grazing ponies just as we were and ride them about together shouting, and about our house and our chestnut tree and how instead of lessons we had primers. He was most interested in every detail of it, so that I quite told him a great many things which I had never mentioned to any outsider before.

Then I wanted to know about how he grew up, and where, and what it was like. He told me that he was orphaned at the age of nine, after which he was was sent away to school on a

Scholarship. He has no family at all, but until the age of 21 he had a trustee.

I immediately thought of poor little half-orphaned Edmund.

"Did you suffer very much in your school?" I asked him.

The question seemed to surprise him slightly, as though he had never asked himself whether or not he had suffered.

"I don't know," he answered rather slowly. "I d-don't seem to remember it particularly. I believe I really shut it out most of the time. My memories of the Greek tragedies and the French Revolution according to Carlyle are much stronger in my mind than any actual memories of my own school life. I seem to have retained only a kind of global consciousness of muddy games, and bustle, and food prepared in enormous quantities slapped onto the plate, and a general sense of permanent capharnaum, from which I escaped as often as possible into the silence of books."

"Were the boys not beaten at your school?" I asked him. "Little Emily, Charles Morrison's niece, tells me that her brother complains bitterly about the treatment meted out to his classmates and himself, and can hardly bear it."

"Well, I never was," he said musingly, "perhaps because I was an orphan, or simply because I never made any trouble of any kind. It was probably for the latter reason; I was not an imaginative or mischievous child, I'm afraid. It certainly happened to others on occasion, but I admit that the reality of it never penetrated my conscious mind. I went all through school as though on a parallel plane, until I went up to College."

"When was that?" I enquired with interest, wondering secretly how old he might be.

"That was six years ago. After I took my d-degree, I obtained this Fellowship; you see, I have not moved about much more than you in my life."

"Well, perhaps not," I concurred, "but still, think how lucky you are to have received such an education. I sorely miss it."

"I think that you possess a treasure infinitely more valuable than any education," he responded seriously, looking at me, then looking away.

"Nonsense! Whatever do you mean?"

"The gift of life," he said, reddening slightly. "You are like a fountain of spring water. No amount of education can teach that secret; quite the contrary, if anything, it probably dulls it. An education which consists mainly in running about the Forest of Arden picking wild flowers and jumping onto grazing ponies is much more likely to provide it, if you ask me!

And this our life, exempt from public haunt,
Finds tongues in trees, books in the running brooks,
Sermons in stones, and good in everything.
I would not change it."

Hmmm. Mr. Weatherburn appears to know his Shakespeare very well.

I have decided to devote my short holiday these last four days to a great course of serious reading. I must improve my mind and study seriously in order to keep abreast of my teaching, especially as the oldest pupils never cease to advance rapidly in their studies! Emily's interests, in particular, are maturing each day, and she needs to read works worthy of them. I have already re-read much of Shakespeare. I have also obtained a very recent novel by a very modern, much disapproved-of — indeed, quite scandalous, writer, Mr. Thomas Hardy. It is called it *The Mayor of Casterbridge*, and within the very first ten pages, an obnoxious gentleman puts his wife up for auction at a public gathering, and finds a taker for five guineas! The wife, poor thing, is only too eager to be sold, as she could hardly chance on someone more disagreeable than her own husband. Still, it is most shocking. The very moment the offer is made, she flings her wedding ring into her husband's face and departs with the purchasing gentleman forever, carrying her baby on her arm. This unusual auction takes place in a tent at a fair, where people come and sit to eat a bowl of something called "furmity". It sounds delicious; it appears to consist in corn and hulled wheat grains, cooked in milk and flavoured with sugar and spices. It is also generously laced with rum in the case of the horrid gentleman, but I shall not heed that addition to the recipe in trying it out for myself at home!

Your delighted

Vanessa

Cambridge, Wednesday, April 11th, 1888

My dearest Dora,

I have not written for several days, as I was caught up, albeit in a secondary role, in some events which have shaken Emily's family to its core. Fate has dealt poor Mrs. Burke-Jones a heavy blow.

It all began the Friday after my tea with Mr. Weatherburn. In the late morning, as I was bent over my desk preparing the lessons for the afternoon, I heard a gentle knock on my door. Such a thing was so rare as to be unheard of, except that Mrs. Fitzwilliam occasionally knocks to complain about something. Imagine my surprise upon opening the door, to see Mr. Weatherburn upon the threshold!

He did not enter, but stood shyly without, and stammering a little as usual, held a magazine out to me, saying,

"I wonder if you have c-come across this new literary magazine which has begun to appear only very lately? I came across it on a trip down to London, and brought it back, thinking it might be of interest to you."

He handed it to me, and I observed the cover and turned the pages. It was called *Woman's World*, edited by a certain Mr. Oscar Wilde.

"He has taken over the m-magazine but recently," Mr. Weatherburn told me; "it seems he has made it literary, when previously it contained articles mainly about fashion. Oscar Wilde's relation with the fair sex appears to be one of frank friendship and sympathy, such as can be felt only by a very special kind of man. The contributions are almost exclusively by women; I enjoyed reading it very much in the train. I particularly recommend the remarkable story by Amy Levy."

I was grateful and moved by his thoughtfulness, and was awkwardly searching for words to express myself, turning over the pages of the magazine, when he continued,

"I thought perhaps we m-might organise a theatre party for London, to see a Shakespeare play, with Morrison and his sister, and Emily, if you would like to join."

London! To see a Shakespeare play!

"Oh, I would *love* to," I burst out. "I have never been to London!"

"No, really? Well then, we must make up for it, there's no time to lose!" he answered, his face suddenly lit up by a warm and cheering smile. "Shall we go tomorrow, as it's a Saturday? I believe they're putting on the *Merchant of Venice*. I shall check if the others agree, and arrange for a box if they do. It will be delightful."

My dear Dora, I could not sleep the whole night for excitement. It seemed like a fairy tale. London — the theatre — things one only reads of!

The very next day, the fairy tale began to come true. Yes, although the day was gray and drizzly, and the omnibus became stuck in the mud and caused a great delay, and our hems became very draggled on the way to the theatre, and our shoes were wet through, still I was carried along in a wave of delight which consisted not only in joyful expectation of the play, but also in the quality of the present moment. There was much laughter amongst us in spite of the bothersome weather; Emily in particular hopped over the puddles, refusing to take shelter under the umbrella, and claiming that

60

the drizzle was sent purposely in order to teach us to appreciate the "gentle rain from heaven".

Arriving in the theatre was heavenly. The luxurious stalls, the plush seats, the gilded decor, the rich curtains; everything was a vision of pleasantness, and the play was magical, thanks to the great effort put into making the dream city of Venice come alive upon the stage. I leaned forward to catch every word, and awaited the most familiar speeches eagerly, trying to guess how they would be spoken. Everyone was in the most lighthearted mood, and all was perfect until the interval.

What happened next was so unexpected as to be almost unbelievable. We had just begun to rise and smooth our skirts in preparation for a short exploratory tour of the hall, when there was a knock on the door of our box, which opened of itself, and there stood a sober-faced gentleman with an air of gloom.

"Pardon me for disturbing you, ladies and gentleman," he said. "I am searching for Mrs. Burke-Jones with a very urgent message."

"I am Mrs. Burke-Jones," she said, stepping forward and growing pale. "What is amiss? Is it about my son Edmund?"

"No, Madam, it does not concern your son," he said. "Step this way, please, I must speak with you alone."

They departed, and our group remained silent with dismay. After some minutes, Mr. Morrison left the box, saying, "I shall go and see if everything is all right."

Not five minutes passed before he returned. He opened the door, and his face bore a strange, hard look. Turning to Emily, he broke the bad news directly.

"I am afraid it is about your father, Emily," he said almost sternly. "He is dead. He died yesterday in a boating accident, together with ... with Mademoiselle Martin."

"Dead! Daddy's dead! Oh, I never saw him again, and I waited so long," she wailed heartrendingly. Then, glancing about her with a look of panic, she suddenly cried "I must see

61

Mother!" She rushed out of the stall, followed by her uncle, who caught her arm and led her away firmly.

I remained alone with Mr. Weatherburn.

"How dreadful," I said, "I had believed that her father was already dead."

"No," he replied softly. "He left several years ago. I believe — no, I know, that he left with the young French girl who was Emily's governess at the time. They had a child very shortly afterwards, and went to live in France, as it was nearly impossible for them to remain together in England."

"I begin to understand," I said, thinking back over some things that had been said or alluded to in Emily's house, which I had not really noticed at the time. "How difficult it must have been for Mrs. Burke-Jones."

"I can imagine it was desperately difficult," he said, "although I did not know the family then. I know that she asked Morrison to leave his College rooms and come to live in her house at that time, and all in all I believe the arrangement suited him capitally. He really is a family man, and loves children."

The lights darkened, as the play was about to resume. Mr. Weatherburn arose, and offered me his arm.

"I do not believe we shall stay for the second half, after what has happened," he said. "It is awkward, one does not want to intrude on the family, nor to seem to abandon them."

The entire audience had by now returned to its seats, and the hall remained nearly empty, so that we soon spotted the small group formed by Mr. Morrison, his sister and her daughter, together with the bearer of ill-tidings. They seemed to be conversing urgently. We approached somewhat; I felt badly uncomfortable and much in the way, although Mr. Weatherburn's calm presence and the fact that he was in the same situation as I reassured me somewhat. However, seeing us at some distance, Mrs. Burke-Jones turned to us and beckoned us to approach.

"We must return to Cambridge immediately," she said, her

face extremely pale and rather stern, much like her brother's. "Perhaps you would prefer to remain here and return independently?"

It was naturally unthinkable. I tried to imagine Mrs. Fitzwilliam's face if I returned alone with Mr Weatherburn from London, late at night. Besides, I believe no one had any stomach for the play after what had happened.

We spent the entire way back to Cambridge in the dark, in almost complete silence. Once there, it was raining heavily, so we took a hansom and directed it first to Mrs. Fitzwilliam's house. Mr. Weatherburn bid Mrs. Burke-Jones goodbye in the gentlest tones, and descended from the hansom, where he waited below to help me alight. But Mrs. Burke-Jones caught my hand in hers before I could descend.

"I travel to France tomorrow," she told me. "My brother will accompany me, and Emily insists on coming also, although I am not sure it is for the best. Please excuse her if you do not see her in lessons on Monday or Tuesday. We will return as soon as our business in France is concluded."

She spoke with dignity, but Emily burst out uncontrollably. "Oh, Mother — how can you call it 'business'! Oh, Miss Duncan, Father left a little boy there, in France, and he is an orphan now — he has no place to go!"

"Emily!" said her mother, perhaps more sharply than she intended. "We must return home now, and begin to prepare ourselves. Good night, Miss Duncan. Please accept my apologies for the sad conclusion of our evening together."

"Please do not even think of apologising," I cried. "If I can be of help to you in any possible manner, do not hesitate to ask me! It would be a great honour."

"Thank you," she said a little more gently. I descended, and the hansom drove off. By this time it was storming. Mr. Weatherburn stood still patiently waiting for me, seeming almost not to notice the rain which poured down upon him and dripped before his eyes from the brim of his hat.

We entered the hall, and I opened my own door, and

turned to bid him goodbye. Instead of which, I was surprised to hear myself say —

"You do look wet and miserable! I should so like to give you a cup of tea!"

"I sh-should love it!" he replied, in a tone of timid audacity which exactly matched my own feelings. Suspecting that Mrs. Fitzwilliam would strongly disapprove, we slipped inside quite silently and took off our wet things, and I built up the fire and put the kettle on, and lit the candles. The tea was soon ready, and we sat on either side of the hearth, avoiding by common consent any talk of the distressing events we had just witnessed. Oddly illumined by the flickering firelight, my cosy sitting room seemed enveloped in secret magic.

We sipped our tea for a moment, looking into the fire, and I searched for words to thank him for the evening, and tell him how beautiful I had found it, in spite of everything.

"It was a marvellous thing for me to see even half a play," I finally said. "My very first visit to the theatre."

"I should like to take you to see the other half," he said a little wistfully. "The very scene following the interval was that in which Bassanio chooses the right casket to win his beloved. Do you remember ..." Slowly turning his intense gaze upon me, he recited, softly and ardently,

Though for myself alone
I would not be ambitious in my wish
To wish myself much better, yet for you
I would be trebled twenty times myself,
A thousand times more fair, ten thousand times more rich,
That only to stand high in your account
I might in virtues, beauties, livings, friends,
Exceed account.

I was deeply confused. Hastily, I turned away, reached down my volume of Shakespeare's plays, and turned to the casket scene. In a moment I had found the speech he was quoting. It was Portia's speech to Bassanio. My eyes followed the lines, and as he paused, I continued it, although it cost me a strange effort.

> *But the full sum of me*
> *Is sum of something which, to term in gross,*
> *Is an unlessoned girl, unschool'd, unpractis'd;*
> *Happy in this, she is not yet so old*
> *But she may learn; happier than this,*
> *She is not bred so dull but she can learn.*

The words were infinitely more powerful than any of our own could ever be. It seemed impossible to add to them. We remained silent, gazing into the fire for a long time, which was yet too short. Suddenly, without warning, he sprang to his feet.

"Of course!" he said. "I have it! How could I not have thought of it before?"

"What, what is it?" I asked anxiously.

"The proof! Yes — it all works!" And he made a sudden dash for the door.

"Wait — your overcoat, your hat!" I called out quickly.

He stopped in his tracks.

"Oh, I am s-s-sorry," he said. "How rude of me to be so absent-minded. I had entirely forgotten where I was — I became lost in mathematical ideas. It is strange — all of a sudden, I saw how to accomplish something which has been eluding me for weeks!" He returned towards me, holding out his hand, and thanked me warmly for the tea.

"I am glad you had a moment to dry before returning to your mathematics, and to your nocturnal pacing," I told him, smiling.

"Pacing? Oh yes. Do you hear me? I am very sorry! I never thought of it. But never fear, I shall not pace tonight. I do it only when my reflections are not proving fruitful. Tonight they are, thanks to you, thanks to Shakespeare." And he slipped out, his head aswirl, I imagine, with theorems and propositions, lemmas and corollaries.

The very next day, Mrs. Burke-Jones departed for France with Mr. Morrison and Emily in tow; they are to return only today. I have thought of them a great deal in these last three days. I shall write to you again, just as soon as something interesting transpires.

Yours ever,

Vanessa

Cambridge, Monday, April 16th, 1888

My dearest little sister,

I have just returned home from tea with Emily; in spite of all that has happened this last week, Mrs. Burke-Jones allowed her to continue our new habit of tea on Monday, as she so strongly wished it. Emily was bursting with the need to pour out her woes; I do not believe anybody really listens to them at home, and she cannot talk to me intimately during lessons.

"Oh, Miss Duncan, Miss Duncan, what do you think? You cannot believe all that has happened," she began almost as soon as I settled down in front of the teapot. "Edmund has been sent home from school; he arrived yesterday, and he is dreadfully ill! But I believe it is not just illness, for the letter said that the school was found to be unsuitable for him, and that he is not to come back ever. Mother is furious, but she does not know what to be furious about really, for no one has told us what he has been expelled for. The letter did not say, and Edmund will not say anything to Mother either, no matter how much she presses him. Oh, Miss Duncan, I cannot help rejoicing really, now that Edmund is home again. I do hope he will stay forever. I believe he will tell me what really happened, sooner or later."

"You must take very good care of him," I told her, thinking of the frail little blond child I had briefly laid eyes on at the dinner party. "It will be a great joy to you, once he gets well again."

"But then, the most dreadful thing happened in France," she went on, unable to contain her emotions. "Oh, Miss Duncan, we actually saw the little boy, Father's son, who lived in France with him! He looks just like Edmund used to ... they look the way I remember my father, too — he was slim and blond. I don't look like him at all; I resemble Mother. The little boy is not even six years old yet. His name is Robert, and he speaks English so sweetly, because Father always spoke English with him. Even though I never saw him before and did not even really know about him, not even his name, I felt that he was my very own brother, just like Edmund. I do so want another little brother! I was so excited, because I thought we were to bring him home! Mother saw lawyers and people for hours and hours. You know, Mademoiselle Martin was my governess until I was seven. She had no family at all, she had grown up in an orphanage and been educated in a convent, and she had come to England all by herself to seek for work, and she used always to say that we were the only family she had ever had. She fell in love with Daddy, you know. I am not supposed to know it, but I do know it, and I think it is very bad, but it could not have been her fault. I would have fallen in love with Daddy myself. I don't know why he had to leave us all and go away with her for all those years, though. He never wrote to me at all after he left. But Mother says that he left me a letter which I will be allowed to open when I am eighteen. It's a very long time from now, and I do so want to know what he says! He left a letter for Mother, too. That's all that he left, for he and Mademoiselle Martin had almost nothing at all to live on; our house belongs to Mother, you know. Papa had not left a testament as people sometimes do, leaving their things to people, because he had nothing, but he had left these letters, in case anything ever happened to him. Mother told me that in the letter he wrote her, he told her how sorry he was about how unhappy he had made her by leaving, and how much he still loved Edmund and me."

I began to feel almost uncomfortable at the intimate nature of the confidences I was receiving, but Emily desperately needed to talk, and the spate of information continued uninterrupted.

"But the most important thing is that he wrote there was no one at all to take care of his little boy, and please could Mother make sure nothing ill happened to him, because she was the only person in the whole wide world that he knew and would trust with his life! Oh, Miss Duncan, I thought we would adopt little Robert straightaway, but Mother would not! We went to see him, and he is living in dreadful rooms, all dirty and smelling of onions, right in the middle of a dirty street in Calais, with washing hanging up everywhere and peeling walls, with a horrible lady who said straight out that she was keeping him only to earn some money, and that the sooner she got rid of him the better. He was the saddest little boy I ever saw — he'd been an orphan for just two days! I tried to play with him, but he asked where Papa and Maman were and cried in my arms. I begged and begged Mother to take him with us; I even tried to order her, sometimes she listens to me and says I am her wise girl. But she *would not listen*, and said to me that she could not bear to see the child, and that she must return home, and think calmly about what to do about him. She gave some money to the lady and said that someone would come to collect the child, and that until then she would send more money. It was like selling him — oh, I cannot bear to think about it. I wanted to talk to her about it again, but she has forbidden me to mention it. Oh, Miss Duncan — what shall I do? What can I do?"

I was compelled to say the truth, that there was really not much the child could do, and that insisting too much might well even harm her case. I advised her gently to leave her mother alone for some time, and then bring up the subject gently and without passion, and listen very carefully to her mother's views. There was really not much else I could say.

"And devote yourself to your lessons, dear, and to taking care of your bro — of Edmund," I added. "I shall give you another of Mr. Lewis Carroll's *Knots* to solve today — mind you reason logically!"

I saw that I had not helped her as much as she had led herself to hope that I would.

"Miss Duncan, please promise you will help me, if I ever really need help," she whispered. "I will do the same for you. Please, let it be a pact between us."

She grasped my hand like a gentleman, and shook it firmly, and I kissed her. I will always help her to the best of my ability, of course, but that is so very limited. I cannot imagine what more she can expect. But I am deeply moved by her determination and her beautiful innate sense of justice.

I leave you now, to prepare my modest evening meal,

Vanessa

Cambridge, Monday, April 23rd, 1888

My very dearest sister,

Today was really a lovely, joyful, sunny day. The legendary English spring has finally made its appearance in full force. The gardens are bursting with flowers, the old walls drowning in wisteria. I had quite a new experience: for the first time, I attended a public lecture!

It was Mr. Weatherburn's idea. He told me that the very important Professor of Mathematics Arthur Cayley — the very one whom I met at Mrs. Burke-Jones's dinner party in early March — was going to hold a public lecture on the teaching of mathematics in a great hall, and that ever so many people were expected to attend, all those who enjoy mathematics or who are engaged in the teaching of it. He added that there would be refreshments afterwards, and if the weather was fine, they would be held in the gardens of Trinity College, where Professor Cayley is a Fellow. I felt extraordinarily honoured; it was my very first entrance within the walls which I can never avoid thinking of as hallowed. And Trinity College, seen from within, is not disappointing. The vine-draped Master's Lodge in the Great Court is the noblest mansion anyone could ever hope to reside in; as for the famous Chapel, a mere human feels almost unworthy of such splendour. They say it rings and echoes with the singing of the choir. I murmured wistfully that I should love to hear it some day, and was almost taken aback when told, in the most pragmatic of tones, that it was open to the public every Monday evening.

I felt shy to attend the lecture alone, and convinced my advanced class of Emily and Rose to join me; Miss Forsyth very kindly replaced me for the afternoon with the little girls. Emily and Rose were enchanted, not by the mathematical lecture, to be sure, but by the change in their usual habits, and the opportunity to spend the loveliest part of the afternoon taking refreshments in splendid gardens, instead of working sums in a schoolroom. There were a great many ladies in the audience; the hall seemed filled with their summery hats, next to which my own appeared sadly modest. Perhaps they are governesses or teachers, or perhaps they are married to mathematicians and wish to have some glimpse of the mysterious activity that occupies their husbands so intensely.

My two pupils were very well-behaved during the lecture; they sat directly behind me, and I tried hard not to wonder whether or not they were paying attention to the illustrious professor, and to ignore the stifled giggles which occasionally reached my ears. I myself listened closely to what Professor Cayley was saying. He sat facing the audience, reading from a prepared text, and looking up rarely; his voice was monotonous, his expression vinegary, and his speech rapid, and it would have been easy to lose the thread, had he not been so powerful in expressing his convictions. I had not realized that the question of Euclid could raise such passions in the breasts of his adepts and his enemies!

Professor Cayley held that the only door to mathematics was through Euclid, that his works attained the highest conceivable perfection of mathematical thinking, and that one could not begin to study them too early. He recommended them strongly to schoolchildren, and said that their study should never be abandoned until all the extant volumes had been completely mastered.

He told us that an Anti-Euclid Association was being founded, and mentioned the many objections that it had brought up against the use of Euclid for students, sternly refuting each one. The texts were archaic in appearance? — they could and should be edited in a modern edition. Their dry reasoning was too difficult for students to master other than by parrot-learning? — good! By memorisation they trained their minds to be familiar with the strategies of geometric proof. They ill prepared the students for the study of Modern Geometry? — false! No student who had not completely mastered the *Elements* should even be allowed to approach the temple of modern mathematics. And on it went, at great length.

After the lecture, we issued outdoors, where long tables had been set up. From the conversations I heard all about me, I realised that Professor Cayley appeared to be rather isolated in his views. Everywhere, I heard Euclid decried and modern texts praised. I ended by feeling quite sorry for poor Euclid, and determining to obtain one of his tomes at all costs and attempt the study of it.

At first, looking about the gardens, I did not espy a single familiar face. However, after some time, I saw someone signalling to me kindly, and recognised Mrs. Beddoes, who had also been a guest at Mrs. Burke-Jones' dinner party. I joined her, and she led me to a shady spot underneath a spreading, low-branched tree, where her circle of friends had gathered. All those whom I remembered from the party were there, and several whom I did not know. Mrs. Beddoes introduced me to some of them.

"You remember Mr. Young, Mr. Wentworth, Miss Chisholm, and my husband, of course," she said. "Let me introduce you to Mr. and Mrs. MacFarlane, Mr. Withers and Professor Crawford. This is Miss Duncan. She teaches Mr. Morrison's little niece."

Mr. MacFarlane and Mr. Withers, the latter an amusing, undersized but aggressive little figure, were bent over a piece of paper, writing something, and hardly nodded to me.

Mr. Crawford was a robust, tall and heavy gentleman with a loud, ringing voice. "So you teach," he said to me, "and have you a particular interest in the teaching of mathematics?"

"I do teach mathematics, or at least arithmetic, to the children in my class," I told him, "but as far as Professor Cayley's lecture is concerned, it is for my own instruction and improvement only. I was not thinking of introducing Euclid to my students."

"I should hope not, indeed," he bellowed, "nor to any students! Faugh! Cayley's ideas are ridiculously backwards. He should leave all notions of teaching to others."

"There is truth to that," intervened Miss Chisholm. "There is something stifling about Professor Cayley's teaching — he sits like a figure of Buddha upon a pedestal, and one feels that a breath of fresh air would be desperately welcome."

At that moment Mr. Beddoes appeared, carrying a cup and saucer, and joined the group.

"Ah, here's Beddoes!" cried Mr. Crawford, in such stentorian tones that all heads nearby turned in his direction, and a few more people approached to join the group. "Well, Beddoes, how have you been? I haven't seen you for a week."

"Quite well, quite well," said Mr. Beddoes, seeming rather

surprised, almost taken aback, no doubt at being thus accosted with almost violent friendliness.

"Now, Beddoes, we're having a debate on Euclid, here — you're a member of the old-fashioned school, of course!" interjected Mr. Withers, a little snappishly.

"Well, I do support the teaching of Euclid, yes," began Mr. Beddoes.

"I don't see how any progress is to made, as long as such people continue to hold teaching responsibilities in our Universities," exclaimed Mr. Withers, turning to Mr. Crawford. "I'd like to know more about that anti-Euclid Society which irked Cayley so much. I'd join it!"

Although his views appeared to correspond with Mr. Crawford's, the latter did not welcome these remarks with any particular ardour. He considered Mr. Withers with some disdain, and said rather loudly, "Before you criticise the teaching methods of better men than yourself, you'd do well to master the mathematics they aim to communicate!"

Mr. Withers responded to this provoking remark with a faint "Ha, ha".

But the words attracted the attention of Mr. Wentworth, who had been listening silently. "Now just a moment," he cried energetically. "Just what are you implying?"

"I'm implying no more than this: those who take decisions and argue the value of teaching methods of mathematics had better be those who master the subject — otherwise the whole University structure may just as well collapse!" answered Mr. Crawford belligerently.

"And how many people, according to you, might belong to this select group?"

"Precious few!"

Although answering Mr. Wentworth, Mr. Crawford continued to address himself directly to Mr. Withers, who became somewhat yellow with annoyance, and hastened off in the direction of the refreshments table.

"Well," intervened Mr. MacFarlane hastily, in a soothing

tone, "few there may be, but I suppose you do at least agree that our most illustrious professors belong to the group?"

"Stagnation, stagnation, that's the whole problem of it!" answered Mr. Crawford resentfully. "Yes, of course I don't deny the fantastic talent of a man like Cayley. But it's not enough! You've got to have the mastery and the originality and then something else, perhaps even more important than those — you've got to have an open mind and welcome new ideas and progress! That's what's missing here in our university. Original minds are held back, unrecognised, stifled by the powers that be!"

These words were greeted by shouts of opposition from those standing about, which soon led to a full-fledged and very lively debate. So much noise was made that I began to wonder what line exactly divides a debate from a quarrel, and whether "your imbecilic preferences" and "that sort of incompetent opinion" could not constitute serious causes of umbrage.

Mrs. Beddoes noted my surprise, and murmured to me in an undertone, "They're always like that, dear, pay no attention. Mathematicians are always so terribly excited about whatever they are doing! Especially Mr. Crawford — he's begun on his favourite theme now. I suppose one has to be a woman, observing it all from the outside, to see how obvious it is that he is really only ever speaking, in veiled terms, of himself and his own resentment at not being sufficiently adulated and rewarded within his community."

And she distanced herself a little from the group and began to talk with Emily and Rose, and ask them questions about themselves, until soon they were engaged in telling her all the details of their lives.

"What lovely children," she said a little sadly, turning to me. "I used to long to have little girls like these, when I was younger, but the time is long past now. Do you think your mothers would allow me to ask you to tea in my house, dears? It would be a great pleasure for me, and perhaps also

74

for you, as my husband has three cats, and one of them has just had kittens. I do not think so very highly of cats myself, and really cannot have them in the house, as they make my eyes water; I find it difficult to go near them. But they are the apple of my husband's eye!"

"Oh, yes, oh, yes, oh, please!" they chorused. "We will ask our mothers, and promise to come very soon!"

"It's time to proceed to a new era," Mr. Crawford was meanwhile still shouting. "No more geometry, no more algebra — mathematical physics is the new force in Cambridge! Why, we've had Maxwell, we've had Airy, we have Stokes — what's all this geometry and algebra! Quaternions — imaginary numbers — hah! Give me truth, give me reality, give me the solar system!"

"Now, now, Crawford," intervened Mr. Beddoes quickly, "there's no need to bring in the solar system, we're talking about Euclid."

"Hah! I suppose you're right. Well, I'll be off then," said Mr. Crawford, changing his tone suddenly, and turning on his heel, as though to dismiss the whole foolish topic. He turned away, and then abruptly turned back. "I need to see you, actually, Beddoes," he said. "What say we dine together one of these days? I'll let you know shortly."

"Why — yes, certainly," said Mr. Beddoes, somewhat taken aback by this welcoming invitation proffered in a tone of barking severity.

Mr. Crawford departed, and I followed his cue, bid good-bye to the company, and went to capture my two protegées, who were gambolling on the lawn, and making occasional forays to the tea table.

"I do believe it is time to walk you home," I told them. They ran about and refused to join me for some little time, enjoying themselves tremendously, but as they saw the company straggling away and the tea-things being collected, they came up to me all twinkling and rosy.

"Well, let us go home, then," said Emily, "can we walk Rose

home first, Miss Duncan? You have never seen her house, it is really very pretty. Rose has a room of her own, and she has ever so many funny things in it. Perhaps she'll play something for you, Miss Duncan, won't you, Rose? Please?"

"Ho," said Rose with her tiny nose in the air, "I don't feel like it today! I ate too much. Maybe another time, I'll play something ... some Bach, some Haydn, maybe something by Mr. Johannes Brahms — we've just received his new sonata. Do-faaaa-la-sooool-re-doooo-si-sooool ..."

And the little elf insisted on being left at her own front door.

'She plays the *violoncello*, Miss Duncan," Emily told me as we continued on towards her own house. "Isn't it strange? I don't know any girls who play anything except piano. It's ever such a big instrument — that's why she always has such wonderful big skirts, to go round it!"

"Oh, that explains the style," I smiled. "I remember how my sister and I used to beg our mother to make ours that way, too. It wasn't for music, though — it was because we used to run about outside, and jump on the ponies and ride them about the fields!"

"Ride them? But didn't you ride sidesaddle?" exclaimed the well-brought up child.

"My dear, we had no saddles at all," I laughingly undeceived her. "I used to be able to ride nearly anything, but I have very little experience of sidesaddles — perhaps I should fall off!"

"Oh, *do* let us go riding together someday, Miss Duncan, when it's warmer," she invited me eagerly as I deposited her upon her doorstep.

It is a tempting idea; I should love to canter along between the hedgerows and pluck the blossoms from the trees in passing, as we used to. But dear me — I do hope I shan't make a spectacle of myself among the other ladies, who unlike me, are probably all experts in the art of moving forwards with the whole lower half of their body perched sideways! The civilised have strange habits, do they not?

Your Vanessa

Cambridge, Tuesday, May 1st, 1888

Oh, Dora, the most dreadful thing has happened — I hardly know how to write about it! Yet I can think of nothing else, and although it is painful and repugnant to me to write to you about such horrors, even less could I ramble on about ordinary things as though nothing was amiss.

In a word — another mathematician has been murdered. It happened yesterday, and the victim is poor Mr. Beddoes, whom I have mentioned to you quite frequently. He was killed exactly like Mr. Akers; by a violent blow to the head, only this time, it happened in the garden just in front of his house. He was discovered by his poor wife; as she found him late returning home, she opened the front door and leaned out to look down the street, and in the darkness saw his huddled form lying near the garden gate.

But that is not the worst. The worst is so very dreadful that I must force myself to remember it, and prevent myself from rushing to bury my head underneath my pillow, hoping that it is all a bad dream.

It is that when poor Mr. Beddoes was struck down, he was returning from having dined out with no other than — once again — my very own poor friend Mr. Weatherburn.

Oh, Dora, it is not possible! He cannot, *cannot* be secretly mad, and in the habit of murdering his dinner companions. No, that sounds funny, and I feel anything but humorous. But then, how can he have such horrid luck? As soon as Mrs. Beddoes had called the police, they came to our house, and although it was very late and everybody had already retired, they knocked loudly upon the door, and Mrs. Fitzwilliam was obliged to rise and unbar it for them. I opened my door a crack, and peered out. Mrs. Fitzwilliam was very angry, but the police paid no attention, and ordered her to go up and fetch down Mr. Weatherburn immediately. He was still up, and came down at once, upon which they squarely told him, "You are under arrest for the murder of Philip Beddoes, Don at Cambridge University."

I never saw a man so amazed. It must have been extremely startling, if he had only just left Mr. Beddoes, fully alive and probably cheerful and well-fed. He turned pale and stepped back, stammering incoherently — "B-b-b-but that's im-im-impossible. I only just left him — why, he was in the p-p-pink of health!"

"Health has nothing to do with it, sir," said the Officer. "The man was murdered. We will trouble you to come along with us, please."

I rushed out into the hallway, although I was rather indecently clad in my nightdress, with my hair all down my back. The police ignored me, and Mrs. Fitzwilliam hustled me back into my room. Still, as the police marched him firmly away, Arthur looked back at me, and our eyes met for one blessed moment. He knows I do not believe a word of it.

I returned to my bed, but could not sleep a wink. I feel as though all happiness and tranquillity have fled forever. All of today I have tormented myself, seeking some issue, some possible action, anything at all to keep from sinking into a state of passive despair. If only, only there were some positive action I could take. Dare I try to visit Arthur in prison? How does one visit a prisoner? Tomorrow morning, I shall waste no time in finding out. Arthur may not be at all pleased — I can well imagine it, but I cannot live in such painful and immobile suspense!

Your loving but desperate sister

Vanessa

Cambridge, Wednesday, May 2nd, 1888

Dearest Dora,

I have done it. It was very strange — I never thought to find myself in such an odd position — visiting a prisoner!

But I cannot yet realise that Arthur is really a prisoner, and neither can he. He thinks it is a foolish mistake that will not fail to be put right in the coming day or two. Nevertheless, this morning's experience falls so far outside of the range of anything I have lived through hitherto, that it will certainly remain etched on my mind for the rest of my life.

Let me recount it to you from the beginning. I arose early, made tea (but could eat nothing), put on my best hat and betook myself to St. Andrew's Street; I knew, from having shopped there often enough, that a large Police Station was located at number 44. Before reaching it, I passed the very store where I had purchased the hat, in a happier moment. I have often stopped to contemplate the pleasing display at Robert Sayle's, and I could not resist a glance at it now. Famous for his travels to the Orient, his shop window contains Chinese silks worthy of the most romantic dreams. For a few moments, I allowed my mind to be invaded by a vision of beauty mingling sunsets, gardens and many-hued raw silk. Then a horrible image of bars and chains obtruded itself upon my brain. I hurried on, and turned into the Police Station, an enormous square building, impressive but excessively heavy in its conception. I felt a little foolish and inconsequent in such a place, but I addressed the Officer on duty firmly, quite as if this were not the case.

"I should like to ask you how I may go about visiting a prisoner who was arrested last night," I said.

He did not appear to perceive anything amiss with my request, and simply and stolidly enquired the name of the said prisoner, after which he informed me that he had been detained in Police Cells for the night, located in the very building where I found myself, and that he was still there, awaiting the van which would transport him to the Castle Hill Gaol.

What could they possibly have against Arthur? He is innocent, and dining with murder victims, even unluckily twice in a row, cannot possibly constitute a real basis for accusation. Well — I suppose they must needs do it, and that I should feel reassured that British justice follows a carefully weighed and balanced process intended to avoid haste and foolish error.

The Officer showed me to a room behind the one over which he presided to receive members of the public, and I sat down and waited. Eventually Arthur was shown in by another Officer. He did not seem overly pleased to see me.

"You should not c-come here," he began, "it is no place for —"

I cut him short rather firmly. I admit that I had expected such comments and previously rehearsed my reply — it came out rather stiffly as a consequence.

"Arthur," I said (it was the first time, I believe, that I used his Christian name aloud), "please, please do understand that no displeasure occasioned by outer circumstances, however dreadful, can compare remotely with the suffering of being forced to stand by, passively and in ignorance, when another person is in danger. If you want to protect me from anything at all, then let it at least be from that which is causing me unbearable torment, and not from mere outward circumstances which cannot possibly touch me!"

He understood what I meant perfectly. His attitude changed, and he took a chair, and leaned towards me, looking into my eyes seriously, unfettered by the discrete but stolid presence of the Officer near the doorway.

"Do not t-torment yourself," he said softly. "I am sure there is no need. It is all a great mistake, and will surely be put right very soon. I can hardly blame the police for making this error; after all, I was rather unluckily placed! But they will not pursue it, I suppose. The true murderer can hardly hope to hide for long."

"Have the police already questioned you?" I asked.

"Oh yes, for hours!"

"What did they ask you?"

"A hundred times the same questions — what were my relations with Akers and Beddoes, why did I dine with them, and so on and so forth. And whether I had hit them over the head with heavy instruments. I grew quite t-tired of replying, always in the same manner, to the fifty different versions of that last question they continued to fling at me. I kept telling them that I dined with Mr. Akers, accompanied him back to his rooms at St. John's, bid him goodnight below, saw him begin to mount the stairs, and departed. I dined with Mr. Beddoes, walked back to his house with him, bid him good night at the gate of his garden, and departed. I realise that it may appear amazing to the point of being positively suspicious, but the fact remains that I heard nothing of any murder in either case!"

"Did they ask you what you had talked about over the two dinners?"

"They pressed me only to admit that there had been quarrels."

"Were there quarrels?"

"Of c-course not! Akers told me that he had had a brilliant idea about a solution to the n-body problem; he almost could not contain himself for pleasure at its elegance and beauty. But after barely mentioning it, and scribbling a formula onto a scrap of paper, he thrust it away in his pocket, and abruptly changed the subject. For the rest, we talked of other things."

"I remember you said that he seemed concerned with Mr. Crawford's reaction," I said.

"Oh, yes, that is true," he answered, "now that I cast my mind back to that evening. He did speak of Crawford — said that his new discovery would be a shocking revelation to him. But he also enjoined me not to mention anything of it to him directly. I believe he wished to complete his work before springing it onto the only other local expert in the field."

"Mr. Crawford is an expert on the same problem — the n-body problem?"

"I suppose so, at least as far as Cantabrigians are concerned," he amended. "England holds no experts like the French and Germans, on these subjects. Anyway, the police then expressed suspicion about why I should walk home with him, as it is not on my way. I told them that I found the Colleges extraordinarily beautiful, and it was a crisp, moonlit night, and it is not so very far out of my way, and that I greatly felt the need of a walk after our copious dinner; I always do."

"How did you come to dine with him at all, Arthur? Everybody seems to have considered him a highly unpleasant sort of fellow."

"Yes, Akers was not well-liked, he was very concerned with himself and his reputation, and his tongue was acid enough. But he never angered me; I thought it was rather amusing, even, at times. He seemed to get along well enough with me; it was he who invited me to dine, on the very same day. I came across him in the mathematics library, actually, and he seemed all pleased and hugging himself, and he said something like 'Ah, Weatherburn, Weatherburn, lovely day isn't it, heh, heh.' And I said 'You seem in a very good mood,' and he said 'I certainly am, got reason to be, heh, heh, heh. Let's dine tonight, what do you say? Meet at eight for dinner at the Irish pub?' And I said 'Why not?' and that was it. It's a nice place; leather booths where one can discuss mathematics and even get out paper and write things down if one wants to, without the people at the neighbouring tables thinking one is quite mad. The police even wanted to know what we ate! I had to tell them that we started with whisky, and then we ordered wine. Akers asked for water as well, as he had to take some medicine or other. Then we had Irish stew. It was quite succulent. I can't think what they were after, though;

perhaps proving I was drunk?"

"Dear me," I said. "It all sounds so pleasant and ordinary. One simply *cannot* realise that poor Mr. Akers died just immediately after it."

"No, I know! I c-c-cannot grasp it myself! And why should I be dining with them always just before? What does it all mean?"

"Well, how did you come to be dining with Mr. Beddoes, then?" I wondered.

"Oh, the police went into that endlessly. Why, it wasn't even Beddoes who asked me at all. It was Crawford. He said why not make up a threesome to dine the following night."

"Really?!" I exclaimed, struck by this piece of information. "But did he not come, then?"

"No, in the late afternoon, he left me a message to say he felt unwell, and shouldn't be able to make it in the evening, and that we two should go anyway and enjoy ourselves."

"So that is how you came to dine with Mr. Beddoes, and find yourself in such a dreadfully compromising position," I said, my mind racing. "I remember now that at the garden party following Professor Cayley's lecture, Mr. Crawford said to Mr. Beddoes that he wanted to dine with him soon."

"Yes, the police got quite excited about this idea of Crawford being involved, I don't know why. They asked me where we were when Crawford spoke, who might have heard us, and so on and so forth. I suppose it might just possibly be an indication of my innocence, although really, I can hardly follow the reasoning; it all seems so absurd. After all, I suppose I might just as well have suddenly decided to murder my dinner partner, no matter who actually proposed having dinner together."

"No!" I exclaimed suddenly. "Perhaps I see what it means — maybe they are not so much thinking about you, but about Mr. Crawford! Is that conceivable? Could Mr. Crawford have done it on purpose?"

"Poor C-Crawford — I suppose he could replace me as a

suspect," he smiled, "but it seems just as ridiculous."

"Well, perhaps it does to you. But that must be what the police are thinking. I expect they will go to see him — and if they don't, I shall! I should like to know what he meant by it, sending you into such a disaster of trouble!"

"Oh, come, he didn't do it on purpose," he said.

"Visiting time is up," intervened the Officer in the doorway abruptly. "The van is here! Come along, sir!"

"They don't have the right to hold me for more than two days without sending me in front of a magistrate," Arthur told me. "That's to happen the day after tomorrow, and the Prosecutor shall present his evidence then. I can't think he'll have much to present, so I am not too worried; one can only be sent to trial if there is some presumption of guilt."

"Come along!" reiterated the Officer.

There was a sharp, rather military echo to his behaviour; I suppose it must be a little awkward to give nasty orders to prisoners who may all the time be perfectly innocent. We are, after all, supposed to presume people innocent until proven guilty (and even that word "proven" is a doubtful one; no mathematician could ever be satisfied with "proof beyond a reasonable doubt"!)

Arthur arose and bid me goodbye with a little twinkle in his brown eyes.

"I really cannot take this seriously," he said. "It shall all be chalked up to experience; nights on prison beds for me, visits to prison cells for you. Let's just hope it does not go on until the charm of originality is entirely lost!"

"Oh, Arthur," I began, but did not continue. His words had suddenly awakened a little pang of fear inside me. Surely it would soon be over — yet the very word "surely" meant there was some doubt. And what if the magistrate should send him to trial? And then?

No — it can't happen!

Still, I feel I simply *must* speak with Mr. Crawford. I shall ask him what he meant by it; he ought to know all the trou-

84

ble he has caused. And for that matter, he may well be the next person upon whom that very same trouble descends!

Well, I do hope I can send you better news in my next letter!

Till then, your loving

Vanessa

Cambridge, Thursday, May 3rd, 1888

My dear Dora,

This morning was the funeral of poor Mr. Beddoes; I saw it in yesterday's evening paper, and decided to attend. I arrived at the cemetery carrying a modest bunch of flowers whose very colours, all to be devoted to the ceremonious celebration of death, seemed sorrowful.

Mr. Beddoes was certainly a man of many friends, for the knot of people who stood around his freshly dug grave as the coffin was lowered was dense and compact. I recognised most of the members of his circle that have become familiar to me over the past month, closely surrounding Mrs. Beddoes, who kept her gentle face hidden under a black veil.

The service ended, and slowly, respectfully, the people began to drift away. I walked near Mrs. Beddoes; a sob escaped her as she turned away.

"My dear Mrs. Beddoes," said the man nearest her, whom I identified as the snappish Mr. Withers of the garden party, "the loss of your husband is a terrible blow for all of us; how much greater must it be for yourself. I wish I could find words to comfort you."

His words were kind, but something about the way he said them was not: he was unctuous, and seemed to be striving to make an impression. He handed Mrs. Beddoes into her carriage as though he took it upon himself to show that he, at least, was filled with noble feelings. Perhaps Mrs. Beddoes felt something of the kind, for she answered him with no more than an indistinct murmur. Mr. Withers turned away and moved off with Mr. Wentworth.

"What a horrible story this is," he said, with the same peculiar emphasis.

"Yes, isn't it," said Mr. Wentworth, in an uninviting tone of voice. But Mr. Withers was not to be stopped so easily.

"A good thing the murderer was discovered so quickly," he said.

"Oh, well ..." mumbled Mr. Wentworth. "I don't know ..."

"I've heard new evidence has turned up," continued Mr. Withers. "I wonder what it is. Well — it'll all come out at the trial."

I speeded my steps to escape from this horrible conversation, in which I detected an edge of distorted pleasure. Espying Mr. Morrison some way ahead, I hastened to his side. He greeted me warmly, and took my arm as we left the cemetery and began to wend our way back to the town.

"So, you too have come?" he asked me. "Beddoes was a Mentor to me, but I did not realise that you were amongst his friends, Miss Duncan."

"I met him twice," I replied. "He seemed a kind gentleman, and his wife was very welcoming."

The small crowd was dispersing along the way; some walked faster, some slower, while yet others had taken carriages back. I quickened my steps somewhat, so as to isolate us a little.

"Mr. Morrison," I said urgently, in a low voice, "I just heard Mr. Withers saying that there is some new evidence against Arthur. What can it be?"

He looked at me with some surprise, and then said, a little coldly, "I really have no idea. But whatever it may be, I fully expect that the police will deal with it adequately."

This response was a blow so unexpected that I could do no more than stare at him in shock. The colour rose in my cheeks.

He became extremely embarrassed. There was a horribly awkward silence. I stared at him, and for a while he seemed to struggle to express himself.

"I perceive what you are thinking, Miss Duncan," he finally began. "But do you think my position is an easy one? Here I am, suddenly informed that my closest friend is a murderer. What do you expect me to do? Condone it?"

"No, I — but Arthur is not — but can you really believe — you think, then, that he is guilty?" I stammered, feeling my initial hot protestation ebb and die on my lips.

"I suppose I believe that the police know what they are doing," he said with a sigh. "And you do not? Are you not letting yourself be blinded by your feelings?"

I found no answer, words failed me. Mumbling a negative, I left him, barely answering his goodbye, and turned towards my own home with feet like lead. I felt desperately tired, and the prospect of the afternoon's teaching weighed upon me. I made my best efforts, but my mind was occupied, and I must have appeared something of an automaton; I can scarcely remember what I did. The evening passed in tormented reflections, and as soon as it was dark, I fell into bed, hoping that sleep would bring me renewed hope. I was unaware of going to sleep, but found myself in the midst of a strange dream. I was walking in delightful gardens, and all around me were people whom I thought to be friends. I did not know them, but I loved them, and my heart was warm and trusting. Then, one by one, they began to turn their eyes upon me, and fix me with strange stares, until the whole crowd held me in its inimical gaze. My joy changed to abject fear and I began to back away from them slowly. But they advanced upon me step by step, until I found myself pressed back against a tree, whose large branches spread above me. Then he who stood in front took out a noose, and cast the rope over a branch. The noose hung down and swayed gently back and forth. He began to speak, and all the others took up the chant, repeating "Hang her by the neck, hang her by the neck, hang her by the neck." He approached me, threw out his hand, grasped my throat. I wanted to scream, but could not — he was strangling me! I awoke then, in a state of terror such that my eyes were starting from their sockets. I lay trembling in bed for many minutes, my forehead damp with fear. A small noise from somewhere within the room caused me to leap upright in shock. It was borne in upon me suddenly, more strongly than before, that *somewhere was a murderer*, who had struck the fatal blows; I verily believed he was there in my room, come to put an end to me. I sat rigid, but everything was silent. After an endless time, I dared to move my hand slowly outwards, felt on my nighttable, seized my box of matches, and struck one. The tiny light flickered and gave me courage. I struck another, and lit my candles; then on shaking legs, I forced myself to search through all of my three rooms. There was no one. I shot the bolt on my door and closed all of the windows, which were open to admit the fresh soft air, then flooded my face with cold water. Too afraid to return to sleep, I lit the lamp and sat at my table with pen and paper to write this letter. The morning light is just appearing now, and I feel better; perhaps I have been quite foolish. I shall return to bed.

I send you several tender kisses; if only you were here!

Your Vanessa

Cambridge, Friday, May 4th, 1888

Oh, my dearest sister,

The most frightful, frightful thing has happened — I must tell you everything, or I shall burst! Indeed, it is becoming such a help to me to write to you, that I don't know how I could do without it. Even as I sit down to write, I feel my tangled thoughts loosening and taking shape, and it seems easier for me to decide whether I should take any action, and what it should be.

The day before yesterday, after lessons, I had given Emily a short note for her uncle, in which I asked him if he could kindly provide me with Mr. Crawford's address, as I needed to speak with him. She had brought an answer yesterday, a sober little note (exactly as though yesterday's scene had not taken place, or perhaps in response to it), containing the directions to Mr. Crawford's rooms in St. John's College: go to the Front Gate of the College in St. John's Street, enter the first Court, he lodges in the tower just to the right. The very first thing this morning, I put on my hat and determined to betake myself there.

I walked along, and the familiar sights along the Chesterton road passed almost in a blur; the purling river caught up to me as I neared the town, and followed me with its song, as though mocking me gently for striding purposefully along a road, while it wended its heedless way through the green. I know, of course, that the town was built around the river, but it strikes my fancy to imagine the opposite; it so often seems to me that the river crosses the town where it will, disrespectful of stone walls and arched gates, be they of colleges or prisons.

As I advanced, I planned and resolved in my head what words I should use, and how I should approach the coming discussion. For I must admit, Dora, that as a form of reaction no doubt, my mind had become completely obsessed and overtaken by the single, dominating idea which had arisen in it during my talk with Arthur: namely, that Mr. Crawford had deliberately arranged the dinner with Mr. Weatherburn and Mr. Beddoes, and then excused himself at the last minute, with the express purpose of making Mr. Weatherburn appear guilty, or at least placing him in a position so compromising that it would certainly take some time before his innocence could be determined. And what could this mean, unless Mr. Crawford had a particular reason to behave so, a very precise reason. And the nature of that reason — I could hardly bring myself to look it in the face! *What might Mr. Crawford have done?*

My steps faltered; I felt a cold wave of fear. Was I about to pay a visit to *the very one who ...* My mind shied away from the thought like a nervous pony, and I began to feel guilty and foolish. Although there is no reason to think that the charm of the garden party where I met him should have the slightest bearing upon the nature of the man (indeed, he had struck me as rather an overbearing character), still, the very fact of having been together with him on that sunny day, and of his being a friend and colleague of Arthur, seemed to raise an almost insuperable barrier between myself and the dangerous supposition which hovered on the fringe of my mind. After a moment, I could not give it any real credence. It seemed to me that could I only see and talk to Mr. Crawford, and question him about the dinner in simple, ordinary terms, everything would be straightened out at once. And I continued on in haste to the College.

I was not entirely sure whether such a stranger as myself, a female to boot, actually possessed any right to enter the sacred quadrangles. I turned into St. John's Street and stopped for a moment in front of the ancient Front Gate of the College, which rose above me, glorious as a cathedral, solid as a brick fortress, mysterious as a medieval castle. I looked up at the strange gilded and painted carvings, and from his niche, St. John gazed down benevolently and encouragingly upon me.

Inside the great gate was a Porter's Lodge, and I went to address myself there for permission to enter. However, the Porter was not within. I stood for a moment, hesitating, looking through into the first Court, where a perfectly square green sward met my enchanted eyes. There seemed to be some little commotion going on, and I even saw people crossing the sacred grass, only to be swiftly accosted by an officious beadle. I daringly advanced, stepped out of the gate into the Court, and turned to the right to locate Mr.

Crawford's tower.

There, right there, immediately, at the base of his very tower, I saw something which afforded me the most fearsome shock — you cannot imagine how my heart leaped and then contracted within my breast! The base of the tower was occupied by a tight knot of policemen and spectators, buzzing like a hive of bees. My stomach sank within me, and I felt a horrible foreboding. I approached the group, and with trepidation, steeled myself to ask what was amiss.

"Someone's dead," I was told.

"Who is it?" I asked, my heart pounding as if to break through the bars of its natural cage.

"Don't know, some mathematician who lives here, they say."

A tremor ran through the tiny crowd, and it parted in front of the door to let out several people who now emerged. These appeared to be policemen, including the high-up kind who wear no uniforms; they carried various kinds of equipment for photography and other measurements. They exchanged words with each other and shook hands, and then moved out, letting two white-clad figures carrying a stretcher pass through. The figure on the stretcher was completely covered over, and the white-clad gentlemen were absolutely expressionless. They were accompanied by a last gentleman, who seemed to be of a medical disposition.

The members of this important-looking group began to take leave of each other and move off. Impelled by an uncontrollable sense of urgency, I rushed up to them and said, thinking that a simple statement of my case would serve better than questions which could be interpreted as idle curiosity, "Excuse me, but I have come here to see a Mr. Crawford on urgent business."

"Mr. Crawford will not be seeing anyone on urgent business any more, Miss, I'm afraid," the medical gentleman told me.

"Oh, please don't say it was he who was just carried away

on a stretcher!" I cried pleadingly.

"I am afraid that it was, indeed, Miss. I am very sorry."

"Is he dead? Whatever happened to him?" I cried, my mind grappling with this new development. Had Mr. Crawford been killed? Then his murderer was still at large, and Arthur was proven innocent! Had he died naturally? Then whatever information he held was lost forever, and Arthur was in danger. Had he committed suicide? Then perhaps the suppositions which had been flirting in my mind were true, and there was some chance of proving them.

"It looks like cardiac arrest," said the medical man. "But we will not know for sure until the post-mortem."

"Cardiac arrest?"

"The heart stops."

"Whyever would it do that?"

"Oh, there are many possible reasons, Miss. The man may have a weak heart, or have had a great shock, or have drunk too much. He certainly seems to have been drinking whisky when it happened. The exact circumstances will become clearer when I do the post-mortem. I'll cut him open, you know, and examine the stomach and bladder contents and things."

"Oh! Oh, dear," I said, momentarily rendered speechless by the graphic image thus depicted. "Oh. I see. Oh. But please ... can I just ask you ... was it a natural death?"

"A natural death? What do you mean?"

"I mean, he was not murdered?!" I burst out of a sudden, amazed and rather ashamed of my own boldness.

"Murdered? How can you murder a man by cardiac arrest? By frightening him to death? Are you thinking of poison? My dear young lady, you have been reading too much Gothic literature. I strongly advise you to return home and repose yourself, and then calmly set about thinking how you can manage your urgent business without consulting Mr. Crawford."

He turned away and joined the others, who were leaving.

The policemen at the tower door were now preventing any-one from entering, and I wended my way slowly towards the exit, left the College and wandered slowly, almost aimlessly, towards the town centre. The blow appeared truly dreadful. My mind spun with possibilities. Could Mr. Crawford possi-bly have committed suicide, weighed down by a double guilt? Perhaps, if so, he had left a note, which would excul-pate Arthur! Could he have been poisoned? What would that mean? If he could not be proved to have been murdered, then what could be done?

I looked around me, and spying a passing hansom, I flagged it suddenly and directed the man to Castle Hill. Entering the gaol, I requested to visit Mr. Weatherburn.

I was led to the door of the visiting room, and caused to stand outside it, looking in through a mesh, while a prison warder stood nearby watching and listening. Arthur entered the room, and faced me through the mesh. He looked a little pale and drawn, but his eyes still twinkled as he looked through at me. I felt a rush of warmth; time and place were momentarily forgotten.

"I shall not tell you that you shouldn't come here," he said smiling. "In fact, I am delighted to see you. I do not want to complain about my lodgings, but I must admit that I am suf-fering rather excruciatingly from boredom. Surely I must be allowed to have something to read, or at the very least paper and pencil! Do you think you could bring me something?"

"Of course," I assured him. "I feel that I will quite soon become an expert on prison regulations. I shall find out everything that can be known about visiting hours and visit-ing rights. Unfortunately, I cannot come in the afternoons, because of lessons."

"Well, I am delighted to see you this morning," he assured me warmly. "But do you know, I c-cannot think that this unfortunate situation will be unduly prolonged. The hearing is to be this afternoon. I can't think what evidence they mean to present."

"This afternoon! Evidence! Oh, Arthur — but there has been a new development — seeing you made me forget it for an instant. Mr. Crawford is dead!"

He started back in amazement, and the warder gazed at us suspiciously, with the heavy stare of a cow watching the plough pass back and forth. Arthur returned to me.

"Crawford dead — good heavens! But there is a rampant murderer out there somewhere. What a horrible thing. Yet as far as I am concerned, I wonder why they do not simply release me at once!"

I saw that he imagined (as I had) that Mr. Crawford had been murdered in the same way as the other two, and that he himself was in consequence quite probably exculpated. I felt annoyed with myself for giving the information in such a misleading manner, and hastened to disabuse him, hating it.

"He was found dead this very morning, of heart failure, and no one knows yet whether he died naturally or not, or whether it was a murder at all," I explained.

His attitude changed somewhat; he drooped, and considered this news without speaking.

"Arthur," I said, "do you not think Mr. Crawford might himself be the murderer, and have died of a heart attack over the excitement of it all, or perhaps have killed himself from remorse?"

"I can't believe it," he answered slowly. "And yet, someone must be the murderer. I don't know what to think."

"Perhaps there is some way of finding out, of proving that it was Mr. Crawford," I said. "Do you not think we could find out exactly what he was doing on the night Mr. Akers was killed?"

"Ten to one he was alone in his rooms, with no witnesses," he sighed.

"Or he might have been the mysterious searcher in Mr. Akers' rooms," I said. "Do you remember how the newspaper article said it looked as though his papers had been disarranged by a search? Can you imagine anything that he might have been looking for?"

"Well, it seems awfully silly, but I suppose he could have been looking for some mathematics, you know. Something about the n-body problem that rumour held they were both working on," he answered. "I mean, pretty much everybody was aware of some slight current of rivalry between the two of them."

"That is very important!" I was beginning, when most suddenly and annoyingly, the warder stepped towards me, and said, "Time's up, Madam."

"Oh, excuse me — I mean, I'm sorry — I mean thank you!" I said confusedly, gathering my things together. But I could not tear myself away. Arthur stood motionless, as though deprived of the energy to return to another day of prison life.

"I will come back tomorrow morning," I told him, "and bring you something to read and write."

"Madam!" said the warder in a peremptory tone.

"Yes, yes, I am so sorry! Goodbye, Arthur, goodbye."

That foolish word did not express one hundredth of what I should have liked to tell him. But no better one came to me.

It is evening now, and I have finished my teaching; from lack of ideas, and secret obsession with the indictment, I spent a large part of the afternoon reading aloud from Oscar Wilde's *Happy Prince*. I must say that I have rarely read anything less "happy"; it did nothing to improve my mood. I cannot help jumping at every noise I hear, thinking that it must be Arthur returning home, released by decision of the magistrate. I can do nothing at all. I must remain patient — it is difficult — and pass the time by writing to you, which soothes me wonderfully and clears my brain.

Oh, if only, only Mr. Crawford had been hit upon the head! Oh, what a dreadful, dreadful thing to say! But he is dead anyway, and perhaps being hit over the head is faster and more painless than cardiac arrest. Well, if I cannot *quite* bring myself to wish that he had been hit over the head, I wish at least that he had killed himself from remorse, and left a note explaining it all. It may yet be so.

Well, I will put a little piece of bread on my plate; I have no appetite at all, but I will *not* give way to weakness. Tea and toast for supper, and audacious investigation tomorrow! I shall model myself on that very famous London detective — what is his name? — who lives in Baker Street.

Please pray for me, and write to me when you can, and all of your own news, and all you think of mine.

Your anxious sister

Vanessa

Monday, May 7th, 1888

Dear Dora,

I discovered on Saturday that the Prosecutor asked the magistrate quite simply for a postponement of Arthur's hearing on Friday, considering that Mr. Crawford's death was relevant. The magistrate granted a minimal postponement, only until the first thing this morning. It is not a public affair, so I could not enter, and was obliged to wait outside the Courthouse. Do you know — I truly believed that I expected to see Arthur emerge, a free man. And yet, it did not end that way, and now I feel as though deep within some secret part of me, I feared and expected this all along.

By eleven o'clock, the proceedings were over. I had not seen Arthur either entering or leaving, and in a great fever of doubt and dismay, I ended up returning to Castle Hill and enquiring as to his whereabouts. As it turned out, he had been quite simply remanded to his cell in the prison. Upon pleading to be allowed to see him in a near panic, I received the placid answer "Why not?" and within a short time we were facing each other as usual through the door with the grille. He appeared pale and dismayed as he recounted the morning's events; oh, Dora, after the presentation of the Public Prosecutor, it was found that there was sufficient evidence against him to warrant a trial! Upon hearing this, I suffocated with all the indignation that Arthur did not seem to feel on his own account.

"What evidence can they possibly have?" I cried.

"I am not sure," he answered wearily. "They must have something special, because I have been formally accused of all three murders, in front of nothing less than a Grand Jury, given the heinous nature of the crime, according to the Public Prosecutor. What really happened today is that the Public Prosecutor convinced the jury that there is enough evidence to warrant a deep and complete investigation into the situation. Because this is all that he is trying to accomplish, only the Prosecutor need speak and introduce witnesses; there is no defence, as I am not considered to be on trial, although I can tell you that it feels very like it in the most unpleasant way. This Prosecutor called the medical examiner as witness and had him tell the Grand Jury how Akers and Beddoes were killed and the usual nonsense about the restaurant. But then he began on Crawford, and explained that *he* was killed by downing a good half-bottle of his own whisky which contained some kind of poison! Then came the strange part: he claimed he could justify that it would have been perfectly possible for me to have murdered Crawford, since the poison could have been introduced into the bottle at any time in the last weeks or months. He said that he would present solid evidence showing that I could have done it — it's a total mystery to me! And then he went on to say that the motive for all these killings was mathematical. He explained at length that although a murder for a mathematical result might be a difficult thing for the layman to understand, the jury should realise that the desire for glory reigned as strong in the breasts of mathematicians as in anyone else's. The jury then unanimously declared that there was sufficient evidence against me to warrant a trial for murder. It's fixed to begin on the 16th of May, and until then I'm condemned to remain here without bail."

In spite of his forced calm, I saw that Arthur's confidence had been shaken, and that he was not at all serene about the upcoming trial. Worse, I did not know how to offer him any comfort, for my own inside seemed wracked with fear at this horrible, unexpected turn of events. When the warder ordered me to leave, I found it difficult to tear myself away, and yet remaining was unbearable also, as it was almost impossible for me to conceal my feelings of fear and distress.

The only drop of comfort in my misery came in the form of a visit from Mr. Morrison, who arrived this afternoon instead of Miss Forsyth, to collect Emily from lessons. He hung about, making conversation, until the usual little melee of pupils, governesses and mothers had departed. I was moving silently about the schoolroom, putting it in order, unwilling to speak to him, but he approached me with a firm step.

"I wish to say something, Miss Duncan," he said.

"I am not sure I wish to hear it," I answered icily.

"Oh, yes, you are, I am sure that you are," he replied undaunted. "I want to thank you, really. You convinced me the other day that you were right; I was being a fool. So I went to visit Weatherburn."

I turned to him in surprise. "You went to the prison?"

"Why not? You have been there, have you not?"

"Yes, I have," I replied, "but I did not think that you ..."

"I wouldn't, normally," he interposed. "Dashed embarrassing, really, doing this kind of thing. You women don't understand what it's like for men; you have all kinds of private conversations all the time, in your homes and over tea and everywhere; you're used to it! But we don't do that kind of thing much between ourselves; we're simply no good at it. We *do* sometimes talk about feelings, you know — but there's a special language to do it with; it's all sort of abstract, or has to seem to be. I'm expressing myself dashed badly. I'm very sorry!"

"No, you aren't. I do understand," I told him.

"And then, behind prison bars, it's worse than ever. There you are, separated by that beastly grille, hearing all kind of people groaning and moaning, children crying, like you've fallen into some Hieronymus Bosch version of hell. And I'm supposed to look him in the eyes in the middle of all this and ask him directly if he has or hasn't actually bopped people over the head."

"But you did it?"

"Well, hang it, yes, I did, actually."

"And what did he say?"

"He was most awfully surprised that I asked him. It was difficult for him to bring himself to come right out and tell me directly that he'd done nothing of the kind. It had nothing to do with the truth of the matter; I saw just how he felt. I'd have felt exactly the same; like the whole idea's so silly one doesn't even like to deny it — it lends it too much seriousness. I did feel like an idiot — it was as though I'd asked the same question to myself! I was wrong, Miss Duncan, and you were right. It's all an enormous mistake."

"But then, you *do* see that we have to do something!" I exclaimed.

"I do see it, and jolly well wish I could think of something to do," he answered, anxiously touching the small moustache which ornaments his upper lip. "But apart from standing by, I don't see much. I just wanted to say this: if you undertake anything at all, do *please* let me know, and count on me. *Don't* go investigating or anything by yourself. It might be dangerous!"

It was nice of him, I'm sure, but if I only had something to investigate, I would certainly rush out and do it at once. There *must* be something. How can I just wait for the trial — and then, even worse, sit through it day after day and *watch*?

I must think. Oh, Dora dear, *do* help me!

Your most worried

Vanessa

Wednesday, May 9th, 1888

Dearest Dora,

The whole of Cambridge is deeply shocked by the death of Mr. Crawford, forming, as it does, the latest in what is now appearing like a series of mysterious deaths of mathematicians. Although no official information about the means of his death has been forthcoming, so that most people really do not know whether the poor man was murdered or not, popular opinion definitely holds it that he was, and that the series of three murders are closely related and were all committed by the same hand. Visions of a secretly insane mathematician, the crazy look in his wild eyes hidden by his heavy eyelids and typically absent-minded demeanor, are rampant in the conversations I have heard in the shops and on the streets. The question of whether the arrested man can now be considered as the obvious murderer is discussed openly.

I cannot seem to think about anything else, and after tormenting myself this morning for some time, I resolved that I must take some action at any cost — anything rather than sit passively by in worry and anguish! But what? My very first decision is that from now on, I will write down every single thing that happens in my letters to you; no detail shall be left out, and I shall put down every idea, every notion that passes through my mind, every word I hear. From this point on, these letters shall be more than letters: they shall be documents to be studied, and you shall read them and re-read them, Dora, dear, and tell me what you think. Somewhere within all this mass of information the truth *must* be hidden, and we must be able to find it!

Having taken this decision, I felt too impatient to sit still, and noting that it does not exclude direct action, I made up my mind to locate the doctor who attended Mr. Crawford at his death, and discover from him if Mr. Crawford's death must necessarily be considered to be a murder or if, after all, there cannot be some other explanation ...

I put this plan into action immediately, by betaking myself to the St. Andrew's Police Station, and enquiring quite directly of the Officer behind the counter, what was the name of the doctor who had attended Mr. Crawford's corpse. He was at first reluctant to discuss the grisly event, but I exercised a little charm and persuasion, until he consented to take out and open a heavy file containing the previous day's log, and produced the name of a certain Dr. Jackson. I then had to discover the address of this Doctor at the Post Office. There were two Doctor Jacksons, but one of them lived extremely near the College where poor Mr. Crawford met his end, and would naturally have been called for. So off I went as fast as I could to his office.

Dr. Jackson must be quite popular, for his waiting room was already full, and I felt that addressing myself to the Doctor out of my proper turn would probably engender some ill feelings towards me in the breasts of my fellow waiters. In spite of this, as soon as the door to the Doctor's private office opened, releasing a patient, I jumped to my feet and hastened forwards.

The Doctor put out his head at the same moment that I put mine inside, so that they met with a bump! We looked at each other for a moment in silent amazement — mine, perhaps, even greater than his, for I saw that he was not at all the gentleman that I expected, the one I had briefly conversed with in the courtyard of the College yesterday. Nevertheless, I seized the moment, and said hastily, "Doctor, I am not at all ill, but I should only like to have a very brief but very urgent word with you."

He hesitated, perhaps somewhat annoyed to be interrupted in his routine, or fearful that his waiting patients would be displeased, as indeed they were, witness the murmurs and grumbling directed at my back. However, he only said, "Let it not be long then, as you can see that I am extremely busy," and beckoning me into his private office, he shut the door.

"Yes, of course," I said. "I have learned from the police that you were the doctor who was called yesterday to see the mathematician who died yesterday at St. John's College, Mr. Crawford."

He acquiesced with a short nod. "Yes. When he was found they sent out immediately to fetch a doctor. People always do it, even though obviously there was nothing I could do."

"I knew Mr. Crawford very well," I began, quite untruthfully, "and was arriving at his rooms to visit him when I learned that he was dead. The police were still present in his rooms. I simply wish to ask you how he died, and above all — *was he murdered*? It is of fundamental importance!"

"Ah, now that, I cannot tell you," he replied simply.

"Why not?" I began, preparing to plead, persuade and cajole.

"Quite simply because I have no idea. He died of heart failure, that is all I know. It may have simply been a heart attack, which itself may have been caused by a shock of some kind, or simply by a weakness of the heart."

"But could it possibly have been a murder? Could such an attack be caused by some poison?" I insisted, wishing to hear the possibilities from his own lips rather than tell him what I knew.

"It could, certainly, although I cannot make any statement to the effect that such was the case."

"What kind of poison could cause such an effect?"

"It could be a derivative of belladonna, or a product of the foxglove, such as the typical heart medicine digitalin, taken in an excessive dose; those would be the most likely candidates, if any poison was used at all."

"Ah!" I cried. "But tell me now; cannot the doctor tell which of these, if any, is the cause of a death by heart failure?"

"It is sometimes possible, for instance if the medicine was taken pure, some smell may remain on the patient's lips. But Mr. Crawford's whole room smelled overwhelmingly of whisky, and there was an open, empty bottle upon the table."

"Could the poison have been in the bottle?"

"It is not impossible."

"But can it be determined?"

"Yes, certainly, and it will no doubt be determined or already has been, by chemical analysis of the remaining drops in the bottle, as well as by a post-mortem of the dead man's body. The case is completely independent of me now; as soon as I saw that the death did not have an obvious, natural explanation, I called in the police, and they of course brought their own doctor, who will perform all further medical examinations."

I understood that the medical man who accompanied the police must have been this doctor. I hopefully asked the Doctor if he knew him personally, but he did not. I was about to take my leave, when suddenly I turned back.

"Doctor, if you could not smell or otherwise detect any trace of poison, what exactly made you think that Mr. Crawford's death was not a natural one?" I asked. "After all, many people die from heart attacks, do they not?"

"Now, that is a tricky question, my dear," he said, and his severe, narrow face actually creased into a somewhat embarrassed smile. "You are certainly of a very enquiring cast of mind. I must admit that under normal circumstances, it is more than likely that I would have simply diagnosed heart failure, made out a certificate for the poor gentlemen, and that would have been the end of the story."

"And what exactly about Mr. Crawford's death constituted abnormal circumstances?" I insisted.

"Oh, well," he hemmed and hawed. "Nothing medical, at all, really. It was just ... well, really, it was the fact of this death of a mathematician following so shortly after the previous ones. Why, nobody seems to be dying at all in Cambridge, lately, except for mathematicians, it seems!"

"Oh!" I said. "I see. But then why should you feel uneasy about your own suspicions? Your reason seems valid enough."

"Oh, well, it makes you wonder, really, how many of the deaths you pass along as normal are really murders, don't you know — only the possibility simply never occurred to you. Now get along, get along, my dear. You are an alarming one for getting things out of people. I really must get back to my patients!"

"Thank you so very much, Doctor," I said warmly. "You have helped me enormously. Good day," and I backed out of the door into the matron whose turn it had been to see the Doctor, and who was on the point of opening it in order to complain about the unjustified delay.

"Oh, I am so sorry!" I said.

"I should hope so, indeed," she answered in high dudgeon.

I took my leave speedily to avoid more scolding, and walked back towards St. Andrew's, this time in the hope of finding out the identity of the other doctor, and anything that was to be found out about the post-mortem. It was not yet ten o'clock, and I felt that the Officer at the Police Station might not appreciate my returning with further questions so soon after he had already helped me. So I compelled myself to stop rushing about, and turning into Petty Cury, I directed myself to my favourite tea room in Peas Hill, where I am presently sitting, writing to you and hoping that if I delay somewhat, another Officer will in the meantime have come to relieve him. My cup of tea sits in front of me, round, kind and comforting, and I stir it slowly, while lending an ear to the conversations going on around me.

Oh, Dora, everywhere I go, street, waiting room, tea-shop, I hear people discussing and gossiping about the murders. And half the time, oh dear, they seem to be saying that fortunately the murderer appears to have been apprehended by the police with lightning speed, and is already under lock and key. I have been straining my ears in vain; not once have I heard a single person respond that the unlucky being under the aforementioned lock and key might be no more than an innocent victim of error. I still cling to the hope that Mr. Crawford's death has some other, more natural explanation. Oh, surely the police will understand this! Yet I feel worried; if only I could find out if what I suspect is right or wrong.

Later

I have just come out of the Police Station, where I drew a terrible blank. They claim that I have no right at all to know anything about the results of the post-mortem, which are communicated only to the lawyers involved in prosecuting and defending the prisoner. There was really nothing to do; the policeman behind the counter was not the same one as this morning, but he was a stolid creature resembling nothing so much as a wall, and there was clearly nothing to be extracted from him. I was compelled to leave gloomily, and now it is midday, and I must post this letter and begin the work by which I earn my daily bread. It is beginning to seem rather irksome to me ...

Write to me soon, dear

Vanessa

Cambridge, Monday, May 14th, 1888

My dearest Dora,

I have spent the whole of this week in a state of intolerable nerves. I cannot sleep, and my teaching suffers, although I try as hard as I can to use it to distract myself from the coming trial.

The Court has appointed Counsel to defend Arthur. He is a rather cold-natured, dry, elderly gentleman named Mr.

Haversham. He has questioned Arthur at length, of course, and has told him that he must base the defence either on lack of evidence, or on an alternative theory. I asked to speak to Mr. Haversham, and he questioned me about Arthur and about the dinner at Mrs. Burke-Jones' home, and about Mr. Crawford, especially his conversation with Mr. Beddoes on the day of the garden party, and how he had expressed the intention of dining with him soon. Rather timidly, I presented him with my theory of Mr. Crawford's guilt and suicide, and asked him if he thought it could not possibly obtain. Not that I want to destroy the poor man's memory, God forbid! But it could hardly hurt him now, whether true or false, and could still serve as an alternative theory. Mr. Haversham said that this theory may provide a valid line of defence, and that he would make use of it. It was odd, however — he did not seem to consider, even for a moment, whether one might care to determine what really happened. It seemed as though all that mattered to him was the possibility that each theory might or might not convince a jury. Such is the nature of lawyers, I suppose. About Mr. Crawford, he said there was really no need to prove anything, but simply to show that it was a possibility just as valid as that presented by the opposition. He says that my memories of the conversation between Mr. Crawford and Mr. Beddoes on the day of the garden party might serve at least as a faint corroboration of Arthur's assertion that his dinner with Mr. Beddoes was planned by Mr. Crawford; he would like to call me as a witness, but he thinks that Mr. Bexheath may do so first. Mr. Haversham says that opposing Counsel, Mr. Bexheath, representing the Crown, is known for his cruel accuracy, and that nothing vague must be put up to him, or he will tear it apart. The Judge, he told us, is Sir William Penrose, who is known, though not for leniency, at least for fairness, open-minded willingness to listen, and lack of prejudice.

Mr. Haversham says that the Prosecution must be developing a theory of its own, which he does not know, but that he will find it out at the Prosecutor's Opening Statement, which begins the trial, and then will be able to develop responses to the various points in the following days. He began to make a list of witnesses he shall call for the defence. Alas, it is rather short, as there is no real line of defence except for the lack of evidence and the unsubstantiated hypothesis of Mr. Crawford's guilt. But he says that his procedure will become clearer after the Prosecution's Opening Statement. He seems a trustworthy man, although distant. I do hope he will handle everything for the best!

I continue to visit Arthur in prison regularly; I have the right to bring books and papers for him, which are examined carefully before being handed to him parsimoniously by the Wardens. The condemned prisoners do not have the right to such things; they are allowed to send or receive a letter or a visit only every three months. Some of the prisoners here are condemned to hard labour, and they spend the day wearily treading on a treadmill; others are confined to their cell, *1888* alone, for 23 hours out of the 24, the remaining hour being spent circulating round and round the tiny courtyard in silence, which is called "exercise". There are quite young children among the prisoners, some no older than Emily, I think! Sometimes we hear them crying as we talk. But the warder never allows me to move an inch from my precisely prescribed path: direct to the visiting door with its grille, and directly back out again. With Arthur, we no longer talk much about the ordeal awaiting him, but of the books we read, and the things we would like to do when this is all over. It has become almost a natural evidence that we will do them together. It is strange, that although the grille divides us, and our every word is overheard by the warder, and the future is clouded, we have drawn infinitely closer to each other; it is as though the circumstantial separation has allowed the souls to come together, whilst they were timid and hesitating when the way was clear.

I remain ever, your

Vanessa

Cambridge, Thursday, May 17th, 1888

Dear Dora,

Arthur's trial began this morning. It will run every weekday until all the witnesses have been questioned. In fact, it really began yesterday, with a great long ceremony of selecting the jury, which took all day, and the continuation, which is really the beginning of the actual proceedings, was then set for this morning.

They are open to the public. Oh, Dora, what a horrible thing it all is — you cannot imagine! There is a public gallery in the Courthouse, and there sit a great many idle people who come there out of pure morbid curiosity. Arthur sits in the dock, and they stare at him, and whisper to each other perfectly audibly. No one seems to believe he might be innocent, and there is constant talk of hanging. Oh, how I hate that loathsome "public"! There they sit, whispering and mumbling and sometimes eating food which they bring in bags so as not to have to leave during the proceedings. I try to sit as far away from anyone as possible.

The very start of the proceedings had nothing to do with Arthur at all; the Judge, a very gracious, *human*-seeming man, for all that he was dressed in the traditional crimson robes and white wig, addressed himself at some length to the members of the Jury, giving them instructions about what it was their duty to know and to do.They must listen to Counsel for both sides, but accept all that they say *only as a matter of opinion*, whereas the sworn testimony of the witnesses must be taken as fact. And he explained to them at some length the matter of "proof beyond a reasonable doubt", and reminded them that the defendant was presumed innocent until his guilt had been convincingly demonstrated. They sat listening and nodding, quite expressionless for the most part. There they are, twelve of them, some fat, some lean, some idiotic, none smiling, and in their nasty hands lies the power to condemn Arthur — even to death. Yes, I write it, although of course it may not — it *cannot* happen. Yet the power is there, unavoidably.

The Judge then explained to the Jury that Arthur is charged with three counts of deliberate, premeditated murder, and that Arthur pleaded Not Guilty. Finally, he announced that the trial would begin with the opening speech for the prosecution, given by Mr. Bexheath, Counsel for the Crown. As I said I would note down every word and every detail concerning this dreadful mystery, in order to scrutinise it and study it with your help, I decided to take down as much as I can of the trial proceedings in shorthand — I am *so* glad I took the trouble to study it, long ago in our little room at home. For I cannot but feel that the secret truth must, somehow, be hidden in the words that will be spoken here.

Case of R. *vs.* Weatherburn

Opening Speech for the Prosecution, by Mr. Bexheath

"May it please you, my Lord, Gentlemen of the Jury. You have heard the charge against the defendant, which is that he deliberately murdered three prominent mathematicians, Mr. Akers, Mr. Beddoes and Mr. Crawford, all of the University of Cambridge. I will show you, Gentlemen, that the prisoner had opportunity, possibility and motive for all three of these grievous murders.

"First let me give you the facts of the case.

"Mr. Akers, a Lecturer at St. John's College, died on the evening of February 14th. After having dined with the prisoner at the Irish pub, they walked, together, back to Mr. Akers' rooms in College, and there Mr. Akers' body was found the next day, lying on the floor of his entrance hall, still wearing his coat and scarf, his hat hung upon the stand.

Barely a moment after arriving home, he was killed, by a powerful blow to the head dealt with the poker taken from his own fireplace, which was left upon the scene.

"Mr. Beddoes was killed in very similar fashion. On the evening of April 30th, he dined with the prisoner, who then accompanied him home. After some hours, as it was drawing late, his wife, surprised that he did not return, opened the front door of her house to look out and see if she could spot him arriving. Instead, she perceived the dark mass of her husband's body lying across the garden path, near the gate. He had been struck down by a blow from a heavy rock, taken from the garden itself; it formed part of the rocky border of the flowerbed, and was pried out from a position almost next to the path leading to the house. Again, the weapon remained at the scene.

"The third murder, that of Mr. Crawford, occurred on the 4th of May. As the prisoner was arrested in the night of April 30th, after the murder of Mr. Beddoes, you may think that he cannot have been responsible for the murder of Mr. Crawford. But, Gentlemen of the Jury, that was a murder of an entirely different type, for Mr. Crawford was poisoned, by drinking half-a-bottle of his own whisky, into which a large dose of the heart medicine digitalin had been introduced, equivalent to several days' worth of normal doses. This digitalin could have been introduced into the bottle of whisky at any time in the past. I will prove to you that the accused had access both to digitalin and to the bottle of whisky in the weeks preceding the murder, and thus that it would have been perfectly possible for him to commit this third murder.

"You may think, Gentlemen of the Jury, that the prisoner must have been a fool, to believe that he could, twice in the same manner, dine with a man and then brutally slaughter him, without being caught. But think again — why not? The first murder had succeeded impeccably. The prisoner was not arrested after the murder of Mr. Akers for the simple reason that not a single trace of proof remained against him. It must

110

have been quite natural for him to decide that a method which had proved so excellent once should work a second time. But the suspicion which surrounded him after the death of Mr. Akers became certainty after the death of Mr. Beddoes. Factual proof is not easy to come by, but we will adduce it little by little; traces of the earth from Mr. Beddoes' garden were found on the prisoner's shoes, he was observed entering the rooms of Mr. Crawford, his conversation over dinner with Mr. Beddoes was partially overheard. The motives of his secret discussions with both Mr. Akers and Mr. Beddoes will be revealed, and the manner of his acts explained.

"You have now already seen that the accused had ample opportunity to kill both Mr. Akers and Mr. Beddoes as they returned home, by the simple expedient of manoeuvering each of them into a position where they were alone together, unobserved, in a quiet place with a heavy object at hand. Before proceeding to discuss the motives for these grievous crimes, let us consider the opportunity and manner of the murder of Mr. Crawford.

"For this, we must enquire into the planning of the manner of death, the possibilities for the prisoner to introduce poison into Mr. Crawford's bottle of whisky, and the possibilities for him to obtain such poison in the first place.

"The first point is a crucial one. For you must know, Gentlemen of the Jury, that the post-mortem examination of Mr. Crawford showed that he had a full half-bottle of whisky in his stomach at the moment of his death, and that this half-bottle of whisky contained a lethal dose of digitalin. But what if the victim had been in the habit of drinking whisky in small quantities, for example an occasional glass before dinner? The amount of digitalin in the half-bottle was naturally spread throughout the liquid, and if such a small quantity were consumed, the only effect would have been a temporary fluttering or quickening of the heart, unlikely to produce death.

"Now, I will call a witness, a friend and colleague of the deceased, who will testify that Mr. Crawford has been seen to consume large quantities of whisky, typically a good half-bottle, on particularly festive or exciting occasions, although he is not known to have consumed it regularly otherwise. As he lived alone, we found no witnesses who could actually testify to the frequency with which he drank in such quantities, but we have some specific, dated examples when he did so.

"Knowing that the dose of digitalin introduced into a half-bottle of whisky was sufficient to kill *only if that half-bottle was consumed in its entirety,* we can conclude that the murderer was someone who was well acquainted with Mr. Crawford's drinking habits; someone who belonged to his rather restricted circle of friends, as the prisoner most certainly did.

"This deals with the first point, that of the planning of the manner of death, and showed that the murderer was undoubtedly one of Mr. Crawford's familiars.

"Let us proceed to the second point, that of the prisoner's access to Mr. Crawford's bottle of whisky. To begin with, we need to determine when the poison was introduced into the bottle. The 4th of May is the latest possible date. What about the earliest possible date? It cannot have been done before the bottle was opened. I will present a witness, Mrs. Wiggins, the charlady who takes care of the daily cleaning of Mr. Crawford's rooms. She will testify that at some time which she estimates as being 'at least two months ago', she cleared away traces of a small party from Mr. Crawford's rooms, washing up whisky glasses and throwing away an empty bottle. This witness will further testify that she has dusted a whisky bottle in its usual place on Mr. Crawford's kitchen shelf every day since that time without noticing traces of any further unusual consumption. We have no proof, of course, that the present bottle, which will be presented in evidence, is the very next one which Mr. Crawford opened, as he *may* well have thrown his own bottles away in the meantime. But it is no matter; what is proved is that the poison may have been introduced into *this* bottle after the witness threw away the previous one, which means *any time within the last several*

112

weeks. As to the actual introduction of the poison into the bottle, that was an easy matter. The accused had free access to Mr. Crawford's rooms at any time, both in his presence and even in his absence, as he was not in the habit of locking his door. We will present witnesses who will testify that the prisoner entered Mr. Crawford's rooms on at least two occasions within the last several weeks.

"We now come to the third point, the question of the prisoner's opportunity to obtain such a poison as digitalin. This question appears delicate at first sight, for the accused is not ill, has no symptoms of heart disease, and has a doctor who asserts that he has never prescribed digitalin for him. Furthermore, this medicine cannot be simply purchased over the counter. However, I will now introduce the crucial clue to the whole affair, which will prove that *the prisoner had knowledge of and access to a bottle of digitalin.*

"Indeed, one of the protagonists of the dreadful story I am unfolding before you *did* suffer from heart disease, and *was* in possession of a bottle of digitalin. That person is the first victim, Mr. Akers. We claim that the prisoner was aware of Mr. Akers' disease and attendant medication, and that he had the opportunity of obtaining some of it for his own use.

"Indeed, according to the prisoner's own deposition, when questioned by police, he saw Mr. Akers take his medicine at the very dinner they took together, before Mr. Akers' brutal murder. He has testified that Mr. Akers began to pour his drops into a glass of water — he does not say specifically that it was digitalin, but we can imagine that he already possessed this knowledge or obtained it naturally in conversation — and then put the bottle of medicine back in his pocket. The accused testifies that he did not lay eyes on the bottle again throughout the evening. *Yet, Gentlemen of the Jury — this is the key fact — the bottle of digitalin was not found in Mr. Akers' pockets after his death!* Does it not seem clear what happened? The murderer strikes, waits for the body to slump to the floor, verifies that it is dead. He then slips his hand into the very pocket where he has seen the precious bottle put away, and seizes it, his mind already possessed by another murder, to be committed on the very heels of the first!

"Now that I have explained to you, Gentlemen of the Jury, *how* the murders were committed, I turn to the problem of *why* they were committed. For this, we need to know something of the personality of the accused. He is a young man, 26 years of age, who was orphaned at the age of nine, and was sent to school and subsequently to University on scholarships, after which his excellent results in his studies enabled him to obtain a Fellowship in Mathematics at the University of Cambridge.

"For his success and settlement in life, Gentlemen of the Jury, this man has no relations to look to, no family, no inheritance, no capital, no annuity, not a single one of those comforting resources which allow a man to follow his vocation in a state of security. His entire future depends on nothing but his very own personal work, and very much on the work he does at this very time, when the University has offered him a temporary Fellowship which may or may not be renewed. Small wonder, then, if he sometimes feared that his abilities may not turn out adequate for such a task. For a Fellowship, Gentlemen of the Jury, is not like a scholarship; it is not awarded for excellent levels of study, but in order to stimulate and support the full-fledged researcher. And research in mathematics is a dangerous terrain, which can lead to disappointment and failure even in the case of those whose studies have been brilliant. It will be impossible to discover and reveal the motive for murder, Gentlemen of the Jury, without making a detour into the unfamiliar world of mathematical research and its psychology.

"The devotion to mathematics, and the reactions to its successes and failures, can lead the mathematician mentally far astray, even to the point of madness. This phenomenon has been observed only too often in the history of the subject; the greatest scientist ever to have frequented our own University,

Sir Isaac Newton, suffered intensely from persecution mania. The monomania of the mathematician, the continual withdrawal into a world of total abstraction, the urge to create, the ever-increasing demands on oneself conjugated with the intense disappointment of failure, only too naturally tend to produce an effect of psychological imbalance. Gentlemen of the Jury, madness lies in wait, ready to strike any mathematician. It may not be visible, but may seethe inside, silently seeking an outlet.

"Outwardly, the prisoner is well-known among his colleagues for his quiet, affable manner, and his ability to preserve friendships with even the most difficult or unsociable members of his profession. He was quite alone, in fact, among all of his colleagues in cultivating close friendships with some of them. I submit to you, Gentlemen of the Jury, that the accused had a reason, and a deep one, for behaving thus. As the only friend of certain important, renowned mathematicians, he was in a unique position to encourage them to talk to him about their researches, and to obtain interesting ideas for himself, which he otherwise might never have discovered. I submit that the prisoner made this technique the basis for all of his mathematical research.

"Let me describe to you how, by carefully observing his behaviour, one naturally reaches this conclusion.

"The accused is quite young, and took his degree only two years ago; since then he has published two articles. Let us consider if those articles correspond to the manner of approach I have described above.

"The first article was published under his name alone. However, the contents of the article stem largely from the doctoral thesis of the prisoner, and that thesis, like any doctoral thesis, was written *under the influence of a director*, in this case the illustrious Professor Arthur Cayley. You may find that this is a very natural state of affairs in what concerns a doctoral thesis, and I certainly do not dispute it. I simply point out that Professor Cayley will testify that he himself was responsible for a significant part of the ideas presented in the article published under the prisoner's name. In principle, young researchers are supposed to use the fact of being helped by their director in their first efforts at research as a springboard to reach independence, and fly with their own wings. The prisoner, instead, appears to have used it as a model for his regularly adopted attitude.

"The second article published by the prisoner bears the name of a co-author, Mr. Charles Morrison, whom we will also call as a witness. Let us consider Mr. Morrison's own list of publications. Although hardly a year older than his friend, you will see, Gentlemen of the Jury, that he has already published six or seven articles of his own. What can we deduce from this? Quite simply, quite naturally, that one of two authors possesses a more fertile mind than the other.

"Apart from Cayley and Morrison, the prisoner had other sources. He carefully cultivated Mr. Akers, a mathematician whose reputation for unfriendliness and unpleasantness was well-known. I will present witnesses who will testify that Mr. Akers was a very skilful mathematician, but that he indulged in the unfortunate habit of freely and snidely insulting those of his colleagues whose minds he considered inferior to his own. There is no reason to suppose that the accused was exempt from such treatment. I submit, Gentlemen of the Jury, that he put up with frequent humiliation, and obsequiously continued friends with Mr. Akers, because of his hidden, deeper goals; those of furthering his career and extending the duration of his Fellowship, thanks to research on ideas produced by Mr. Akers' powerful mind. The same underhanded motivation lay behind his apparent friendship with Mr. Beddoes and Mr. Crawford.

"Why should he resolve on the murders of these three mathematicians, since they were all three useful to him? To answer this question, it will be necessary to question some mathematical experts, who will testify that these three particular mathematicians were all working in and around the very same problem, known as the n-body problem. They are not, however, known to have been collaborating. I submit, Gentlemen of the Jury, that by dint of his frequent secret discussions with these three mathematicians, by putting various ideas of theirs together, perhaps, the accused came to realise that he could produce some research work of a very high value, which would ensure his reputation for a long time to come, but that he could not, of course, do so if they were all three present to lay claim to part of the credit. Therefore, he decided quite simply and brutally to eliminate them. Such, Gentlemen of the Jury, is the motive I claim to lie behind the series of horrendous murders you have heard described, and it is no negligible one, involving, as it does, the entire financial and professional future of a man without resources. Murder has been committed for far less. Please bear this in mind, when listening to the opening statement of my learned friend, and the various declarations of the witnesses who will be summoned and questioned one by one."

I hardly dared look at Arthur throughout this dreadful speech, which became increasingly devastating as it advanced. Although I could easily see him simply by glancing up, it seemed a cruel thing to do, and I tried to keep my eyes firmly glued to Mr. Bexheath. Oh, it makes me boil, the whole procedure! I suppose that if a person is guilty of a crime, they somehow forfeit the right to proper treatment on the part of Society — but it seems very hard that a perfectly innocent person should be subjected to this public pillory, to sit exposed, in enforced silence, and be stared at by curious idlers who listen eagerly whilst all these falsely righteous, insulting, humiliating accusations are thrown at him. Even supposing that justice does not miscarry, and that one is acquitted and discharged, as they say, without a stain on one's character — that does not begin to make up for the needless suffering thus undergone! When I think that every acquittal follows such a scene of torment, the hair rises upon my scalp.

Tears of indignation burned my eyes as that horrid man, whose neck I would willingly have wrung, invented his perfectly nasty motive, and I could not resist casting a tiny glance in the direction of the dock. Arthur was sitting motionless, with his forehead pressed in his hand, which was hardly surprising. At least nature provides us with this one final screen against the stares and mockery of the world, when all others have been torn away.

It was an incredible relief when Mr. Bexheath sat down; the tension in the Courthouse lightened sensibly, and the Judge then requested if Mr. Haversham wished to rise and make his Opening Statement, before any witnesses should be called. I thought that he would have put it off, so as to prepare his answer to the hateful accusations, but barristers think quickly, no doubt, and he had taken notes and completed the preparation of his answer even as the other was still speaking. He rose to his feet, and began.

Opening Speech for the Defence, by Mr. Haversham

"May it please you, my Lord, Gentlemen of the Jury. You have heard the charge of triple murder levelled against the prisoner, and you have heard the reconstruction given by my learned friend, of the manner in which the murders were committed, and of the motive thereof.

"I will now undertake to show you two things. First, that the manner of the murders as described by Counsel for the Crown is merely an interpretation laid upon the very few facts which the police investigation has been able to obtain, and that it is possible to construct at least one other equally plausible interpretation, fitting the known facts equally well. As you know, Gentlemen of the Jury, as long as no further concrete evidence can be brought forth in favour of the Crown's interpretation, this means that the prisoner's guilt has not been proved beyond a reasonable doubt, and he therefore must be acquitted. Second, I will show you that the argument as to motive submitted by my learned colleague is no more than a twisted tissue of inventions.

"When listening to the opening statement of Counsel for the Crown, Gentlemen of the Jury, I am certain that you were attentive at all times to distinguish facts from opinions. I will now give a completely different interpretation of the events surrounding the murders, which fits with all the known facts as well as that of opposing Counsel.

"My friends, it is well-known that a mathematician's force diminishes with age. Imagine, now, a mathematician, known for his tremendous ability and originality of thought, who finds, as he grows older, that he is no longer as able as he used to be, of bringing his own ideas to fruition. He still has brilliant ideas, but something is lacking which did not use to lack; the precision, the memory, the persistence in overcoming obstacles. Such a mathematician may well turn to others for aid, and receive it, for mathematicians, by and large, are a generous race, much given to assisting each other.

"Now, imagine that such a mathematician produces a truly remarkable idea — the idea of a lifetime! Imagine that he burns to develop it and to complete it, but is blocked, perhaps, by technicalities which he does not master, and turns to others for help. Suppose that they are able to provide exactly the little missing detail which makes everything work, and the final *Quod Erat Demonstrandum* is appended to the proof of the grand theorem. May not the author then well feel that the contributions of his colleagues is of far less importance than his own, being merely of a technical nature, while his was the founding and driving idea? And would it not then be natural for him to feel that his helpers have not merited the forthcoming honour and glory to the same degree as himself? And yet the joint publication of mathematical articles makes no distinction between the different authors. Such feelings may easily give rise to jealousy and resentment, and this may

119

easily swell into a burning desire to obtain and keep the glory for oneself, by whatever means, the more so as the glory is greater.

"Gentlemen of the Jury, I submit that such were the feelings of the mathematician Mr. Crawford, and that, as some ideas of his, thanks to the occasional help of his two friends Mr. Akers and Mr. Beddoes, were blossoming into a work of tremendous importance, he determined to eliminate them, and to allow himself alone to be crowned with the laurels he felt he richly deserved.

"I claim that Mr. Crawford planned the death of Mr. Akers, concealing himself in his rooms when he knew that his friend was dining out, holding his poker in his gloved hands, awaiting his return, and that when Mr. Akers entered his own doors, the blow fell, powerful and immediate. Mr. Crawford then dropped the poker, searched the pockets of the deceased, removed the fatal bottle of digitalin which we know to have been there, and departed, unseen and unsuspected. Recall, Gentlemen of the Jury, that Mr. Crawford was a hefty and powerful man, and that he was a close familiar of Mr. Akers.

"I claim that Mr. Crawford, having waited for some weeks and seen that no one was accused of the murder he had thus secretly perpetrated, then planned to eliminate Mr. Beddoes in a similar manner. This time, he ensured his absence from home by himself organising a dinner invitation, together with a third person, namely the prisoner, who will testify to this fact. Why Mr. Crawford should have chosen the prisoner to make up a third party is not difficult to imagine; he must have seen that the third party would automatically come under suspicion for the murder, and all the more so if he had already been associated in some way with the previous murder. Mr. Crawford then recused himself from the dinner on the grounds of feeling unwell. There is no witness to his acts of that evening, but I claim, Gentlemen of the Jury, that he hid himself among the great lilac bushes which shield Mr. Beddoes' garden so effectively from the street, took up a large and heavy rock which lay to hand in the garden border, and waited. The fact that Mr. Beddoes did not return alone, but was accompanied by the prisoner, may have momentarily annoyed him, but the prisoner took his leave of Mr. Beddoes at the gate and turned away down the street, leaving Mr. Crawford time to put his sudden, evil plan into execution. As for my learned friend's allegation that the prisoner carried earth from Mr. Beddoes' garden upon his shoes, this follows naturally from the brief moment during which he stood within the open gateway shaking hands, and it is perfectly absurd to adduce it as evidence against the prisoner.

"Gentlemen of the Jury, I submit to you that after several weeks of rumination upon these deeds, Mr. Crawford could not bear the realisation of what he had done, and that seeing no further obstacle between himself and the glory he sought for, or perhaps — and this is even more likely, as no particular theorem has actually come to light, left behind by any of the three protagonists — suddenly realising that his brilliant result suffered from a fatal flaw which rendered it utterly false, and which had escaped even the careful eyes of his colleagues, he poured the poison into his bottle of whisky and drank it down, impelled by the sufferings of a guilty conscience to make an end of everything.

"I beg you to take note, Gentlemen, of the striking lack of concrete evidence against the prisoner in this case. There are no traces of fingerprints on the poker nor on the rock, no traces of blood upon the prisoner's clothes — in short, no hard factual evidence against him at all! It is up to you, Gentlemen, to decide whether the events I have described are plausible, in which case the prisoner's guilt can certainly not be considered as proven.

"I turn now to the question of motive, and submit to you that the prisoner would have had no motive whatsoever to commit the triple murder of which he stands accused. The motive described by opposing Counsel does not hold water for a moment; the very witnesses called by the prosecution will disclaim it utterly. They will tell you that the motive described above is quite simply non-existent, a purely fictitious invention on the part of my learned friend.

"No proof of manner, no proof of motive — Gentlemen of the Jury, I fully expect that you will acquit the prisoner!"

I find that Mr. Haversham's speech was short and pointed, but something about it troubles me. I cannot lay my finger on exactly what, but it lies in his reconstruction of the Crawford theory. I myself suggested this theory, but somehow, his way of telling it strikes me as curiously unconvincing. Yes — I know what it is! Why, why on earth would Mr. Crawford have bothered to remove the flask of digitalin from Mr. Akers' pockets? What could it possibly mean? Could he have been envisioning using it for another murder? Surely not to kill himself with! It is all so confusing, and the speeches by the barristers do not help. How they are allowed and encouraged to indulge in inventions — almost in lies — in the interest of their client! What a peculiar profession.

The Court has adjourned, and I have come away. This afternoon, the Prosecution will begin to call its witnesses; rumour says that the first to be called will be the medical examiner, who will testify as to the details of the manner of death met by the three victims. But I cannot attend; I shall return tomorrow morning, and write you everything that passes. It somehow gives a little relief to my anguish, and some trace of hope, when I write down everything black on white and share it with you.

Your most affectionate sister,

Vanessa

Cambridge, Friday, May 18th, 1888

Dear Dora,

I am here in the Courtroom, following what is now going to become installed as my daily routine: Court in the morning, lessons in the afternoon. I can no longer visit Arthur or speak to him at all, as he must spend his entire day in Court.

Today, however, I am no longer in the public gallery. Strange as it may seem, I have learned that I am to be called as a witness for the prosecution! Mr. Bexheath will certainly obtain no evidence for the prosecution from me, whatever he may think. But then, he knows nothing of my feelings, of course. The whole collection of witnesses for the prosecution must sit together along a special bench while we are in Court. I am allowed to leave in the afternoons to teach my lessons, but I am under strict injunctions to discuss the case with nobody. On the bench with me are several mathematicians: Mr. Morrison is sitting next to me, and although we may not communicate, his eyes twinkle at me occasionally (and he can even be heard emitting indignant remarks under his breath, in full defiance of orders!). Next to him are Mr. Wentworth and Mr. Withers. Professor Cayley will be called tomorrow. Mrs. Beddoes and Mrs. Wiggins, the charlady, are also present, as well as two or three other people with whom I am not acquainted; I cannot imagine who they might be. If all these people are going to be as ineffective, as witnesses for the prosecution, as I intend to be, their testimonies will not go far to help Mr. Bexheath!

Mr. Morrison says that he means to attend the trial for the whole of every day, and that he will keep me abreast of what goes on in the afternoons. He told me that yesterday, the entire afternoon was devoted to the examination and cross-examination of the medical examiner, but that apart from graphic descriptions of the explicit manner of death of the three victims, nothing was elicited which was in any way surprising or unexpected. Mr. Morrison says that when his testimony was not gruesome, it was boring. He told me that Mr. Akers' personal doctor was also heard; his testimony concerned only the fact of Mr. Akers' heart disease, and its attendant medication. He testified that judging by the last time he had prescribed for Mr. Akers, and given his regular dose of ten drops three times a day, Mr. Akers' medicine bottle must still have contained at least three weeks' worth of medicine.

In contrast, I must admit that I found the court procedure of this morning to be — it sounds heartless, but at certain moments it was almost amusing! Mr. Bexheath put Professor Cayley and Mr. Morrison on the stand, in order to support his theory of Arthur's motive. But I do not think he obtained from them exactly what he wanted.

Professor Cayley was called first. He stood at the witness stand, with his stern, thin-lipped face and indrawn cheeks showing much the same disapproving expression he had worn for his lecture on the teaching of mathematics, except that the disapproval now seemed to fix upon Mr. Bexheath rather than upon the enemies of Euclid. His voice was nasal, his tone chilly, and his answers brief. Rather than describe the scene, I have written out my shorthand notes in full, and will continue to do so every day.

Direct examination of Professor Cayley, by Mr. Bexheath

The witness was sworn in by the Court Clerk.

Mr. Bexheath: You are Professor Arthur Cayley, sixty-six years old, Sadleirian Professor of Pure Mathematics at the University of Cambridge?

Professor Cayley: Yes.

Mr. Bexheath: The prisoner wrote a doctoral dissertation under your direction?

Professor Cayley: Yes.

Mr. Bexheath: Who decided on the subject of that dissertation?

Professor Cayley: I did.

Mr. Bexheath: Did you provide guidance throughout the time during which the prisoner wrote the dissertation?

Professor Cayley: Certainly.

Mr. Bexheath: How often did you meet with the prisoner during the course of his doctoral research?

Professor Cayley: I met with him once a week precisely, as I do with each of my doctoral students.

Mr. Bexheath: Did the prisoner subsequently write and publish an article in the *Cambridge Mathematical Journal* based on the research done for his doctoral dissertation?

Professor Cayley: Yes.

Mr. Bexheath: The article in the *Cambridge Mathematical Journal* was signed by the prisoner alone.

Professor Cayley: Certainly.

Mr. Bexheath: Yet he benefited from your guidance during the entire course of the preparation of his dissertation, whose contents then went into the article?

Professor Cayley: That is the case.

Mr. Bexheath: Thank you very much, Professor Cayley. I have no more questions.

Cross-examination of Professor Cayley, by Mr. Haversham

Mr. Haversham: Professor Cayley, you have said that you meet with each of your doctoral students regularly once a week.

Professor Cayley: I have said so, yes.

Mr. Haversham: Therefore you devote more or less the same amount of time to each one. But can you say that you also devote the same amount of mathematical guidance to each one?

Professor Cayley: No, certainly not.

Mr. Haversham: Some students show more independence than others?

Professor Cayley: Yes indeed.

Mr. Haversham: Was the prisoner one of the more independent or the less independent-minded amongst your students?

Professor Cayley: Arthur Weatherburn was one of the most independent-minded students I have ever had.

Mr. Haversham: Yet you did provide him with some guidance.

Professor Cayley: Very little apart from indicating a suitable problem to him.

Mr. Haversham: What transpired during your weekly meetings, then?

Professor Cayley: Weatherburn told me what he had worked on during the course of the elapsed week, and I listened and made comments.

Mr. Haversham: Would you say that Mr. Weatherburn is a highly creative mathematician?

Professor Cayley: Undoubtedly.

Mr. Haversham: Now, as to the publication of an article drawn from research done as part of a doctoral dissertation under your guidance. Would you say that that is normal procedure?

Professor Cayley: Certainly.

Mr. Haversham: All students do it?

Professor Cayley: All those who succeed in writing a doctoral dissertation containing material original enough to warrant publication.

Mr. Haversham: So that it cannot be used to conclude that Mr. Weatherburn is not an independent mathematician, or makes abusive use of the help of others to advance in his profession?

Professor Cayley: Absolutely not.

Mr. Haversham: Thank you very much, Professor Cayley. I have no more questions.

The Judge invited Professor Cayley to stand down, with flowery expressions of respect, and the Bailiff appeared to usher him politely to the exit. He was not required to waste a single moment of his precious time more than was necessary for the taking of his deposition.

I considered Professor Cayley's testimony to be highly positive for Arthur. But the stolid and impassive faces of the members of the Jury did not seem to reflect such feelings. Perhaps it should be considered a draw.

Following Professor Cayley, Mr. Morrison was called to the stand.

Direct examination of Mr. Morrison, by Mr. Bexheath

The witness was sworn in.

Mr. Bexheath: Please state your name, age and occupation for the benefit of the Jury, sir.

Mr. Morrison: My name is Charles Morrison, I am 27 years old, and I hold a Fellowship in Pure Mathematics at the University of Cambridge.

Mr. Bexheath: When, where, and under whose direction did you write your doctoral thesis?

Mr. Morrison: I completed it three years ago, here in Cambridge, under the direction of Professor Arthur Cayley.

Mr. Bexheath: How many articles have you published in professional journals since that time?

Mr. Morrison: Six, some under my name alone, others in collaboration.

Mr. Bexheath: How many of these articles were written in collaboration with the prisoner?

Mr. Morrison: One.

Mr. Bexheath: How many articles has the prisoner published?

Mr. Morrison: Two, but it doesn't mean anything!

Mr. Bexheath: Mr. Morrison, please confine yourself to strictly answering my questions. Your opinions are not required here. Now, let us turn to the article you published jointly with the prisoner. I would like to ask you some questions concerning your contributions to that article, as compared with those of the prisoner. I wish to discuss the procedure of writing an article jointly. How is it possible for a mathematical idea to germinate in more than one mind?

Mr. Morrison: Well, what usually happens that conversation with another person, possibly more of an expert than oneself in some aspect of the material under discussion, stimulates the idea.

Mr. Bexheath: That is a very interesting answer. So, before writing this article together, you and the prisoner had mathematical discussions?

Mr. Morrison: Oh, yes.

Mr. Bexheath: Frequently?

Mr. Morrison: Oh, yes, quite frequently.

Mr. Bexheath: And one day, these discussions caused a new idea to germinate?

Mr. Morrison: Yes.

Mr. Bexheath: Mr. Morrison, how would you say that the ideas contained in those articles which you published alone germinated?

Mr. Morrison: Well, you think about something by yourself, looking at it, turning it over from all angles, trying to figure out what it looks like and how it works, until suddenly you see the light.

Mr. Bexheath: So mathematical ideas can be stimulated either by conversation or through deep and tenacious personal reflection?

Mr. Morrison: Yes.

Mr. Bexheath: Now, let us take the situation you have described; two mathematicians are talking about some problem in mathematics, and all of a sudden, some remark made by one of them, whom we can imagine to be a well-educated mathematician who has recently completed brilliant studies, causes the other one, whom we can imagine to be an imaginative and fertile mathematician with several original publications to his credit, to "see the light", as you put it; to perceive, say, a solution to some problem. What would the procedure of publication be in a case like that? Would the two mathematicians publish jointly, or only the one who actually came to the solution?

Mr. Morrison: It all depends on how big, how necessary the help given by the other one was, and what kind of relations they had with each other.

Mr. Bexheath: If they are close friends and peers, for example.

Mr. Morrison: Well, there is no rule.

Mr. Bexheath: But it is quite likely that they would publish together?

Mr. Morrison: It certainly could happen. But my collaboration with Arthur Weatherburn wasn't at all like that.

Mr. Bexheath: Mr. Morrison! You will confine yourself to answering the questions.

Mr. Morrison: That whole story of motive you invented was just arrant nonsense, Mr. Bexheath!

Mr. Bexheath: Mr. Morrison!

Mr. Justice Penrose: Mr. Morrison, you will please cease these extraneous remarks. That last one will be struck off the record.

Mr. Morrison: Strike it off, but it doesn't make it any the less true. Arthur is a first-class mathematician!

Mr. Justice Penrose: Mr. Morrison! Desist immediately. That last remark will also be struck off the record.

Mr. Morrison: This is all wrong!

Mr. Bexheath: My examination of this unruly witness is terminated.

Mr. Morrison: I still have a lot of things to say.

Mr. Justice Penrose: Mr. Morrison! You are not in Court to express your personal opinions! Please be quiet at once. You will now be cross-examined, and I pray that you CONFINE YOURSELF TO ANSWERING COUNSEL'S QUESTIONS, otherwise you will be held for Contempt of Court.

Cross-examination of Mr. Morrison, by Mr. Haversham

Mr. Haversham: Mr. Morrison, I would like to ask about the joint article published by yourself together with the prisoner.

Mr. Morrison: Yes, and I should greatly like to answer.

Mr. Justice Penrose: Mr. Morrison!

Mr. Haversham: Would you say that that article contains a valuable mathematical idea?

Mr. Morrison: Frankly, it contains what I believe to be more than just an idea; the beginnings of a fascinating new theory.

Mr. Haversham: In a joint article, it must often be extremely difficult, if not meaningless, to try to discern which author is responsible for what concept. Would you say that this is the case for the article in question?

Mr. Morrison: No, actually.

Mr. Haversham: No?

Mr. Morrison: Well, no. In the case of our article, it is actually quite clear.

Mr. Haversham: Would it be possible for you to give some description of the nature of your collaboration with the prisoner, and of your respective contributions to the joint article?

Mr. Morrison: Yes. Arthur has a theoretical mind which grapples with vast concepts, whereas I like to solve problems using techniques, often adapted from those developed by Professor Cayley, in interesting ways. I was showing Arthur how I solved some technical problem or other, writing on the blackboard, and he was listening. All of a sudden, he said to me something like "What you're doing is just the tip of the iceberg!" He realised what I hadn't realised; that I was just working on a special case of a grand theory which could be applied to solve a great many different problems by a coherent, general expression of my technique. I thought his idea was fantastic.

Mr. Haversham: So you do not agree with my learned friend's evaluation of the process of the collaboration between you.

Mr. Morrison: It's plain ridiculous! Arthur's just talking mathematics all the time with people, because they always want to talk to him, seeing that he knows so much about practically every subject. As for trying to imply that having published more articles or less articles is a reflection of one's mathematical creativity, it's all rot. One deep article can be worth a bushel of little ones.

Mr. Justice Penrose: Mr. Morrison, you will immediately cease to employ insulting terms. This is a Court of Justice. Behave yourself accordingly!

Mr. Morrison: Yes, my Lord. Let me express myself better. (*Pinchedly*) The arguments submitted by the Counsel for the Crown, tending to indicate that the value of a mathematician's depths, originality and creative power can be measured by a yardstick as crude as the positive integer denoting the quantity of published articles is a mistaken point of view, which bears the risk of misleading the members of the Jury, who are unfamiliar with the nature of mathematical research, into unfortunate errors of judgement.

Mr. Haversham: (*hastily*) My cross-examination is finished, my Lord.

Mr. Justice Penrose: In that case, this wearisome witness would do well to stand down immediately. Court is adjourned.

Oh, Dora — even the Jury smiled sometimes during this deposition! When Mr. Morrison came back to the witnesses' bench, I could have kissed him! I found it inside me, for the first time, to forgive him for having been convinced of Arthur's guilt in the first days. If only things continue this way, then Mr. Bexheath's horrible arguments will all fall apart. Oh, if only it could happen so!

Your very own, some what more optimistic

Vanessa

Cambridge, Saturday, May 19th, 1888

My dearest Dora,

Some days ago, I met poor Mrs. Beddoes in a shop, and she stopped to speak to me. She seemed pleased to see me, if one can use the word pleased of someone who seems inexorably separated from the outer world by a barrier of inner mourning. We spoke for a moment, and she asked after Rose and Emily, and invited me to bring them to tea; she told me that the silence of her lonely house was full of sorrow, and I felt that she would like to chase it away, however briefly, with the voices of children.

Today, I had no lessons, and felt reluctant to remain alone, and I do not know exactly what faint feelings drew me towards her; I felt the need to talk to her, because she was placed so near the centre of my troubles. I went to see her, therefore, this morning, and she welcomed me with pleasure — no; again, the word is not applicable, but she said that it would *give* her great pleasure to have Emily and Rose for tea, and spend a moment in the company of their adorable pink cheeks and gaiety. I then called on the girls' mothers and obtained their permission, and at four o'clock this afternoon, the three of us made our way together through the garden gate and up the pretty path, half-smothered in flowers, where poor Mr. Beddoes met his death less than two weeks ago.

When Mrs. Beddoes perceived our approach, her sad and rather tired face lit up with a kind smile. She (or her cook) had prepared sundry scones, sandwiches and cakes, of which we partook with a distressing lack of moderation. The little girls then went to romp outside in the garden back of the house, which runs long, rich and green down to the fence behind. They soon discovered the tiny wooden shed which Mr. Beddoes had built at the end of it to lodge his cats, as Mrs. Beddoes could not bear them in the house. She smiled as she saw the girls, through the glass door, chasing and playing with the animals, of which I made out at least six.

"The little kittens have grown now, they dearly love a romp," she said. "We meant to give them away; my husband had already written out a list with their descriptions." She showed me the neatly printed little list, in which each kitten was identified by a fanciful name, together with its colour and description.

"Now I feel that I should keep each and every one of them," she went on, "they may have been the last thing which gave my husband joy before his death. I cannot really abide them, but they do not need much care; I simply put food out for them. Mr. Beddoes used to visit those kittens several times a day, when they were tiny things still in their basket."

She wanted to talk a great deal about Mr. Beddoes, and I

wanted nothing else, hoping against hope to learn something, anything at all that could help some new understanding develop in my mind. The house was so fresh and pretty, the garden so blooming, and she herself so kind and welcoming — yet, behind the scene lay the pale echoes of other images; a dark night, a creeping, hiding person, a dead man lying across the path, a widow weeping alone.

"Everyone perceived my husband as a gentle and accommodating man," she told me. "And indeed, he was; he did not like disputes of any kind. Yet his feelings and opinions were strong, although he was very private about them. I believe no one really knew how much he thought about most things, to hear how casually he mentioned them. And although he was friendly with everyone, he did not have many real friends."

"Who were his closest friends?" I asked.

"Oh, he talked most often about Mr. Crawford," she smiled. "They were really a pair, those two — so very different from each other! You saw Mr. Crawford — he was so very loud and strong-minded! Their friendship was all full of ups and downs on account of it. Philip always avoided quarrels — he used to say that they were no way to solve any problem of any kind. But as Mr. Crawford did not avoid them, they did occasionally happen; Mr. Crawford would shout, and Philip would come home most annoyed. It happened just a month or two ago. He visited Mr. Crawford, and something must have come up between them, for he came home and told me they'd had a most disappointing discussion, and Crawford was furious on account of it. Philip was not pleased himself, by any means, but it was not his way to quarrel. He would ruminate alone, and see how to obtain what he wanted by his own means."

"Did they make up their quarrel afterwards?"

"Oh yes, they did. We saw Mr. Crawford at the garden party after Professor Cayley's lecture, do you remember? And he behaved as though nothing was amiss. Philip was happy enough to let it go at that. They always did make up their quarrels sooner or later."

"Yes, I remember," I said. "Mr. Crawford suddenly greeted Mr. Beddoes, and even said that he wanted to dine with him soon, and Mr. Beddoes seemed quite surprised."

"Yes, he was, for Mr. Crawford had quite a temper. I never could take to him really. Yet he and Philip had something in common, I know, though we rarely spoke of it. Their profession is a difficult one, my dear. You cannot imagine what it is to live for so many years among mathematicians. It seems as though the striving and disappointment and frustration which must naturally accompany any kind of scientific research must constantly struggle within them, against the joy and elation of discovery. Mr. Crawford was a bitter man, really. He was truly brilliant, I believe; at least Philip often said so, but because he made one or two serious errors in the last decades, publishing results which turned out to be flawed, he lost some of the consideration of his colleagues, and he felt that his true worth was unjustly unrecognised. It seemed to me sometimes that he blamed the whole world for it, he was so very aggressive. My husband was also bitter at moments, though not for the same reason. He admired the ideas of others, but his estimation of his own work was a permanent disappointment to him; he often felt that something great had come nearly within his grasp, and he had let it escape. I believe this perpetual resentment and bitterness is the curse of many mathematicians; certainly Philip worked and sought and studied as hard as any."

Her eyes filled with tears as the memory of her loss arose in her, and she changed the subject suddenly. "Let us go out in the garden," she said. "My husband always used to walk about in it while he was working. And he had been working so very hard these last months, upstairs in his little office; there were days when he seemed absolutely delighted, and others which were rather terrible. All of the mathematical papers he left upstairs have been sorted and studied by his colleagues and students; several of them came here, and they looked at everything so carefully, and did a lovely job. It can't have been very difficult; Philip's handwriting was as clear as print."

We went out, and joined the girls, who were playing with the kittens, and dancing about with twinkling eyes.

"We cleaned out the kitties' house!" they told us proudly. I bent my head to peer inside the little wooden structure, which Mr. Beddoes had built with his own hands for his beloved cats, and admired how the girls had swept it out with a branch and shaken out and plumped up the colourful quilted morsels which cosily lined each basket.

"Thank you so much, my dears," Mrs. Beddoes told them. "I should do it myself now and then, but the cats do so make my eyes water! Perhaps you will come again some day and do it for me."

She bid us goodbye kindly, and we went on our way, the girls discussing cats and giggling violently over some shared secret, and I walking along absently, my mind on the quarrel between Mr. Beddoes and Mr. Crawford, which had taken place "some days" before the garden party of the 23rd of April. What could it have been about, I wonder? I am sure it is a clue.

I must ponder it all in solitude,

Your loving Vanessa

Cambridge, Monday, May 21st, 1888

Dear Dora,

The third day of the trial has begun. It appears less favourable than yesterday, and yet I still find that Mr. Bexheath is not succeeding in providing anything like a proof of his case that eliminates the Mr. Crawford theory, in spite of all his leading questions and the answers he elicits. On the other hand, although Mr. Haversham makes some progress in spoiling the coherent impression that Mr. Bexheath would like to give, he makes very little in eliciting any useful positive information in support of the alternative theory ... and nothing at all *which could help us to determine whether or not it is true.* Yet it must be true. For what else, what else is possible?

The first witness called this morning by the Prosecution was Mrs. Wiggins.

Direct examination of Mrs. Wiggins, by Mr. Bexheath

The witness was sworn in by the Court Clerk

Mr. Bexheath: Please give your name, age and occupation.

Mrs. Wiggins: Alice Wiggins, fifty-one, charlady of St. John's College.

Mr. Bexheath: Were you responsible, until his death, for cleaning the rooms in College of Mr. Geoffrey Akers?

Mrs. Wiggins: Yes, I was, less luck to me.

Mr. Bexheath: Can you describe the situation of Mr. Akers' rooms?

Mrs. Wiggins: They was up one flight of stairs from the base of the north-east tower.

Mr. Bexheath: Was anyone living below, or on the same level as Mr. Akers?

Mrs. Wiggins: No, the other rooms are above.

Mr. Bexheath: Can you tell me if Mr. Akers ever received visitors in his rooms?

Mrs. Wiggins: I believe 'e never did. At least they left no trace. 'E was a very unsociable man.

Mr. Bexheath: Did you never see the prisoner in or about Mr. Akers' rooms?

Mrs. Wiggins: No, thank God, I never.

Mr. Bexheath: Can you describe the general state of Mr. Akers' rooms?

Mrs. Wiggins: 'E was a dirty man, sir. I cleaned good and regular, but he dirtied it all up just as fast. Papers everywhere, all mixed up, and he angry if I so much as touched any. Cigar ash, 'e was a one for smoking, and dropped the ash down just anywhere. Food and drink left about. 'E was a man of irregular 'abits. But visits and friends 'e did not 'ave.

Mr. Bexheath: Now, Mrs. Wiggins, one of the main questions I have for you is this. Can you describe any changes that you noticed in Mr. Akers' rooms, between the time that you last cleared up there, on the 14th of last February, and the following day, when you were called into his rooms by the police?

Mrs. Wiggins: Well, as I've already told you, sir, there was a mess that was not there when I left the previous day. The papers was all messed about, and the drawers in the study open.

Mr. Bexheath: The room appeared to have been searched?

Mrs. Wiggins: Well, it might have been Mr. Akers messing about, looking for something 'isself. If 'e did that, 'e would leave the drawers open as well. That'd be typical. 'E would never think of closing a drawer to save an elderly woman's back.

Mr. Bexheath: Yes, of course. But somebody searched the room, whether Mr. Akers himself, or the person who lay in

139

wait for him in his rooms.

Mrs. Wiggins: Or somebody else.

Mr. Bexheath: Quite. Did Mr. Akers frequently dine out?

Mrs. Wiggins: 'E may have dined in College, or out, but certainly not in 'is rooms. Didn't fancy 'isself as a cook, I'd say; I wouldn't 'ave either.

Mr. Bexheath: Did he ever spend a night away from home?

Mrs. Wiggins: Not that I know. 'Is bed was always undone and a right mess every morning. Sundays I wouldn't know.

Mr. Bexheath: Thank you. Now let us pass to another subject, namely the rooms of Mr. Crawford, in the same College. Can you describe them?

Mrs. Wiggins: They weren't nigh so bad as Mr. Akers'. Mr. Crawford was a big, rough man but 'e 'ad a good 'eart. 'E'd pass the time o' day with me, like as not, when 'e was in. Mr. Akers never.

Mr. Bexheath: Did Mr. Crawford occasionally receive visitors?

Mrs. Wiggins: Yes, sometimes.

Mr. Bexheath: Frequently? For meals?

Mrs. Wiggins: No, not for meals, but for drinks now and then. Not too often, I'd say. Maybe every couple o' months or so 'e'd have some friends by.

Mr. Bexheath: Did you see them?

Mrs. Wiggins: No, they'd come after I was done. I did 'is rooms in the morning. But they'd leave glasses and things about for me to wash up the next day.

Mr. Bexheath: So you have no idea who Mr. Crawford's occasional visitors might have been.

Mrs. Wiggins: No, I don't.

Mr. Bexheath: How many came at one time?

Mrs. Wiggins: Oh, just a couple, one or two. Mr. Crawford didn't 'ave no grand parties in 'is rooms!

Mr. Bexheath: Can you remember any time when Mr. Crawford received visitors who drank whisky?

Mrs. Wiggins: It's been some time, but there was some, because the bottle was out and the glasses and all, and it smelled whisky that strong I had to air out the rooms.

Mr. Bexheath: When was that?

Mrs. Wiggins: That was months ago.

Mr. Bexheath: How many months?

Mrs. Wiggins: Oh, three or four. Yes, that'd have been back in February, that would have been. Round about the murder of Mr. Akers, it was.

Mr. Bexheath: Before or after his murder?

Mrs. Wiggins: I don't rightly remember, but I think it must have been just before, because I was cleaning up and I hadn't got any thoughts about Mr. Akers in my head right then, as seems natural I would have had, if I'd heard about him already.

Mr. Bexheath: What did you do with the whisky bottle that day?

Mrs. Wiggins: I put it back on the shelf; it was still near half-full. Then I washed out the glasses.

Mr. Bexheath: Did Mr. Crawford generally have a bottle of whisky about his rooms?

Mrs. Wiggins: There was always a bottle o' whisky on Mr. Crawford's shelf, along with other bottles. 'E was a one for a drink.

Mr. Bexheath: Did you ever notice if the bottle of whisky on the shelf was full or empty?

Mrs. Wiggins: No, I never paid attention, just flicked my duster and went on. It might 'ave been the same bottle or changed twenty times as he drank it down, I never noticed.

Mr. Bexheath: All right. Now, Mrs. Wiggins, can you remember any other specific times that Mr. Crawford received visitors?

Mrs. Wiggins: Not specific. O' course, there may have been visitors any time who didn't drink. Last month some time, there was someone for certain.

Mr. Bexheath: Someone? One person visited Mr. Crawford?

Mrs. Wiggins: Yes, I remember that.

Mr. Bexheath: You cannot recall when?

Mrs. Wiggins: No; it was more than a month ago, though.

Mr. Bexheath: But less than two months ago?

Mrs. Wiggins: Oh yes, it'd have been right around the middle of April.

Mr. Bexheath: And how do you know there was a single

visitor?

Mrs. Wiggins: Well, I remember washing up two glasses, and putting away the bottle.

Mr. Bexheath: Oh, so they drank whisky?

Mrs. Wiggins: No, it was red wine.

Mr. Bexheath: I see. Red wine, indeed. You remember that.

Mrs. Wiggins: Oh yes, I aired, because it smelled. Mr. Crawford don't — didn't, poor gentleman — open his windows much. It was always easy to say what 'e'd been a-drinking of.

Mr. Bexheath: Thank you, Mrs. Wiggins.

Cross-examination of Mrs. Wiggins, by Mr. Haversham

Mr. Haversham: When you said there was a single visitor to Mr. Crawford's rooms some time in the last month or two, do you have any idea whom it might have been?

Mrs. Wiggins: No sir, except it was someone who drank red wine.

Mr. Haversham: Do you know what time of day that person visited Mr. Crawford?

Mrs. Wiggins: No sir, except it was not in the morning when I was there.

Mr. Haversham: I see. So someone who can be identified exactly by the two facts of his being acquainted with Mr. Crawford, and his accepting a glass of red wine, visited Mr. Crawford sometime, on an unknown day, at an unknown hour. Do you think we can draw any conclusion from this?

Mrs. Wiggins: No sir.

Mr. Haversham: The mysterious visitor could have been Mr. Beddoes as easily as it could have been Mr. Weatherburn, or some other person.

Mrs. Wiggins: For aught I know, sir.

Mr. Haversham: Thank you. You may stand down.

Mr. Justice Penrose: Have the police made an effort to trace this person?

Mr. Haversham: Yes, my Lord, without success. His visit was not witnessed by anyone on Mr. Crawford's stair.

The second witness called was Mrs. Beddoes. I felt sorry for the poor lady, as I saw her take the stand, and my heart was wrung with fear that her statements, probably filled with resigned conviction of Arthur's guilt, would have great weight with the Jury on account of her mourning, and her gentle, sorrowful face.

Direct examination of Mrs. Beddoes, by Mr. Bexheath

Mr. Bexheath: Mrs. Beddoes, I am very sorry to call you here. I deeply sympathise with your mourning, and I shall try to trouble you as little as possible.

Mrs. Beddoes:(*with a wavering voice*) Thank you, sir.

Mr. Bexheath: I would just like to ask you a few questions about the relations between Mr. Akers, your husband, Mr. Crawford and the prisoner.

Mrs. Beddoes: Yes?

Mr. Bexheath: Was your husband the friend of each of the other three men?

Mrs. Beddoes: Yes, sir, he was a good friend to all three of them.

Mr. Bexheath: Can you describe the nature of his friendship with Mr. Akers?

Mrs. Beddoes: My husband was not as close to Mr. Akers as he was to the other two. They talked mathematics sometimes, however, and my husband admired Mr. Akers. He often said that Mr. Akers had a wonderful talent for calculating things by wise methods, which no one else would have been able to calculate ever.

Mr. Bexheath: Can you tell me where they discussed mathematics? The testimony of Mrs. Wiggins appears to indicate that they did not discuss it in Mr. Akers' rooms.

Mrs. Beddoes: Nor did they discuss it in our house. I do not know, sir. It must have been in their offices at the University, or in the Library, or in other rooms, or at dinner.

Mr. Bexheath: Did they actually collaborate? Work on mathematics together? Or did they just talk about it?

Mrs. Beddoes: I don't know, sir. But I believe they never went so far as regularly working together.

Mr. Bexheath: Now, can you describe your husband's relations with Mr. Crawford?

Mrs. Beddoes: They were close friends. Mr. Crawford had a strong personality, and my husband was sometimes put off by his ways, but their friendship was a deep one. They had a difference back in April, but Mr. Crawford forgot it and my husband kept no rancour, so they became friends again.

Mr. Bexheath: Was your husband in the habit of visiting Mr. Crawford's rooms?

Mrs. Beddoes: I really don't know, but I do not remember his ever mentioning it.

Mr. Bexheath: Did they dine together?

Mrs. Beddoes: Yes, occasionally they did.

Mr. Bexheath: Can you remember if they were to dine together on the night of your husband's death?

Mrs. Beddoes: No. I've been asked that many times already. I am very sorry, but my husband did not tell me whom he was dining with that night, or anything at all about Mr. Crawford. He only — he only left me a message to say he would not be dining at home.

Mr. Bexheath: I see. Now, let us proceed to the relations between your husband and the prisoner.

Mrs. Beddoes: My husband was very fond of Mr. Weatherburn. He spoke very highly of him and said he would go far. They met regularly to talk. Mr. Weatherburn was very friendly with me also. I thought he was a nice young man. I had no idea ...

The witness burst into tears.

Mr. Bexheath: Now, now, Mrs. Beddoes. Please calm yourself. I will not ask you any more questions.

Mr. Haversham: I have no questions for this witness.

The witness was led away sobbing into her handkerchief, to the accompanying sympathetic murmur of the public gallery.

Mr. Haversham: I would like to point out to the members of the Jury that the evidence of this witness as to the existence of a quarrel between Mr. Beddoes and Mr. Crawford is of fundamental importance. It ties in with the mysterious, red-wine drinking visitor to Mr. Crawford's rooms; this could have been Mr. Beddoes, and it might have been the occasion of the quarrel. Or else the quarrel took place on another occasion, but in any case, it undoubtedly took place. Please do not omit to note this important fact.

Oh, Dora — poor Mrs. Beddoes. I wonder if she really does think Arthur is guilty. She said ... but no. If I were she, I would hardly care what happened in the world around me, after the bitter loss. I shall go and visit her. I continue to listen carefully to everything that the witnesses say, for *somewhere within it the truth must be hidden*. I read my notes over and over. But I cannot see anything. Can you? We *must* find something!

Your very own

Vanessa

Cambridge, Tuesday, May 22nd, 1888

My dearest Dora,

As the witnesses arrived and took their places this morning, I asked Mr. Morrison in a whisper what had transpired yesterday afternoon. He told me that every one of Mr. Crawford's neighbours had been interrogated, and no less than two of them had testified to being acquainted with Arthur, and having seen him enter Mr. Crawford's rooms on at least one occasion, though no dates were made explicit.

This morning, Mr. Bexheath called Mr. Withers as a witness. I had already observed him to be sharp and unkind, but in his testimony he showed himself to be a vile man. That weasel-faced betrayer — his heart must resemble a shrivelled walnut! I would not exchange mine for his for the universe and my happiness besides.

147

Direct examination of Mr. Withers, by Mr. Bexheath

Mr. Bexheath: Please give your name, age and profession.

Mr. Withers: Edward Withers, thirty-two years old, Lecturer in Pure Mathematics at Cambridge University.

Mr. Bexheath: You were acquainted with the three murder victims, Mr. Akers, Mr. Beddoes and Mr. Crawford, as well as with the prisoner?

Mr. Withers: Well, hardly. I saw them occasionally, of course, but couldn't say I knew them very closely. I would like to say that I really have no connection with this whole story.

Mr. Bexheath: Mr. Withers, were you at all familiar with Mr. Crawford's drinking habits?

Mr. Withers: I was not familiar enough with him to describe his regular habits. But I must say I have seen him, on occasions at which he was extremely excited, down a great quantity of whisky, without apparent losing his faculties by doing so.

Mr. Bexheath: How often have you seen him doing so?

Mr. Withers: Not more than once or twice. I do not believe he did it frequently; only on particular occasions of excitement or rejoicing, when he seemed to lose count of the quantity consumed.

Mr. Bexheath: Thank you. Now, the second point I would like to raise is that of the relations between the prisoner and each of the three murder victims. Did you have occasion to observe them?

Mr. Withers: Yes, I observed them at various public occasions, and at some common meals.

Mr. Bexheath: How would you describe them?

Mr. Withers: Well, Weatherburn always acted very friendly with all three of them.

Mr. Bexheath: Would you say that he sought their friendship?

Mr. Withers: Yes, absolutely. He went out of his way to obtain their attention.

Mr. Bexheath: For what purpose?

Mr. Withers: I imagine he had purposes of his own in behaving thus.

Mr. Bexheath: Yes indeed, I imagine so too. Would you say that the prisoner went out of his way to cultivate their friendship and arrange to meet with them regularly?

Mr. Withers: Yes, he did.

Mr. Bexheath: Were you aware of the habit attributed very frequently to Mr. Akers, and in a lesser measure to Mr. Crawford, of directing quite insulting, sarcastic and offensive remarks to his colleagues in public?

Mr. Withers: Certainly.

Mr. Bexheath: Can you describe such an episode?

Mr. Withers: Well, I remember once Wentworth talking to a bunch of fellows, and Akers came along and stopped by to listen, and then he turned to Wentworth and said "Pretty presumptuous for a fellow who's never proved a theorem worth a grain of salt in his life. I'd aim lower if I were you."

Mr. Bexheath: Can you describe Mr. Wentworth's reaction?

Mr. Withers: He told Akers to go boil his head.

Mr. Bexheath: And was he subsequently again on friendly terms with Mr. Akers?

Mr. Withers: Certainly not.

Mr. Bexheath: Would you say that was a normal reaction?

Mr. Withers: Absolutely. A man has to have some pride.

Mr. Bexheath: Was the prisoner ever the butt of such remarks in your hearing?

Mr. Withers: Oh, yes.

Mr. Bexheath: Can you describe his reaction?

Mr. Withers: He only smiled.

Mr. Bexheath: In other words, he endured the insults without taking offense. Would you describe his attitude of deliberately not taking offense as sycophantic?

Mr. Withers: It struck me as obsequious.

Mr. Bexheath: Quite so. Now, Mr. Withers, I would like to turn to the mathematical aspects of the case. Do you know what mathematical topics the deceased gentlemen worked on?

Mr. Withers: Rumour had it they were interested in the n-body problem. I myself heard Crawford mention it elusively when somewhat tipsy.

Mr. Bexheath: Do you know if the prisoner worked on that topic?

Mr. Withers: I don't know it, no. But I certainly heard him discussing the problem at table.

Mr. Bexheath: With just the ordinary interest that any mathematician might evince in a difficult open problem, or with personal interest?

Mr. Withers: He was fairly enthusiastic. I would say personal interest.

Mr. Haversham: My Lord, I strongly object to this question and its answer, to say nothing of the previous ones, and request that they be struck from the record. The witness' opinion is of no value.

Mr. Justice Penrose: Members of the Jury, be aware that the last response given by the witness expresses his personal opinion, and should not be treated as an established fact.

Mr. Haversham: Why, you might as well ask him if he believes the prisoner to be guilty!

Mr. Justice Penrose: Let us remain reasonable. That is not at all the same.

Mr. Bexheath: Well, Mr. Withers, can you perhaps tell us exactly what, in Mr. Weatherburn's manner of talking about the n-body problem, might have led you to form your opinion? Then we shall be on a basis of fact.

Mr. Withers: Let me see. I remember one day back in the first part of April, just a while after Easter, at high table, a number of people were discussing the n-body problem, and Weatherburn was among them. I was just listening, myself. I know nothing about the n-body problem, and really have no idea what Akers and Crawford might have been doing with it. I certainly never asked them. I would again like to stress that I really have no connections with all of this. However, a day or two later, I came across Weatherburn in town, and he was very excited about some wonderful result he claimed he had just proved. He was extremely pleased with himself. I didn't ask for details, but given the previous day's discussion,

I naturally must have assumed it had to do with the n-body problem. This must be at the basis of the impression I mentioned before.

Mr. Bexheath: Thank you very much, Mr. Withers. This is highly interesting. Can you possibly remember the precise day on which the prisoner talked about having made a mathematical discovery?

Mr. Withers: Let me think. I left Cambridge for some days after Easter. I came back on a Thursday. High table would have been on the Friday. So I met Weatherburn ... yes, it was on a Sunday. So it must have been Sunday, April 8th.

Mr. Bexheath: This is very useful. Thank you very much for your helpful testimony, Mr. Withers.

Mr. Withers: You are quite welcome.

Cross-examination of Mr. Withers, by Mr. Haversham

Mr. Haversham: Mr. Withers, you say that you were not particularly acquainted with Mr. Akers, Mr. Beddoes and Mr. Crawford.

Mr. Withers: Yes, not particularly.

Mr. Haversham: Did you attend Mr. Beddoes' funeral?

Mr. Withers: Yes, naturally.

Mr. Haversham: Did you take it upon yourself to accompany Mrs. Beddoes to her carriage afterwards?

Mr. Withers: I did.

Mr. Haversham: Have you ever been invited to their house?

Mr. Withers: Yes.

Mr. Haversham: How many times?

Mr. Withers: I really didn't count them.

Mr. Haversham: So it was sufficiently often for you to lose count. Not in the nature of two or three times only, then.

Mr. Withers: Well, a little more than that.

Mr. Haversham: Your acquaintance with Mrs. Beddoes and her husband does not appear to have been so very slight.

Mr. Withers: Well, I knew Beddoes a little better than the other two.

Mr. Haversham: And yet you would use the words "slight acquaintance" to denote your relations with a man who had invited you to his house numerous times?

Mr. Withers: It was a little more than slight.

Mr. Haversham: Oh, thank you for the rectification. Now, Mr. Withers, I would like to return to the subject so interestingly raised by my learned friend: that of the insulting attitude frequently adopted by Mr. Akers, and also occasionally, although in a lesser measure, by Mr. Crawford, in public.

Mr. Withers: Yes, what about it?

Mr. Haversham: Were you yourself ever the butt of such remarks?

Mr. Withers: I don't remember.

Mr. Haversham: But there are witnesses who remember such an occasion perfectly well. The event occurred at the garden party following a lecture delivered by Professor Arthur Cayley on the subject of the teaching of mathematics. The witnesses claim that you made a remark about joining an anti-

Euclid Society, and that Mr. Crawford said to you, "Before you criticise the teaching methods of better men than yourself, you'd do well to master the mathematics they aim to communicate!"

Mr. Withers: I have no recollection of the event.

Mr. Haversham: You have no recollection of your reaction?

Mr. Withers: None at all.

Mr. Haversham: One witness claims that you laughed weakly.

Mr. Withers: Well, it must have been a joke, not an insult, and the witness did not understand it.

Mr. Haversham: The witness claims that those around did not take it as a joke, and that Mr. Wentworth rose to your defence, demanding of Mr. Crawford to explain exactly what he meant, upon which he continued to insult you, and you departed.

Mr. Withers: I don't recall any of this. And at any rate, I did not butter up Mr. Crawford.

Mr. Haversham: Quite so. Nor did you tell him to go boil his head, although you described it as the only natural reaction of a man with pride.

Mr. Withers: Humph.

Mr. Haversham: My cross-examination is finished, my Lord.

Mr. Justice Penrose: You may stand down.

Throughout this testimony, Arthur showed no sign of the sorrow or disgust that this man's ignoble description of his actions must have engendered within him. Yet his whole aspect appeared desperately tired and hopeless, as though at this point, he wished only for an end to the weary proceedings, whatever it might be. Merely from his demeanour, I perceive that he feels none of the surging hope of being acquitted that I feel for him, none of the indignation, not even the waves of terrible fear that sweep through me whenever I recall that Mr. Bexheath's tendentious questions are not just misleading, infuriating and untruthful, but death-dealing. Arthur's very life-blood seems to flow otherwise than mine; mine rushes in tumults, driving me to action, while his is a dreamy little brook, in which he floats absently, like Ophelia "incapable of his own distress".

Oh, how I seethe within at Mr. Withers' nastiness. No matter what the outcome of this trial, I shall certain never address a single word to Mr. Withers again. By now I am used to the fact that Mr. Bexheath is able to elicit exactly the information he wants from the various witnesses, but Mr. Withers appears to positively burn with the desire to aid and abet him in his nefarious, mistaken goals. Perhaps *he* has his own purposes. Ha.

Yours ever

Vanessa

Cambridge, Wednesday, May 23rd, 1888

Dear Dora,

That horrid Mr. Bexheath would tear the waters of untruth from the driest stone! I was this morning's first witness, and was so upset after his horrid examination that I had to leave the Court in order to hide my tears of rage.

Before being called, during the few minutes that it takes us to arrive and settle on our witnesses' bench, Mr. Morrison kept me up to date, by informing me in a whisper that yesterday afternoon, Mr. Bexheath interrogated the waiters at the Irish pub, who recalled serving dinner to Arthur and Mr. Akers on the first occasion, and Arthur and Mr. Beddoes on the second. One of them recalled the whisky, wine and water ordered by Mr. Akers at the first meal, and Mr. Bexheath picked up his testimony and addressed himself to the Jury, stressing the fact that *the prisoner is fond of red wine*, like Mr. Crawford's mysterious visitor, who would have had such a perfect opportunity to pour the poison into the whisky bottle on the day of his friendly visit, and that *the victim had ordered water*, in order to take his medicine, which proved that Arthur was familiar with the bottle of digitalin he kept in his pocket. The waiter testified that Arthur and Mr. Akers were always together throughout the entire meal, except for one brief journey of Mr. Akers' to wash his hands, and they left together. Oh, how *can* they think that these stupid remarks prove anything!

I was then informed that I was to be the first witness called today, and prepared myself stubbornly inside to resist the tooth-baring, fire-breathing dragon that I perceived behind Mr. Bexheath's bland features. Alas, more like a serpent than a dragon, he twisted the things I said into their very opposite meanings, and spoiled my reputation in doing it.

Direct examination of Miss Duncan, by Mr. Bexheath

Mr. Bexheath: Please give your name, age and occupation.

Vanessa: Vanessa Duncan, 20, schoolteacher.

Mr. Bexheath: Miss Duncan, I have spoken to your landlady, and she has told me that you have rooms on the ground floor of her house, and the prisoner's rooms were just above yours. Is this true?

Vanessa: (*through clenched teeth, and determined to be as monosyllabic as possible*) Yes.

Mr. Bexheath: She tells me that you spoke to her of your upstairs neighbour's habit of continually pacing back and forth at night. Is this true?

Vanessa: Yes.

Mr. Bexheath: The prisoner paced a great deal, alone in his rooms at night?

Vanessa: Well, he paced sometimes.

Mr. Bexheath: It is well-known, of course, that sleeplessness and nocturnal pacing are signs of a troubled conscience.

Vanessa: (*forgetting to speak in monosyllables*) What nonsense! He paced because he was thinking about mathematics.

Mr. Bexheath: Quite. So, Miss Duncan, eventually you became acquainted with the prisoner socially?

Vanessa: Yes. We met at a dinner party given by the mother of one of my pupils.

Mr. Bexheath: Did you once have tea in Grantchester with the prisoner?

Vanessa: Yes.

Mr. Bexheath: You went alone together to Grantchester?

Vanessa: Yes.

Mr. Bexheath: You are aware that this constitutes very suggestive behaviour?

Vanessa: No.

Mr. Bexheath: Oh, you are not aware. Then perhaps you should become aware, for your good name is threatened by such behaviour. Did you ever visit the prisoner in his rooms?

Vanessa: Never.

Mr. Bexheath: Did the prisoner ever visit you in your rooms?

Vanessa: Yes. Once he came down to my rooms to give me a magazine edited by Mr. Oscar Wilde and to invite me to the theatre in London with a party of friends.

Mr. Bexheath: Did he enter your rooms?

Vanessa: No, he stood at the door.

Mr. Bexheath: Very correct, I am sure. And that is the only time he ever visited you in your rooms?

Vanessa: No.

Mr. Bexheath: There were other times?

Vanessa: One other time. He briefly took tea in my rooms after returning from the theatre where we had been, as I said, with a party of friends.

Mr. Bexheath: Your friends of course joined you for this tea?

Vanessa: No.

Mr. Bexheath: Only the prisoner came into your rooms?

Vanessa: Yes.

Mr. Bexheath: What time of day was it?

Vanessa: It was near midnight.

Mr. Bexheath: You and the prisoner were alone in your rooms together at midnight?

Vanessa: Yes, for a short time. We only —

Mr. Bexheath: I AM LEARNING most interesting facts about the prisoner's attitudes in his personal life. Nocturnal pacing is now followed by nocturnal visits to the rooms of young ladies living alone. You, Miss Duncan, hail from the countryside, and may be unaware of the social consequences of such actions as you have been engaging in, but Mr. Weatherburn is most certainly aware of them. If you did not previously, do you at least now realise how he has compromised you?

Vanessa: No.

Mr. Bexheath: You would do better to realise it, and modify your future behaviour accordingly, if it is not already too late. However, Miss Duncan, you are not on trial here. You are young and inexperienced, and I give you this advice in a fatherly and not in a judgemental spirit. The case of the prisoner is an entirely different one. Your testimony paints a most relevant picture of the prisoner's very personal manner of flouting noble feelings in the pursuit of his own pleasure and advantage.

Vanessa: No, it does not!

Mr. Bexheath: Miss Duncan, I counsel you to abandon your stubborn attitude, and to reflect carefully and deeply on what I have told you. I have no more questions for you. This was my last witness, my Lord. It is unfortunate that there are no witnesses to the actual deeds of which the prisoner is accused, but that is only to be expected. One tends to avoid committing murder in front of people. The witnesses I have questioned here have attested, as you have heard, my Lord, and Gentlemen of the Jury, to a mass of details which build up to form a coherent picture which I will summarise fully and completely in my closing speech.

Mr. Justice Penrose: Thank you. Would Counsel for the Defence like to cross-examine?

Mr. Haversham: Most certainly, my Lord.

Mr. Haversham: Miss Duncan, what day was the fatal midnight visit to your rooms upon which my learned colleague has made so many insinuations?

Vanessa: It was on the 7th of April.

Mr. Haversham: And how long did Mr. Weatherburn remain in your rooms at that time?

Vanessa: About fifteen minutes.

Mr. Haversham: How did he come to enter your rooms?

Vanessa: We came in from outside, where we had stopped in a hansom. It was raining extremely hard. We were wet. I invited him in for a cup of tea.

Mr. Haversham: What did you do during his visit?

Vanessa: We sat in front of the fire and had tea and talked a little about the play we had just seen and the friends we had just left.

Mr. Haversham: How did Mr. Weatherburn come to take his leave?

Vanessa: He jumped up quite suddenly and said that some mathematical proof had suddenly struck him, and dashed off upstairs, almost forgetting his overcoat.

Mr. Haversham: It does not strike me that such a brief neighbourly call can be considered to destroy anybody's reputation, nor to constitute a flouting of noble feelings nor a defiance of social conventions, I am glad to say. Furthermore, I take it that the mathematical discovery which caused the prisoner to precipitately leave Miss Duncan's room is one and the same as that which he mentioned to Mr. Withers on the following day. There are no grounds to conclude that it had any relation whatsoever to the famous n-body problem; it is more likely to be related to his own personal research. We will return to this question later. In the meantime, Miss Duncan, I would like, if I may, to ask you some questions about serious matters. Do you recall the garden party following Professor Cayley's lecture on the teaching of mathematics, which took place on the 23rd of April?

Vanessa: Yes, very well.

Mr. Haversham: Did you hear some words exchanged between Mr. Beddoes and Mr. Crawford?

Vanessa: Yes.

Mr. Haversham: Can you recall them?

Vanessa: There weren't many. First, Mr. Crawford was standing with the group of people around Mrs. Beddoes, and when Mr. Beddoes came up, Mr. Crawford simply said something like "Here's Beddoes, I haven't seen you for a week, how have you been?"

Mr. Haversham: That seems normal enough. How did Mr. Beddoes respond?

Vanessa: He seemed extremely surprised. I did not know then that they had quarrelled, but that would explain his surprise. He only said "Quite well". Then the mathematicians standing about went on arguing, and then Mr. Crawford left, but just as he was leaving, he turned to Mr. Beddoes and said that he needed to see him soon, and that they should dine together, and that he would let him know. Mr. Beddoes seemed surprised and rather pleased at this invitation.

Mr. Haversham: So Mr. Beddoes had quarrelled with Mr. Crawford and they had not spoken until the garden party at which Mr. Crawford appeared to wish for a reconciliation, and spoke of a dinner invitation. Might he not have been actually preparing the dinner invitation which he did extend to Mr. Beddoes a week later, as part of a plan to murder him?

Mr. Bexheath: I object to all this, my Lord! A flighty young lady's interpretations of the moods of those around her cannot be introduced as evidence, and neither can my learned colleague's unsubstantiated hypotheses!

Mr. Haversham: Everything the witness has described was observed by several people, some of whom will be called as witnesses for the Defence. For that matter, it can be confirmed by Mrs. Beddoes, my Lord, who was also present. But I do not wish to trouble her unnecessarily in her distress.

Mr. Justice Penrose: Quite so. We accept the witness' statements subject to corroboration by subsequent witnesses for the Defence.

Mr. Haversham: In that case, I have no further questions.

Oh, Dora, wasn't Mr. Bexheath awful? I do feel afraid that if word of this gets out of this Courtroom, some of the mothers of my pupils may not appreciate it at all. What if my school fails because of it? Oh dear, am I ruined? It does seem *so* very stupid, for a lovely cup of tea! How *can* society be so absurd, so suspicious? It's odd — people are all trying (or at least, they it seem to be trying) as hard as they can to be decent and moral, but *seems* to lead to all kinds of extra, unnecessary suspiciousness and nastiness. Oh well. If Arthur is hung I hardly care whether I am ruined or not. I might as well be. I shall return home, and we shall be two old maids and live by netting.

Your loving although ruined twin

Vanessa

Cambridge, Thursday, May 24th, 1888

Oh, Dora —

This morning I woke up, and the memory of yesterday's disaster swept over my consciousness, and I wanted to hide under the covers and remain there forever. How difficult it was to oblige myself to rise and dress, and bend my steps towards the Courthouse. I loathed to go, yet I had to go, and could not have stayed away, though I felt that I must have earned the general contempt of everyone in the room (or perhaps only my own, which is heavy enough).

I hardly dared look at Mr. Morrison, but he sat down next to me immediately, exactly as though nothing untoward had happened, and gave me his usual news bulletin: I had been the last witness for the Prosecution, and in the afternoon, the Judge invited Mr. Haversham to begin calling the witnesses for the defence. Mr. Haversham called Arthur, and led him with careful questions through his contacts with all the mathematicians of his acquaintance, and the murdered men in particular, and then elicited full details of the evenings spent with Mr. Akers and Mr. Beddoes, and everything possible concerning the quarrel between Mr. Crawford and Mr. Beddoes. Mr. Morrison said that the story which emerged was simple and coherent, and appeared to ring true. But as it was drawing late, his cross-examination had been put off until this morning. I braced myself to silently endure the unavoidable wave of horridness.

Cross-examination of Mr. Weatherburn, by Mr. Bexheath

Mr. Bexheath: (*addressing himself to the members of the Jury*) Let me make my intentions clear. In interrogating the prisoner, my goal is to clarify details of how the murders actually took place.

Mr. Haversham: My Lord, I object to my learned colleague's statement! It implies a presumption of guilt.

Mr. Justice Penrose: No, it does not. Counsel's sentence is perfectly clear: he wishes to clarify details of how the murders took place.

Mr. Bexheath: Thank you, my Lord. Now, sir, let us begin with the first murder, that of Mr. Geoffrey Akers. You dined with Mr. Akers on the evening of February 14th?

Arthur: Yes, I d-did.

Mr. Bexheath: Before discussing the actual events of that dinner, I would like to deal with two points: your relations with Mr. Akers, and the question of how you came to be dining with him at all. How would you describe your relations with Mr. Akers?

Arthur: I would describe us as being friends.

Mr. Bexheath: You are 26 years old, and Mr. Akers was 37. The difference in age, and consequently in outlook upon life, is considerable. What interests did you share with Mr. Akers which would make such a friendship possible?

Arthur: I enjoyed his sarcastic humour. As for him, I suppose that like every human being, he needed to talk, to express himself, at least sometimes, and had very few opportunities of doing so.

Mr. Bexheath: Why so?

Arthur: Because his sarcastic and contemptuous nature drove many people away from him.

Mr. Bexheath: Why should that be? All of us enjoy a little witty sarcasm.

Arthur: Yes, b-but Mr. Akers often aimed his barbed shafts at those around him.

Mr. Bexheath: Quite so. And people might feel diminished, humiliated or insulted by such remarks being aimed at them.

Arthur: People felt that in order to protect themselves from having to undergo such unpleasant feelings, they would act safely in keeping their distance from Mr. Akers.

Mr. Bexheath: Please explain, sir, how it comes about, that in your particular case, you were exempt either from such treatment, or from such feelings?

Arthur: I never felt Mr. Akers' remarks about myself to be in the least bit offensive; I found them amusing.

Mr. Bexheath: Ah, so his habit of making snide remarks was not suspended for your sole benefit?

Arthur: Oh, no.

Mr. Bexheath: And you remained almost the only one among all of his colleagues whose pride was not affected by this.

Arthur: My pride was not affected.

Mr. Bexheath: Perhaps that is because you have very little.

Arthur: (*silence*)

Mr. Bexheath: Or perhaps you smothered the natural reaction of pride, in order to cultivate his acquaintance to your own advantage.

Arthur: (*silence*)

Mr. Bexheath: You do not appear to disagree.

Arthur: *"The silence often of pure innocence Persuades when speaking fails."*

Mr. Bexheath: My dear man, if you have nothing to say, do not fill the gap with Shakespeare.

Arthur: (*shrugging*) As you say.

Mr. Bexheath: Let us now turn to your dinner with Mr. Akers. Can you recount how you came to be dining together?

Arthur: I met him in the mathematics library in the afternoon, and he seemed very p-p-p — very pleased about some mathematical result, and wanted an opportunity to talk about it, so he suggested we dine.

Mr. Bexheath: The suggestion came entirely from him, you say.

Arthur: Yes.

Mr. Bexheath: Were there any witnesses to your conversation?

Arthur: I suppose not. P-people whisper in libraries.

Mr. Bexheath: So that there is no one can actually testify that the idea really originated with Mr. Akers and not with yourself.

Arthur: Except for myself.

Mr. Bexheath: Quite so. And so you met at the Irish pub.

Arthur: Yes.

Mr. Bexheath: Now let us consider the question of Mr. Akers' medicine bottle. How did you become aware of its existence? Please describe very exactly every single thing that Mr. Akers did with his medicine.

Arthur: We had whiskies to start with, and then ordered a bottle of red wine and Irish stew. The wine was brought at once, and Mr. Akers turned to the waiter and asked for a p-p-pitcher of water as well. The waiter brought it, and he poured out a glass and said, "Have to take my medicine." He then took out a little square flask made of thick glass, and removed the stopper. The opening was in dropper form. He turned the flask upside down and measured out a drop or so into his water, and shook the flask a little. Then he said something like "Dash it, what am I doing?" and stopped it up and put it away into his pocket. I never laid eyes on that medicine bottle at any time after that.

Mr. Bexheath: Did he drink the water?

Arthur: Yes, complaining. He did not like water.

Mr. Bexheath: You say that he put only one drop into the water?

Arthur: One or two.

Mr. Bexheath: You are aware that his regular dose was of ten drops?

Arthur: No, I was not aware of that.

Mr. Bexheath: Can you explain why he would have taken less?

Arthur: Perhaps he remembered that he had already taken his dose earlier.

Mr. Bexheath: Then why would he have drunk the water?

Arthur: I really d-don't know. Perhaps he didn't want to waste the drop.

Mr. Bexheath: And were you not surprised to see a medicine given in a standard dose of one drop?

Arthur: I d-didn't think about it at all.

Mr. Bexheath: You did not ask him about it?

Arthur: No.

Mr. Bexheath: You felt no interest?

Arthur: No.

Mr. Bexheath: A man is struggling with his dropper bottle in front of you, and complaining about having to drink water, and you do not even ask him about it?

Arthur: No, I did not. I hardly noticed. We were talking of other things.

Mr. Bexheath: What things?

Arthur: Mathematics.

Mr. Bexheath: Ah, mathematics. What about them?

Arthur: About the n-body problem. Suddenly, Akers began to tell me about his new idea for a complete solution. He seemed agitated and excited, as though he could not restrain his desire to talk about it.

Mr. Bexheath: Restrain his desire? Why should he restrain his desire?

Arthur: At the same time, he wanted to keep his solution secret.

Mr. Bexheath: Why so?

Arthur: I g-guessed that perhaps it was not completely written yet, and he wanted to keep it a secret until he should have a manuscript submitted.

Mr. Bexheath: Why was such secrecy necessary?

Arthur: Akers felt that he had rivals in the subject.

Mr. Bexheath: Are you implying that he feared his interesting result risked being stolen by someone else, and made use of for their own advantage?

Arthur: It is p-possible.

Mr. Bexheath: But surely then he would keep the secret only from those rivals. Why should he keep it from a trusted friend?

Arthur: He probably thought that word would get around if he talked about it at all.

Mr. Bexheath: There you were, across from each other, in a leather booth in a noisy restaurant, in complete privacy, where no one could possibly overhear you, and he desired to talk about it. Could he not simply have bound you to silence?

Arthur: He could have asked me to keep quiet, of course.

Mr. Bexheath: But he did not do so. Perhaps he did not trust you.

Arthur: He did not trust anybody, I think.

Mr. Bexheath: I submit that he must have trusted you to start with, since he began to communicate his results with you. What transpired to make him suddenly change his mind?

Arthur: Nothing transpired at all. He suddenly felt he was saying too much.

Mr. Bexheath: Suddenly, for no reason at all?

Arthur: Because of his natural discretion.

Mr. Bexheath: Or because you, sir, showed him by some sign that your interest in his work was more than purely friendly — in other words, that *the thief he feared was no other than yourself*. What did you say to him, sir, which caused him to suddenly change his mind and cut short his explanations? Did you show excessive interest? Did he see by your expression that his discovery had awakened your covetousness?

Arthur: I can't — no. Surely not.

Mr. Bexheath: Well, well. Now, did you and Mr. Akers remain together all the time after that?

Arthur: Yes, we finished dinner together and walked back to his rooms.

Mr. Bexheath: You never separated for a moment?

Arthur: I d-don't remember that we did.

Mr. Bexheath: This proves that the digitalin bottle was still in his pocket at the time of his death, does it not?

Arthur: I suppose so.

Mr. Bexheath: You suppose so. Do you not *know* so?

Arthur: Not of my own knowledge.

Mr. Bexheath: Logical reasoning is not sufficient to convince you, a mathematician?

Arthur: Hum.

Mr. Bexheath: Well, well, now, perhaps mathematicians are not so rigorous as we might have supposed, when it is a matter of personal advantage!

Tittering in the public gallery.

Arthur: What advantage? That of being hung for something I didn't do?

Mr. Bexheath: That is a matter for the Jury to decide.

Arthur: That may be difficult for them, given the complete lack of evidence.

Mr. Bexheath: Oh, I think there is plenty of evidence.

Arthur: I fail to perceive it. It is like using a conjecture to prove another conjecture.

Mr. Justice Penrose: Your perceptions are not the issue here, sir. Please confine yourself to answering Counsel's questions.

Mr. Bexheath: You are aware that the medicine bottle was not found in his pocket by the doctor who examined the corpse?

Arthur: Yes, I have heard that.

Mr. Bexheath: So the bottle must have been taken by the murderer.

Arthur: It seems likely.

Mr. Bexheath: Now, sir, you are on oath to tell the truth, the whole truth, and nothing but the truth. DID YOU TAKE THE FLASK OF DIGITALIN FROM MR. AKERS?

Arthur: N-N-No. N-No. No. I did not.

Mr. Bexheath: Are you certain?

Arthur: Yes!

Mr. Bexheath: DID YOU KILL MR. AKERS?

Arthur: No!

Mr. Bexheath: Hmph. Very well. Now, sir, I would like to recall and interrogate you about a point raised in previous testimonies. We have heard that you allowed yourself to visit Miss Duncan alone in her rooms, late at night. I suppose you consider destroying the reputation of a young and defenceless girl as natural as smiling when you are insulted in public?

Arthur: (*silence*)

Mr. Bexheath: Well? May I take it that this behaviour is perfectly acceptable to you?

Arthur: I c-c-cannot think that my v-visit could have any effect on Miss Duncan's reputation. What c-could have an effect is your way of insinuating things which d-d-did not occur.

Mr. Bexheath: I take your statement to mean that as long as no one knows about such nocturnal visits, no one's reputation is destroyed.

Arthur: N-no, that is not what I mean. I mean that on a rainy night, I took a cup of t-tea in Miss Duncan's rooms which she very k-k-kindly offered me, and then returned to my rooms upstairs. You p-pretend to be concerned about her reputation, and instead you insinuate falsehoods with "*the shrug, the hum or ha, these petty brands that calumny doth use.*"

Mr. Bexheath: I see. So according to Shakespeare, I myself am responsible for the harm done to Miss Duncan's reputation.

Tittering in the public.

Mr. Bexheath: I imagine that point of view is extremely serviceable, when applied to one's own conduct.

Further tittering in the public. The Judge tapped his gavel lightly upon his desk.

Mr. Bexheath: Now, sir, is it true that you told both Miss Duncan upon that evening, and Mr. Withers on the following day, that you had come upon a new and exciting proof of some mathematical result?

Arthur: Yes, it is true. How long ago it seems!

Mr. Bexheath: I submit that you proved a result connected with the n-body problem, and that your proof was based on information obtained from Mr. Akers.

Arthur: No, absolutely not.

Mr. Bexheath: Then what was the result which you proved?

Arthur: It was about normal forms of matrices, whatever that may signify to you.

Mr. Bexheath: Have you any proof of that? Have you written something?

Arthur: Not yet.

Mr. Bexheath: Ah, not yet. Quite. So you cannot prove your assertion. As far as proof is concerned, you may well have proved something concerning the n-body problem, in which case you would have every reason to keep it secret.

Arthur: That could be true, but it happens to be false.

Mr. Bexheath: Let us now turn to the murder of Mr. Beddoes. Recall your dinner in the Irish pub. What did you eat?

Arthur: We had the same thing as the other time. It is the speciality of the house.

Mr. Bexheath: Upon what subject did your conversation with

173

Mr. Beddoes turn, during your dinner together?

Arthur: Upon mathematics and other mathematicians.

Mr. Bexheath: Did you discuss the famous n-body problem?

Arthur: Not directly. Beddoes asked me a rather technical question, how one formula should imply another, and we tried to work it out together, but we did not succeed. He wrote down the formulae; they looked to me as though they had some relations with the partial differential equations involved in the n-body problem, but he did not actually say anything about it.

Mr. Bexheath: Did you ask him about the source of the formulae he was trying to understand?

Arthur: I did, but he did not really answer. He said they had come up in discussions with others. He mentioned Mr. Crawford, with whom we should have been dining in any case.

Mr. Bexheath: Ah yes, that famous story. You claim that the original dinner invitation of that evening, the 30th of April, actually originated with Mr. Crawford, who then in the early evening claimed an indisposition and sent a note to Mr. Beddoes and to yourself inviting you to go without him.

Arthur: Yes.

Mr. Bexheath: Do you have the note?

Arthur: No, I d-did not keep it.

Mr. Bexheath: Quite so. So that your statement cannot be independently established.

Arthur: It seems not.

Mr. Bexheath: After dinner, you then accompanied Mr. Beddoes to his garden gate.

Arthur: Yes.

Mr. Bexheath: But you did not enter the garden?

Arthur: He opened the gate, and we stood in the gateway, shaking hands.

Mr. Bexheath: You are aware that the traces of earth on your shoes prove that YOU WERE IN THE GARDEN?

Arthur: I must have picked them up standing just inside the gateway.

Mr. Bexheath: But the gateway opens onto a path leading to the house, and the path is paved.

Arthur: In a garden, I suppose earth frequently lies over the flagstones.

Mr. Bexheath: Mrs. Beddoes keeps a well-swept path.

Arthur: There is no real answer to that.

Mr. Bexheath: So, were you actually within Mr. Beddoes' garden?

Arthur: Just inside the gateway.

Mr. Bexheath: DID YOU, SIR, TAKE UP A HEAVY ROCK EMBEDDED IN THE EARTH NEAR THE PATH, AND STRIKE MR. BEDDOES WITH IT?

Arthur: N-N-No! No. No. No.

Mr. Bexheath: Very well. Very well, then. Very well. In that case, let us turn to the death of Mr. Crawford. Is it true that you visited him on occasion in his rooms?

Arthur: I have entered his rooms on two occasions within the last few months.

Mr. Bexheath: Did you have anything to drink there?

Arthur: No.

Mr. Bexheath: No red wine?

Arthur: No.

Mr. Bexheath: Can you recall the dates of your visits?

Arthur: I went once in March, after a lecture of Mr. Crawford, to bring him a book which he had accidentally left in the lecture room. I do not remember the exact date. I went another time in April, to collect Mr. Crawford on the way to high table.

Mr. Bexheath: On both occasions, Mr. Crawford was in his rooms?

Arthur: Yes.

Mr. Bexheath: Did he keep his door locked?

Arthur: No.

Mr. Bexheath: Did you knock, or simply enter?

Arthur: I knocked, and he opened.

Mr. Bexheath: DID YOU POUR THE DIGITALIN INTO HIS BOTTLE OF WHISKY UPON ONE OF THESE OCCASIONS?

Arthur: No!

Mr. Bexheath: You are on oath, sir.

Arthur: I know it.

Mr. Bexheath: In that case I have nothing more to say.

Arthur sat down in the dock and my heart went out to him, in a great turmoil and commotion of distress and tenderness. That monstrous Mr. Bexheath tried every underhanded way, even making use of Arthur's unfortunate (although endearing) stammer, to influence the Jury's thinking. I stared miserably into their dull faces, but could read nothing of their reactions. The things that are happening in this Court do not represent anything like law and justice! I am so worried. Can they possibly find something incriminating in Arthur's statements?

Your fearful

Vanessa

Cambridge, Friday, May 25th, 1888

Oh, dear Dora —

The trial has taken a disastrous turn! I have a horrible feeling, which is positively physical: watery bones.

All began much as usual. Judge and Jury filed to their places, the barristers sat at their tables, the witnesses along their benches, the public in their gallery, and last but not least, Arthur appeared between two policemen and was escorted, like a dangerous criminal, into the dock. Our eyes met briefly, but he looked down directly; sometimes I suspect that my presence here, observing the unendurable, must make it even worse for him, but I could not bear not to be here, and such is the nature of things.

The Judge began by turning to Mr. Haversham, and asking him if he wished to continue presenting the witnesses for the defence, when Mr. Bexheath arose from his place, and intervened, addressing the Judge respectfully.

"I have a request to make, my Lord, which I hope the Court

will look upon favourably."

"Yes, what is it?" enquired Mr. Justice Penrose.

"My Lord, in principle, I have finished presenting the witnesses assembled in support of the Crown. However, my personal researches upon the important questions of facts raised here have led to the discovery of two new witnesses, who are able to provide a *capital* piece of evidence in favour of the Crown."

A great murmur and commotion ran all around the Courtroom, as everybody wondered what this new, revealing piece of evidence could be. I felt my breast contract and tighten with strain, and looked anxiously at Mr. Morrison. Instead of smiling encouragingly at me, he stared back at me with dismay.

"Counsel for the Defence, do you accept the interrogation of these new witnesses for the prosecution, before continuing with the regular series of your own witnesses?" the Judge asked Mr. Haversham politely.

I dearly hoped he would refuse, but of course, the question was a mere formality, and he had no real possibility of doing so. He acquiesced as graciously as possible, and Mr. Bexheath said, "Then I would like to request Miss Pamela Simpson to take the stand!"

A door opened, and the Bailiff ushered a young lady into the Courtroom, and guided her to the witness stand, where she stood, her head thrown back, an air of frank curiosity and amusement upon her face.

Dora, dear, I really do not know how to describe such a person! if I dared, I would imagine that she is the exact type of what certain ladies of our acquaintance would have termed "a creature". Bold, brazen, laughing, daring, hard, devil-may-care, every word and every movement betraying a conscious desire to produce a specific effect — she seemed as out of place in the solemn Courtroom as a brilliant bird of paradise. She stood, half-smiling, in a position of insolent ease, in her bright clothes, and waited. The Court Clerk appeared with his Bible and swore her in. Her hand upon the Bible, she took the oath with clear, ringing tones, so that it did not seem that the suspicion of incorrectness naturally aroused by her appearance need necessarily apply to her veracity.

Direct examination of Miss Pamela Simpson by Mr. Bexheath

Mr. Bexheath: Tell us your name, please.

Miss Simpson: Pamela Simpson.

Mr. Bexheath: Your age?

Miss Simpson: Twenty-two last January.

Mr. Bexheath: Where do you reside, Miss Simpson?

Miss Simpson: In London, just behind King's Cross.

Mr. Bexheath: Miss Simpson, were you acquainted with the late Mr. Jeremy Crawford, Lecturer in Mathematics at the University of Cambridge?

Miss Simpson: Yes, I was acquainted with him. He was a nice man. I'm very sorry he's dead.

Mr. Bexheath: Can you tell us if you saw Mr. Crawford on February 14th last?

Miss Simpson: Yes, I did.

Mr. Bexheath: Are you aware that that was the day of the murder of the mathematician Mr. Geoffrey Akers?

Miss Simpson: Well, I wasn't then, but I know it now.

Commotion and murmuring in the Court. The Judge banged his gavel until silence was restored.

Mr. Bexheath: Can you tell us what part of the day of February the 14th you spent with Mr. Crawford?

Miss Simpson: The whole evening, from eight o'clock, and the whole night, until the next morning.

Commotion and murmuring in the Court. The Judge banged his gavel and said "If silence is not kept I will clear the court!"

Mr. Bexheath: Where did you spend those hours with Mr. Crawford, Miss Simpson?

Miss Simpson: Well, in my rooms, except when we dined.

Mr. Bexheath: You are referring to your rooms in London, behind King's Cross Station?

Miss Simpson: Yes.

Mr. Bexheath: And where did you dine?

Miss Simpson: We dined at *Jenny's Corner*, a small restaurant situated near to my rooms.

Mr. Bexheath: *Jenny's Corner* is run by a Miss Jenny Pease?

Miss Simpson: Yes.

Mr. Bexheath: She is a friend of yours?

Miss Simpson: Yes.

Mr. Bexheath: You are aware that Miss Pease is present today, and will be examined with a view to confirming, for the benefit of the Jury, the veracity of your statements?

Miss Simpson: What, sir? Excuse me?

Mr. Bexheath: You know that Miss Pease is here, and that she will be questioned as to your dinner of February 14th?

Miss Simpson: Oh! Yes, I know that, of course. We came up here together.

Mr. Bexheath: Now, Miss Simpson, do you know how Mr. Crawford came from Cambridge to London?

Miss Simpson: Yes, I know that. He came down by the train, for I fetched him myself at the station at about seven thirty, and we came home together.

Mr. Bexheath: And did you and Mr. Crawford separate for any length of time during the evening of February 14th?

Miss Simpson: No, sir, absolutely not. We were stuck together like two peas in a pod the whole livelong evening, and the night, too.

Mr. Bexheath: So there is no possibility whatsoever that Mr. Crawford could have been assassinating a man, in Cambridge, on the evening of February the 14th.

Miss Simpson: Absolutely not!

Mr. Bexheath: Remember now, Miss Simpson, that your testimony is of vital importance, and you are on oath. You are absolutely certain of what you are saying?

Miss Simpson: Oh, yes. I realise that what I'm saying shows that Mr. Crawford did not kill that Mr. Akers, and that makes it seem like it must be the poor young man in the dock over there that did it. I feel very sorry for him and hope it wasn't him, but I can't help what I'm saying, as it is true.

Mr. Bexheath: Thank you very much, Miss Simpson.

Mr. Justice Penrose: Mr. Haversham, would you like to cross-examine this witness?

Mr. Haversham: Most certainly, my Lord.

Cross-examination of Miss Pamela Simpson, by Mr. Haversham.

Mr. Haversham: Miss Simpson, may I enquire what your profession is?

Miss Simpson: (*absolutely undecomposed*) I'm afraid I've got none, Mr. Barrister.

Mr. Haversham: But you must have money to live on, don't you? How do you pay for your rent, and your meals?

Miss Simpson: Oh, I get money where I can, as gifts, often enough.

Mr. Haversham: And who gives you such kind gifts?

Miss Simpson: Friends.

Mr. Haversham: And what service do you render these friends, that they are so kindly disposed towards you?

Miss Simpson: Mr. Barrister, if you're trying to shame me, it won't work. For I'm ready to say right out that I take good care of my gentlemen friends, and they takes good care of me.

Mr. Haversham: Oh! I see. So you have come to a satisfactory arrangement with your gentlemen friends?

Miss Simpson: You're right I have.

Mr. Haversham: And how many of these friends do you have?

Miss Simpson: I've never counted them!

Mr. Haversham: So there are too many to estimate, say, on the fingers of one hand.

Miss Simpson: Oh Lord, yes.

Mr. Haversham: Quite. Now, let us discuss your acquaintance with Mr. Crawford.

Miss Simpson: I'm ready to when you are.

Mr. Haversham: Can you tell us when and how you first met Mr. Crawford?

Miss Simpson: I met him in London, some years ago. It's hard for me to remember exactly when — probably three or four years ago.

Mr. Haversham: And where did you meet him?

Miss Simpson: In the train station.

Mr. Haversham: Would you like to tell us the circumstances of that meeting?

Miss Simpson: Well — he come out of the train, with his bags, and I see he looks like a nice kind of man, so I goes up to him and says "Hello, sir, looking for a nice place to stay while you visit London?" and he smiles at me and says "Well, that might be, my dear, it might be." So he did.

Mr. Haversham: So he did what?

Miss Simpson: Stay at my place. It's a nice place, isn't it?

Mr. Haversham: And at that time, you already had a number of friends, as you call them?

Miss Simpson: Not as many as now.

Mr. Haversham: Yes. And was that your regular method for making new friends?

Miss Simpson: Well, I've never been shy about speaking to people I see that look nice.

Mr. Haversham: And how often did you see Mr. Jeremy Crawford?

Miss Simpson: Oh, he'd come down to London and see me fairly regularly.

Mr. Haversham: How regularly?

Miss Simpson: Maybe every month or so. Pretty much every month. It's hard for a man to be alone all the time, they risks turning into dry sticks. You ought to know that, by the look of you.

Laughter in the Court. The Judge banged his gavel.

Mr. Haversham: Miss Simpson, did Mr. Crawford have a regular date or day of the week on which he would come down to see you?

Miss Simpson: No.

Mr. Haversham: So how can you be so sure that the day he came to see you last February was exactly the 14th?

Miss Simpson: Oh, that's easy. For one thing, it was Saint Valentine's day. That's a romantic day, you know. We joked about it. But anyway, I have his letter.

Mr. Haversham: What letter is that?

Miss Simpson: Well, when he thought he had a free day to come down, you know, he'd simply write me, and I'd write back, if it was all right.

Mr. Haversham: You mean, if you were not busy with another friend on that day?

Miss Simpson: You've hit it on the nose, Mr. Barrister. So he wrote me about the 14th of February, and I wrote back it was all right, and here is the letter.

Mr. Haversham: This is the letter he wrote to you?

Miss Simpson: Yes.

Mr. Haversham: But we do not appear to be in possession of your affirmative answer, so this does not really constitute a proof that he came on that day.

Miss Simpson: No, I doubt he kept my notes, but there's this letter, and there's what I remember and have sworn to, and Jenny remembers too.

Mr. Haversham: So our establishment of the date depends essentially on your memory and your ability to distinguish between your different friends, and the different days upon which you received them.

Miss Simpson: Oh, no, Mr. Barrister. Don't try to make out that I'm all confused. I remember rightly about the 14th, and this letter says so too, and Jenny will as well.

Mr. Haversham: Very well. You may stand down.

Then Mr. Bexheath called Miss Jenny Pease to the stand. She was a buxom lady, quite a bit older than Miss Simpson, and not so garish, but equally sure of herself. She was sworn in by the Clerk, and her direct examination began.

Direct examination of Miss Jenny Pease, by Mr. Bexheath

Mr. Bexheath: What is your name?

Miss Pease: Jenny Pease, sir.

Mr. Bexheath: Please state your profession.

Miss Pease: I have a little restaurant nearby King's Cross, sir, down in London.

Mr. Bexheath: You are acquainted with Miss Pamela Simpson?

Miss Pease: Oh yes.

Mr. Bexheath: For how long have you known her?

Miss Pease: Oh, she comes to the restaurant regular, sir, been coming for the last couple of years, or thereabouts.

Mr. Bexheath: Does she come alone?

Miss Pease: Sometimes alone, sometimes with friends.

Mr. Bexheath: Do you clearly remember whether Miss Simpson came to eat in your restaurant on the 14th of February last?

Miss Pease: Yes, sir.

Mr. Bexheath: She did come?

Miss Pease: Yes, sir.

Mr. Bexheath: Did she come alone?

Miss Pease: No, sir. She came accompanied by a gentleman friend, Mr. Crawford.

Mr. Bexheath: You were previously acquainted with Mr. Crawford?

Miss Pease: Oh, yes, sir. He and Pam had come to the restaurant any number of times already, before then.

Mr. Bexheath: Now, Miss Pease, can you tell me how you can be absolutely certain that the day Miss Simpson and Mr. Crawford had dinner in your restaurant was precisely the

14th of February, and no other day?

Miss Pease: Oh, I remember well enough. We joked back and forth about its being Saint Valentine's day, like, and so Mr. Crawford must be Pam's real sweetheart. Also, it was a Tuesday, that's my mutton chop day, and they had it.

Mr. Bexheath: Your mutton chop day?

Miss Pease: The dish of the day, sir. There's one for every day of the week: Monday liver, Tuesday mutton chop, Wednesday T-bone, Thursday fowl, Friday fish ...

Mr. Bexheath: Yes, yes, Miss Pease, we understand. And the order of the dish of the day never varies? It is the same from week to week?

Miss Pease: Has been for years. The regulars likes things regular, if you know what I mean, sir. They likes to know what to expect.

Mr. Bexheath: Of course. Well, this concludes my examination.

Cross-examination of Miss Jenny Pease, by Mr. Haversham.

Mr. Haversham: Now, Miss Pease, I have heard your testimony, and there is really only one thing in it I would like to ask you about.

Miss Pease: What's that, then?

Mr. Haversham: Your memory. You claim that you remember the exact day upon which Miss Simpson and Mr. Crawford came to your restaurant, three and a half months ago.

Miss Pease: Well, I do, then.

Mr. Haversham: May I conclude that you remember every

187

day that every single one of your clients came to the restaurant?

Miss Pease: No. But I'm specially friends with Pam.

Mr. Haversham: Oh, I see. So then, you are simply able to remember each and every day upon which Miss Simpson came to dine in the restaurant, and whom she was with each time. Could you please give me a complete list of those dates, going back over the last four months?

Miss Pease: No, you know right well I can't do anything of the kind!

Mr. Haversham: Oh, really? No, I am quite surprised. So, after all, your memory of Miss Simpson's various visits is not so perfectly clear.

Miss Pease: Not every one of her visits, but the one on the February 14th is pretty clear.

Mr. Haversham: Pretty clear? But not completely clear?

Miss Pease: Well, it's completely clear that she was there, and that she was with Mr. Crawford, that I already was acquainted with, and that they ate mutton chops and we chaffed about Saint Valentine's day. Those things are clear.

Mr. Haversham: Miss Pease, may I ask you who first questioned you about this important date of February 14th, and then brought you to this Court?

Miss Pease: It was police, sir. What with Pam seeing that her friend Mr. Crawford had died, she was talking to her friends and all about how she knew him, and it got to police, and they came and questioned her about these two dates: February 14th and April 30th. Pam didn't know anything about April 30th; she hadn't seen anything of Mr. Crawford on that day. But she remembered about being with him on February 14th, and remembered about coming to the restaurant that day. So then they came to ask me about it.

Mr. Haversham: And how did they ask you about it? Was the date of February 14th suggested to you? Or were you asked to recall it yourself?

Miss Pease: They reminded me back in February, and said had I seen Miss Simpson and her Mr. Crawford, and I really couldn't bring it to mind at first, as I sees her so often. Then they had us together, and she reminded me about Saint Valentine's day, and I remembered.

Mr. Haversham: I see. That is very helpful. They reminded you about what to remember, and then you remembered it.

Miss Pease: I see what you're saying, sir, but it isn't that way. I really remembered it, they just jogged my memory, like.

Mr. Haversham: Very well, they jogged your memory, and then you remembered the date of February 14th which previously you had not remembered. You may stand down.

Mr. Haversham certainly tried everything he could to shed doubt upon the testimony of these two ladies, but I am afraid he did not succeed in convincing the Jury. I must admit frankly that he did not even succeed in convincing me; the ladies' statements really did ring simple and true. They may have been bribed or threatened or simply cajoled into inventing the story, but the police themselves would have no reason to do it ... it would have to be the true murderer himself. *But why should he care* whether Arthur or Mr. Crawford was convicted for his own crimes — OH — unless ... oh! What if Arthur himself was the intended next victim, and this is the murderer's cunning way of disposing of him? What a horrible idea! But ... it means that if Miss Simpson and Miss Pease are not telling the truth, then they must know who the murderer is. I *must* try to meet them. Perhaps, after lessons, I could catch a train to London and eat at *Jenny's Corner*.

Late at night.
I have done it. The two ladies were sent back to London by train, as Miss Pease was very anxious about her restaurant being locked up unexpectedly even for a single evening. I myself hastened home to teach my little class — how difficult it is becoming, now that my mind is so dreadfully elsewhere! The moment the last little pupil had disappeared around the corner, I put on my hat, snatched up a bag, put all my available money into it, and rushed to the railway station, where I purchased a ticket to London and found myself quite soon swept off by a rattling locomotive. It was not so difficult, really; I just did the same as the day we all went to the theatre. When the train pulled into London, I got out, and addressing the driver of a hansom waiting in the road, I asked him if he knew of a restaurant called *Jenny's Corner* in the neighbourhood. He did not, but by dint of wandering about the streets and asking continually, I eventually discovered it. It was dinner time, and the restaurant was already quite full. It is a small, dingy hole, rather dirty, with little tables set close together, but it was warmly lit nonetheless, and the buxom Miss Pease with her apron, emerging frequently from her kitchen to banter with the customers, and aided by a scrap of a girl taken in off the streets, by the look of her, lent a welcoming atmosphere to the whole.

I was quite out of place in the restaurant, my dear; I was most unlike anybody else there, and felt that they looked at me with some hostility. However, I entered, and the scrap of a girl showed me to a tiny corner table. There was no menu; she simply stopped in front of me and breathlessly recited a list of dishes, ending with "dish-of-the-day's-fish-mum, if you please, a nice baked haddock it is". I said I would have baked haddock please, and could I speak with Miss Pease.

The girl went into the kitchen through the swinging baize

door, and came out carrying plates and mugs. She was followed by Miss Pease, who looked suspiciously over at me. She stared for a moment, and then her face broke into a smile.

"Oh, I recognise you," she said. "You was at the trial this morning, up on the witness bench, along of us."

"Yes, I was," I told her. "I have come to see you because of the trial." My voice became unsteady, and Miss Pease waxed motherly.

"P'raps you'd better come in here and talk private for a moment," she said. I got up and followed her into the fuming kitchen, and from there, into a small, cluttered back room.

"Miss Pease," I said, "I'm a friend of Arthur Weatherburn, the man accused of murdering Mr. Crawford and the others."

I meant to go on, but suddenly and quite unexpectedly, I burst into tears. In a moment I found myself pillowed on Miss Pease's ample breast. She put her arms around me, and said,

"Dear, dear, it must be very hard for you."

"Yes," I sobbed. "Oh, Miss Pease, he didn't do it!"

"Well, poor Mr. Crawford ain't done it either, seems now, so then I don't know who it might have been," she said.

"I came to ask you about that," I told her, suddenly feeling that perfect directness was possible with this kindly soul. "I wanted to know if it was true, what you said. I mean, really true — do you really remember all that? Or was it just the police or somebody else wanting you to say it, so as to incriminate Arthur?" And the tears began again, harder than ever.

"La, la," she said, patting me on the back. "I'm so sorry, dear. I do wish I could help you. It's a nasty situation you're in, isn't it? I truly wish I could tell you that I don't remember really about that poor dead Mr. Crawford, and that mayhap he was the murderer after all, and not your young man. But it can't be done. They was really here that night, the two of them. I know it well as can be, what with the mutton chops that was his favourite dish, and the Saint Valentine jokes about sweethearts and all. There ain't no doubt about it, dear. It came back to me when Pam reminded me, and that's how it happened, that's all. Now, now, don't take on so, dear. If your young man's innocent, why they'll acquit him, won't they? Now, you take this handkerchief, and sit down, and have your bit of fish." And I did, and then a comforting cup of tea, before which I sit as I write to you.

Oh, dear. Oh, dear. Oh, dear. I can no more bring myself to believe that this kind and sincere woman is lying than that Arthur is the murderer. What *shall* I do?

Your miserable

Vanessa

Cambridge, Saturday, May 26th, 1888

My dearest Dora,

Last night, upon returning from my sad little dinner at *Jenny's Corner,* I had a terrifying experience.

I was walking back to the station, to return home. My mind was filled with the disaster which has befallen Arthur, and the devastating kindliness of Miss Pease. I could not conclude anything other than that she and her friend Miss Simpson had told the truth, the simple truth, *and this means the murderer is still at large*. Who can it be, Dora?? More strongly than ever, the thought was borne in upon me *that the murderer exists in flesh and blood*. I had felt that same feeling in the first days when I went to visit Arthur in prison, but afterwards, I believe I had convinced myself so completely that Mr. Crawford must be the murderer, that I quite forgot my original fears. They began to return in force, as I ran over the familiar faces of Arthur's many colleagues whom I had met over the last months. One of them must be secretly mad. Who was it? Where was he now? What was he planning, presently, at this very minute? Who would be the next victim? Was he trying to systematically eliminate the entire group of mathematicians associated to Mr. Akers and Mr. Crawford? Arthur was undoubtedly one of them. I could not help feeling that even if a condemnation awaited Arthur, at least while the trial lasted, he was safely in prison, where the murderer could not get at him.

But is not the murderer afraid, Dora? Does he not feel his entrails burn with fear and guilt as the trial takes its daily course? Does he follow it? *Is he sitting in the Courtroom, day after day*? I felt my hair rise upon the back of my head, and at the same moment, I became aware that I was being quietly followed, down a dark and empty street.

My heart pounded wildly, as I forced myself to continue on steadily towards the corner, where a dim glow showed me that the perpendicular street was gaslit. I dared not turn and look at my pursuer, nor quicken my pace to alarm or attract him. I tried to tell myself that it was simply another quiet foot passenger, like myself, walking along innocently on business of his own. Or even an ordinary footpad, pickpocket, thief, attacker of any kind — anyone at all — *but not the Cambridge murderer*! Of course, that could not be. Why should he have followed me here?

The more I walked, the more I felt that if I should suddenly turn around, I would see a familiar face, and if so, I would *know*. Yet I was too afraid. I decided to do it exactly when I had very nearly reached the street corner. I fixed my eyes upon the point I meant to arrive at when I should suddenly whip around, and advanced steadily towards it.

But before I reached it, my unknown follower suddenly broke into a run. His footsteps pounded behind me. My heart leapt, my eyes started out of their sockets, I turned around and saw him bearing down on me, his collar up and his face muffled by a dark scarf, and involuntarily I also began to run wildly towards the corner, screaming. I was hindered by my skirts, and he reached me before I could come to the lighted section, and seizing me violently from behind, pulled me into a doorway. I wrenched loose and struggled and screamed.

193

Then came running footsteps, and a man and a woman together came hurrying round the corner from the lighted street. The man shouted out, "What's happening?" My assailant dropped me and raced away like lightning, down the street the other way, and I fell into the arms of the lady, my heart knocking as though to burst. They scolded me a great deal for walking alone in such a dangerous neighbour-hood, and hailed a hansom to take me to the station. I cried in the hansom, partly from relief, partly from distress, and also because I had not been able to identify my attacker in any way, not even to guess his age; simply that he was not an eld-erly man because he seemed so strong and fast. It could have been *him*, or it could have been a perfect stranger, a criminal lurking in the dark London streets, waiting to rob or kill any vulnerable victim who should walk by. Perhaps I will never know. But fear has invaded me now.

When I arose this morning, I found that last night's experi-ence had left me weak and shaking, and I had no desire to be alone. I decided to visit Emily and offer her to accompany me on a walk. But the maid informed me that she had gone to visit Rose, so I went hither.

The girls were delighted to see me. Emily at once began to wrap her arms around her friend, and ask her if she would not invite me in for a moment, and play something for me.

"Oh, I don't know," said Rose capriciously, dancing about. "Have you already played for Miss Duncan?"

"No," said Emily.

"Well, then I don't have to," began Rose, but Emily inter-rupted her.

"Oh, I only learn piano with Miss Forsyth," she said, shrugging her shoulders. "Everybody plays piano. Anyway, I don't like it nearly as much as other things. It's not like you, Rose. You get to play what you want."

As we entered Rose's house, I was immediately struck by its loveliness and taste. Her mother greeted me warmly and asked if I would like a cup of tea. As soon as I was provided with it, Emily began to cajole again.

"Could we please, please just take Miss Duncan to see Rose's room? It is so pretty, and she has never seen it."

"Why, of course," she said, and I was towed upstairs by two eager hands and made to admire Rose's bed, her curtains, and her toys, all of which appeared to have been lovingly fabricated by her mother and herself, in the fluffiest and tenderest possible manner.

"Rose made ever so many of these," Emily said, showing them to me. "But this one is the biggest toy of all," and she reached underneath the high bed, extracted a very large box, and opened its clasps.

Out came a great musical instrument made of dark, burnished wood — a *violoncello*. From watching Rose, Emily had understood a little bit of how to play it, and she took up the bow, rubbed something on it and sitting on a chair, took the 'cello in front of her and began to make sounds with it, using her left hand to change the notes, while Rose danced about the room, dimpling, and pretending that there was no relation at all between herself and the enormous instrument. Emily continued on, purposely teasing her friend by making uglier and uglier noises, until Rose could finally stand it no longer and snatched the bow from her.

"No, let me show you!" she began, meaning only to guide Emily's hands, but Emily jumped up with alacrity, pushed her into the chair and planted the instrument firmly in front of her. Only her head and shoulders appeared behind it from above, while her ample skirts enveloped the sides of it below. She began to play a little bit, slowly, as if testing the strings, and turning the keys. Then the music grew and soared in a great wave of rich, vibrating sounds. It was slow, deep and heartrending, seemingly with a great many voices, as the strings sounded simultaneously, bringing to mind a noble forest, where the very trees join above to form a natural cathedral, arching in worship to the sky. Then, after a little pause, the instrument, as though singing of itself, launched into something gay and humorous — a jig. A final chord, a pause, and it slipped to a dramatic, desperate plea which reached out wrenchingly, tormentingly. The succession of moods was so extreme, the voice of the music so absorbing, the changes so sudden, so unexpected that my heart seemed pulled this way and that and I quite forgot about Rose herself; it was a great shock to me when the plaint came to an end and the violoncello's wild voice was replaced by her own little chirp, as she flung the 'cello on her bed, saying, "There, the end!"

Her mother was standing in the doorway, listening. I turned to her as the two girls chatted together, and said, "How beautifully, how unexpectedly she plays."

"Unexpected, indeed!" she concurred, laughing. "My husband and I hardly know what to do about it. It began when she was barely five years old; I began to teach her the piano, and to take her to concerts, and within a month she had refused to touch so much as a black or white key, and was demanding only to play a 'cello like those she had seen in great orchestras. And she has never stopped since. It is really awkward for a girl to play such an instrument — she has to have all her dresses made specially. We are quite taken aback by it all; I don't know what will come of it. She is often quite reluctant to practise, or to play for friends, and behaves in every way like a perfectly normal little girl, so that we feel reassured, and then she picks up the instrument, and it seems as though an entirely different person is playing; someone strangely old, and deeply versed in every human emotion. Her father did not mind satisfying her when he thought it was the caprice of a tiny child, but now he is especially worried that it might eventually occur to her to wish to appear on a concert stage — I'm afraid he would find that truly unacceptable!"

I felt a little sorry for Rose, if her hopes were destined to be blighted. I glanced over to her, but it seemed that no one could have been less interested in the question of a possible future career on or off the stage. She was extremely busy with her family of dolls.

"There is plenty of time!" I said. "She is enjoying herself greatly for now."

"Oh yes, she dearly loves her friends, and her school, and her dolls. What a delightful mother she will be some day. She is an odd little being, however. She can be extraordinarily bold and stubborn at times! I do hope she is not so in class."

"Oh, no indeed," I laughed. "She is charming, and I could not do without her."

Rose's mother descended, and I turned to Rose.

"How beautifully you played," I told her. "The very wood of the instrument seems to call out of itself!"

"Oh yes, it talks — it's my big baby," she said happily, taking it in her arms. "Let me put it back in its bed. It has a lovely bed, look — all with velvet inside."

I looked.

"Oh!" said Rose, her cheeks becoming a little pink. "What are these? I forgot!" She extracted a slightly crumpled bundle of papers from the luxurious, dark rose-coloured interior of the large box.

"Rose — what are those papers?" I asked her in amazement. "Look — they have mathematics written on them. Wherever did you get them?"

"It was a secret," she said a little guiltily. "We found them, Emily and I, and we thought it was a clue. But then we forgot all about it."

"Found them? Where?"

"They were in Mr. Beddoes' cat house, in one of the baskets, under the mattress. We found them when we shook them all out and fluffed them up. We thought they must be an important clue to the mystery, and we took them, and I hid them in my petticoats and brought them here. We meant to give them to you, really, Miss Duncan. We just forgot!"

I took the papers, and scanned them eagerly. They were neatly written, line after line of mathematics in Mr. Beddoes' small, regular handwriting, which I recognised from the list of kittens Mrs. Beddoes had shown me. The margins were carefully annotated with question marks and even tiny questions. They were well-thumbed, as though they had been often turned over and read and worked on, as well as being a little crumpled, perhaps from their journey in Rose's petticoats.

"Whatever can they be?" I said. "What a strange place to keep them! Shall we go to your house, Emily, and ask your uncle what they might mean?"

I drew Emily away by the arm, and we took our leave of Rose and her mother. Emily did not want to leave, but she was also greatly interested by the idea of finding out about the suddenly rediscovered clue.

"Rose is such fun," she told me, "She has a hundred ideas, she makes things all by herself, all the time. Sometimes I'd like to go and live in her house! I wish Edmund was more like that, but he isn't. He needs me to tell him stories and cheer him up. It's a secret," she whispered in my ear as we arrived at her door, "but he's very sad. He won't really tell me why, though. It is a secret — please don't mention it to Mother."

At the door of her house, she eagerly enquired if her uncle was within, but we were informed that he had gone out for the evening. Emily kissed me affectionately.

"Do, do come back tomorrow morning," she said. "Uncle Charles will be back then, and we will show him the papers!" And she entered, hopefully to shed a ray of sunshine into the gloomy atmosphere of care which seems to reign in her house ever since the tragic moment in the theatre.

I felt afraid when I found myself once again alone in the streets. I slipped along warily, and each footstep made me start. I was relieved when I entered my own rooms and barred the door behind me. I hid the papers carefully.

I do hope that tomorrow will reveal something of importance!

Your loving

Vanessa

Cambridge, Sunday, May 27th, 1888

Dearest Dora,

What a lovely long letter I received from you! For a few moments, while I read it, I was transported to home, and forgot everything about my current circumstances. So much so, that suddenly, after reading about Mr. Edwards' beautiful letter and his offer of marriage, I felt my heart rejoice, and wondered briefly why it seemed so very much heavier than usual. Memory had momentarily disappeared, but not pain.

Oh, Dora, how exciting, how beautiful! Dear Mr. Edwards. I've always wondered, when sayings and aphorisms are so contradictory, how one can possibly use them to determine anything? When he left, who could ever have said whether it was going to be "Out of sight, out of mind" or "Absence makes the heart grow fonder". But oh, Dora, will you have the courage to wait so long — more than a year for him to return on leave, and then maybe several until he may return to England forever? Or would you have the courage to envision such a plunge into unknown regions as joining him in India would represent? But then, a voyage to India — a mere country — cannot be half so mysterious and so frightening as that other voyage, into the wilderness of marriage and husband, and that with a man whom you know so little as yet. Yet how should I talk, when one cannot control one's dreams....

One's dreams, so easily shattered, so far from reality! And (as far as I am concerned) what dreadful, what fearsome, what unthinkable reality! Day after day I struggle in vain to make sense of the confusion of events surrounding the dreadful murders, and succeed only in learning one piece of seemingly meaningless information after another. Earlier this evening, I betook myself to Emily's house, in the hopes of meeting Mr. Morrison, and obtaining his opinion on the papers discovered by the girls in Mr. Beddoes' garden. He was within, and we mounted to Emily's nursery, where I speedily spread them out in front of him.

"What do you think of them?" I asked him.

He scanned the papers one by one, in order, stopping here and there, reading carefully, peering closely at the tiny marginal notes. He began to become quite excited.

"You know, I am really no expert on the famous n-body problem," he told me, "but like everybody else, I am more or less familiar with the basics of the topic, from hearing people lecture on it. This paper is dealing with that problem. Look, here it says 'let n=3'. Yes, indeed, I recognise these differential equations as those expressing the three-body problem. Whose manuscript is this, Miss Duncan? Where does it come from?"

"It was written by Mr. Beddoes," I told him, "and found by Rose and Emily, in a place where he had hidden it very secretly."

"Rose and Emily!" he exclaimed, gazing more closely at the page in front of him, his face gleaming intensely. "My niece is beginning her mathematical career very young, then, if she has found the lost solution to such a famous problem. For look — this manuscript purports to contain a solution! See this heavily underlined formula here? It is the central point of the manuscript, I would say. And what follows looks like a sketchy proof that it is the sought-for solution to the mysterious differential equations. My word, this *is* exciting. So, of all people, *Beddoes* would be the one to have been in possession of a solution, all along, when people were all thinking that either Akers or Crawford must be looking for one!"

"Might they not have been working together?" I asked.

"I really don't know — I suppose they might have."

"What do these notes in the margin mean?" I asked him.

He bent over the sheets and turned them over one by one,

deciphering the tiny letters.

"They are odd," he remarked. "They are very odd, really — what a strange mentality Beddoes had. He must have objected to crossing things out. Look at this one here! On the page it says (A) => (B), that is, A implies B, and in the margin is a question mark. He must have written down A implies B, and then come to question the implication while rereading it."

"Could it not be that he wrote down what another person explained to him?" I asked. "Then perhaps he could not understand it later, when he looked it over."

"Yes, I guess that is not impossible," he said consideringly. "Except that the writing is so extraordinarily neat — it really doesn't seem like someone taking notes, does it? It looks like a fair copy."

"Well, he could have copied out the rough notes, I suppose."

"Sounds strange, but maybe." He looked up at me, his eyes brilliant with interest. "Yes, I guess I can imagine that. The three of them closeted secretly together, working for the grand prize. One of them — Akers or Crawford — gets up to the blackboard and begins to explain his idea. Beddoes writes it all down. Then he goes home and, being a precise sort of fellow, goes over the notes again, copying them out neatly and trying to make sure that he understands the logical process behind each and every line. Whoever was explaining the idea must have been a little careless about going into the details, because Beddoes has marked a good three or four places he doesn't understand."

Something that Arthur had said during his testimony came back into my head.

"Do you remember how Arthur said in Court that at his dinner with Mr. Beddoes, Mr. Beddoes wrote down a question about some differential equations that he didn't understand, and Arthur tried to help him with it?"

"Yes!" he answered excitedly. "You're right! It must mean that Beddoes was working over this manuscript then, trying

201

to understand every bit of it. No, but wait. Why wouldn't he have just asked Crawford?"

"Perhaps this manuscript holds notes of work by Mr. Akers, and he was already dead!" I cried. "But then, it would still have made more sense to discuss it with Mr. Crawford, if they were working together. Oh, no! I remember now — they had quarrelled! It is true that Mr. Crawford had said that he wanted to dine with Mr. Beddoes, but perhaps Mr. Beddoes was waiting for the invitation to speak with him about it. Yes, of course. He expected to have dinner with Crawford that very night, but since he did not come, he asked his questions to Arthur instead. He must have had the formulae in his head, for he certainly did not show this manuscript to Arthur. If he hid it so carefully, it must have been a great secret."

"Well, I should think it would be, if it is really a solution to the grand old problem," he said. "But it seems that they never had time to write it up and submit it for the prize, since they were both dead within a few days after Beddoes asked his question to Arthur."

"I don't know," I said slowly, gazing into the fire. It dimmed into confusion before my eyes, and seemed filled with whirling images. Mr. Akers, writing down a formula and thrusting it into his pocket. Mr. Beddoes, holding a glass of wine, arguing with Mr. Crawford, a manuscript on the table between them. A blow with a poker — a blow with a great rock. A gloved hand, carefully, silently pouring drops of digitalin, in a little stream, into a bottle of whisky, and Mr. Crawford throwing glass after glass down his throat, exclaiming in triumph. A killer, seeking for a manuscript, perhaps even finding one — but *who*?

Fear invaded my limbs once again, as I visualised the gloved figure. Faces flitted in front of its formless visage — those of all my mathematical acqaintances — Mr. Withers, Mr. Wentworth, Mr. Young, even Mr. Morrison himself. I became faint with anxiety — I felt myself to be surrounded by murderers! Then the flames took shape, and became flames once again, as I heard Mr. Morrison saying,

"You don't look too well, Miss Duncan. Are you all right?"

"Oh, yes," I said confusedly. "Thank you so much for your help. I should go home now."

"I will accompany you," he said with alacrity, rising.

"No — no! Oh, no, thank you," I said in dismay, recalling my momentary, flickering vision.

He looked at me intently.

"It may be a little dangerous for you, to wander about the streets alone, do you not think?"

"I need to be alone!" I cried, and hastily shaking his hand, I made my way down the stairs and out of the door.

Dora, no one can have made the road homewards longer than I did! For protection, I resolved never to be within less than a few yards from some other person, preferably of the male sex. But each time I fixed upon someone and carefully matched my pace to his, he persistently took a wrong turning, so that I arrived home only after a making a remarkable number of squares and rectangles. And even at home, I hardly felt reassured. I barred the doors and windows, yet fear assailed me, and even trying to write to you did not bring me the usual feeling of calm. I got into my bed, and lay rigid, listening to every sound, but after ten minutes I could not bear it any more.

I got up, lit a candle, and holding the candlestick and my letter, very silently, in the silent house, I made my way to my front door, opened it, and slipped outside, closing it silently behind me. Noiselessly, I climbed the stairs to Arthur's rooms — perhaps his door was not locked, for Mrs. Fitzwilliam often went in and out, to dust, and also, at various times (somewhat grumblingly and against her will) to fetch articles of his that I then transported to him in prison. I tried the door quietly. It opened, and I slipped inside — and here I am.

I have never been in Arthur's rooms before, or even seen them. By the light of my candle, I am looking around me. They are harmoniously bare and simple; a little monastery.

An antique urn sits in a niche, mathematical papers are scattered on the desk, a worn volume of Shakespeare lies upon the table. If Mrs. Fitzwilliam finds me here, she will be really very annoyed. I must rise very early, and slip down the stairs. But now ... Arthur's bed is calling me, and I shall finish this letter, which I am writing with his pen in my hand and his eiderdown pulled about me. In spite of everything, I feel swept up in an unreasonable wave of warmth and safety, and so I shall bid you goodnight.

Your loving

Vanessa

Cambridge, Monday, May 28th, 1888

Dear Dora,

Last night, I slept deeply and beautifully, and woke up somewhat later than I had meant. I slipped downstairs with tremendous trepidation (really, I cannot understand exactly what Mrs. Fitzwilliam does to provoke such fear!) and, seeing no one, reached my own door with a great sense of relief. There, I found that she had already pushed the daily post under the door, and your very own letter awaited me on the carpet. I tore it open eagerly.

I read it again and again, struck above all by this extraordinary sentence: *There appears to me to be a strange parallel between the famous three-body problem, and that which you are so desperately trying to solve. I see two satellites, Mr. Akers and Mr. Beddoes, orbiting around the larger-than-life figure of Mr. Crawford, struggling with the laws of gravity binding them to him inexorably, and wishing, as it were, to go "spiralling off" to the "infinity" of independent glory.* Oh, Dora, what do you mean? Can you mean what I think you mean? Can the preposterous, unbelievable idea which flooded into my mind on reading and rereading that sentence possibly be true? Is that what you are trying to tell me? — you, my twin, who sometimes know my mind better than I know it myself!

The more I think about it, the more I feel convinced. Yet can it be? The thoughts and images which whirled in my head yesterday seem to fall into place, and form a new picture, one I had never thought of before ...

I have written down a list of the main events and details, as I recall hearing about them, in order to study whether what I now guess (what *you* guessed, Dora?) makes sense.

Mid-February: Three people met and drank whisky in Mr. Crawford's rooms (according to Mrs. Wiggins).

February 14th: Mr. Akers dined with Arthur and talked about the n-body problem, showed him a formula, mentioned a manuscript. Strange behaviour with his medicine: he began to pour it out, stopped after only a drop or two (the usual dose being ten drops) and stuffed the flask back into his pocket. He was killed upon returning home by someone waiting in his rooms. The bottle of digitalin was not found on him. His rooms may have been searched, the manuscript may have been taken; in any case it was never found. Mr. Crawford spent this same evening in London.

Mid-April: Someone visited Mr. Crawford in his rooms and had a glass of wine (according to Mrs. Wiggins). Also at this time (so perhaps on this occasion?) Mr. Crawford and Mr. Beddoes quarrelled (according to Mrs. Beddoes).

April 23rd: Mr. Crawford addressed Mr. Beddoes at the garden party, asking him to dine with him some day shortly. Mr. Beddoes seemed surprised (as well he might) but not displeased at this gesture of reconciliation.

April 30th: Mr. Crawford organised a dinner with Arthur and Mr. Beddoes together, but excused himself at the last minute because of ill-health. So Mr. Beddoes dined with Arthur. He showed him a formula and tried to ask him for help with understanding it. Arthur thought it had to do with the three-body problem though Mr. Beddoes did not say so. Mr. Beddoes was killed upon returning home, by someone waiting for him in the garden (so someone who knew, somehow, that he would be returning in the evening).

May 3rd: Mr. Crawford dies after drinking whisky containing digitalin which may have been put there any time in the previous weeks.

May 19th: Emily and Rose find a strange manuscript in Mr. Beddoes' handwriting, with questions and annotations in the margins, purporting to solve the three-body problem. Relation with Mr. Akers' lost manuscript ...

Dora — it all comes together! I am still not sure exactly what happened and how it happened, but in any case I am sure that *what you are saying is right*.

What shall I do? What *shall* I do?

Should I rush to the Courtroom, that terrible Courtroom, and pull Mr. Haversham aside, or plead for an audience with the Judge, and pour out to him all that has occurred to me? But I can imagine him only too well, wearing a patronising smile, and saying to me, "You have not the shadow of a proof, my dear young lady, whereas we are now all aware that you have every reason for inventing such a fairy tale." And then, how can I tell him what happened, when I am not completely sure yet myself?

Proof, proof! Is everything to collapse because of proof? *I must have proof*. What do I have? Nothing, nearly nothing — only the manuscript, and the meaning that it holds. A manuscript which I felt immediately to be the fundamental hinge on which the whole mystery turned, and yet whose sense I did not understand until this very moment.

No, I need more, I need evidence. Where can I find it? In Europe, on the mainland — in Belgium —in Stockholm!

It is the only answer. I must leave at once. Vanessa

Calais, Monday, May 28th, 1888

Dear Dora,

I am writing to you, not in a moment of leisure, but in a terrible moment of forced inactivity, late in the evening of a day so strange, that I never imagined I would live through one like it. To think that this very morning, I wrote you another letter, in another world — it seems so long ago! No sooner had I concluded my letter to you, than I leapt up, fired by the urgent desire to depart. But for someone whose greatest journey was from the countryside of Kent to the town of Cambridge, and from the town of Cambridge to the great city of London, the prospect of a European journey held something rather terrifying. I hardly knew how to begin. To calm my nerves, I bent my mind severely to a few simple thoughts.

All that is necessary is to purchase a ticket to London, thence take a boat to Europe ... and then continue to purchase tickets and take trains until my destination is reached.

Surely many people in these foreign countries must speak English, and be kind and helpful. Miss Chisholm will fearlessly leave her country to study in an unknown land, for the love of mathematics.

Arthur risks his life if I do not act.

The last thought sent me scuttling out of the house to the small railway station where, quivering with dismay, I forced myself to ask for a ticket to London in a calm voice. It was not so difficult; I purchased a one-way ticket (to the great surprise of the gentleman behind the counter, and somewhat to my own surprise, but heaven alone knows where my adventure will end — I dared not make any assumptions about the date of my return).

Then I sped home to my rooms and taking out a small valise, rather than the great trunk I had when I first arrived here, I packed only my best grey dress and as many under-things as I could fit in with it. Then I put on the dark brown travelling dress. Shortly before the departure of the train, I grasped the valise firmly, put on my small brown hat, stepped out of doors, filled with resolution, and walked per-haps twenty paces. Suddenly, I remembered something. I stopped and turned around — I thought I saw a surreptitious figure dart behind a corner, and my heart contracted momen-tarily with fear. But I turned back firmly, re-entered my rooms, took up a large piece of paper and wrote upon it "Lessons are cancelled for some days", pinned it to my door with a severe gesture, and departed once again.

Taking the train would not have been bad, Dora dear, if I had not been so fearful of all that was to follow. I sat down, and observed my fellow travellers, and waited, trying to con-trol my racing thoughts and consider my next step, until the train drew up in the London station. Then I stepped forth and went to the nearest counter, to inquire as calmly as possible how I could get myself on a boat to Europe. I stood behind a British family who asked as though it were the most natural thing in the world for a boat-train to Calais, and I found myself asking for the same thing. Later, I discovered I could have travelled directly to Ostend in Belgium. But what hap-pened was perhaps meant to be, as you will see.

I was sent to another counter, purchased a ticket, boarded a train to Dover, stood in various lines, always clutching my valise, and after what seemed like an endless time of trains, stations, lines and waiting, I found myself upon a boat, for the first time in my life.

The day was fine, the boat lifted and slopped gently in the water; a great many people got on it before and after me, some gabbling away in French, but many as British as you and I. I felt reassured by the presence of these friendly people, and resolved to converse with some of them, to ask if they could indicate a modest but agreeable hotel in Calais, for evening would be drawing in by the time I reached the shores of France, and I thought I should spend the night there, and begin my journey to Belgium as early as I could tomorrow morning.

I hung over the railings on the deck, looking out over the water, and as the boat slowly pulled away from the shore, and England began to recede, I understood for the first time what is meant by "the white cliffs of Dover", and my heart was torn with emotion at leaving England and all that it held for me — leaving it in danger, as it seemed to me. I felt suffocated with fear that I was making a dreadful mistake, travelling away to no purpose, abandoning Arthur. And yet, as a mere observer, a daily witness to his passive misery, I was so useless — worse than useless! I was walking about the deck, miserable and quite hungry, tormented by the inactivity of travel, when all of a sudden I received a great shock — a shock so fearfully unexpected you can hardly imagine it. Two tender arms were flung about my neck, and Emily — my dear Emily — was in my arms, clinging to me, and talking at a great speed, as though afraid to let me say a word.

"Oh, Miss Duncan, dear Miss Duncan," she cried, "please help me! Oh, you must help me — no one in the world can help me except you! I have followed you here all the way from Cambridge, but I dared not allow you to see me before, I was so very frightened you would take me back!"

"Emily — Emily, what are you doing here?" I gasped. "Your mother — she must be out of herself with distress. How could you, Emily — why, whatever are you thinking of? Oh, what can I do with you, oh, what shall I do, what shall I do?"

My distress was as great as hers, for the idea of turning back from my mission, losing not only time, effort and money but also the courage and the impulse, was dreadful to me.

"It is for Robert, Miss Duncan," she told me, her white little face looking into mine, all framed by her soft dark hair, her eyes like pools of sadness, *we must save him*, you *must*, you *must* help me to save him!"

"Robert? Your father's little orphan? Why, what must we save him from, pray?"

"From Mother!" she cried dramatically. "Mother does not want him, Miss Duncan, she says she cannot bear to have him home, and she will send him to — oh, to boarding school, to boarding school — it is too horrible, and he is only six, only six years old!"

"But my dear child, a great many little boys of six are sent to boarding school, and they are all the better for it," I began. "Just because your poor brother had such a very dreadful experience there does not mean ..."

But she interrupted me imploringly. "Oh, Miss Duncan, it was not just my brother! Every boy in the school suffered so, only Edmund is more fragile and cannot bear it. Oh, you cannot imagine all that he has told me, and some of the things he cries out in his sleep! He cannot bear to go to sleep, it was so dreadful in school; he said he began to be frightened after dinner, and it went on growing all the evening until bedtime. Don't you understand? You can't do that to a little boy, especially one who only just became an orphan! Miss Duncan, shall I tell you a story Edmund told me once? It was about his best friend, a boy called Watkins. Watkins was given a message: he was called to see the Headmaster. That meant he was to be punished for something. He was so afraid he cried. Edmund thought it would be worse if he didn't go, so he went down with him, and waited outside the door, listening. He said he was very surprised to hear nothing — no screams. Then Watkins came out, and he was smiling with relief. And he said to Edmund 'Thank God — I'm not to be punished!' Edmund said 'Why did he call you?' And Watkins said — 'He told me my mother had died.' Oh, Miss Duncan, can you imagine it? Can you? It is worse than a prison! Edmund *shan't* go back if I can help it, and neither shall Robert!"

In spite of my emotion, I compelled myself to express the voice of reason.

"But Emily dear, if your mother has decided that Robert

210

must be sent to a school, what exactly do you hope to obtain by following me to Europe?"

"Oh, first I wanted to run away, and send a telegram to Mother saying that I should come back only if she promised to keep Robert. But now, I believe Heaven itself has sent you here, for we are on our way to Calais, and I believe that we must fetch Robert ourselves, and bring him home."

"My dear child, I haven't the least notion where he is, and we could not possibly simply arrive and carry him off! And then, I cannot, I cannot go back — I must travel to Stockholm, Emily. It is more important than anything."

"No!" she cried. "I know why you are going — you are going for Mr. Weatherburn! Oh, Miss Duncan, of course whatever you can do for him is important — but not more important than anything. Please, please think for a moment if he were here, if he could be here for just one second, and you asked him what you should do now — what he would say? I know he would say that we must get Robert — he is so kind! We cannot leave Robert — you don't know where he is, but I do! He is with that horrible Madame Bignon, whom I saw when Mother and I travelled here — that horrible woman who is keeping him for money, right in Calais, where we are going. He was the saddest little boy I ever saw, he clung to me so when Mother decided we had to leave. I only left because she said we might arrange for him to come home, although I had wanted him to join us there and then, but she said it was impossible! He loved me so, and cried terribly when I left ... and oh, *he looked so much like Father!* Please, Miss Duncan — I won't make you travel back to England with me — we will travel together to Stockholm, and bring Robert — I will take care of him all the time, just like a mother, and we will be as good as gold and help you in everything you do! We will help each other — you will see! I have travelled often, and can speak French, and some German, too, you know. And — Miss Duncan, look — I have brought ever so much money with me — all that I have ever received since I was small, and

Edmund's as well, and some more which I begged Uncle to lend me for an urgent secret reason. He did it, and didn't ask me a single question!"

I hesitated, and was lost. Emily is so lovely, so firm in her gentle way, so tall and ladylike for her thirteen years, so decisive and able and just, that she brought me infinite consolation, and I felt that her presence would be precious to me. Already I knew that were I to send her back, I would desperately miss her loving company. I was so afraid of the long trip into unknown places, but Emily had already taken boats and trains and spoken foreign languages, and she was filled with courage and the desire to do right. I reflected as these thoughts went through my mind, and then turned to her.

"We must send a telegram to your mother the moment we arrive in Calais," I said. "Then, we will find a small hotel. And if the little boy truly lives in the town, we can call on him. But I believe you may be too hopeful. Why should they allow him to leave with me?"

"They will! I will say that you are my governess and we are calling to fetch him. They know me. And if they want money, we shall pay them," she said, and her very voice vibrated with the force that makes things happen. She turned to me, put her two hands on my shoulders, and looked up into my eyes.

"We are really trying to do the same thing," she said seriously. "You are doing it for Mr. Weatherburn, and I for Robert. You will see — together we will succeed."

And Dora, it may well be that without her loving help and presence, I would have despaired. Calais was a scene of indescribable confusion; oh, the motley crowds that invaded the place! Sailors, Frenchmen and foreigners of all descriptions, dirty children and beggars swarmed all about the area of the port, which was loaded high with stacks of boxes and bags of goods of all sorts being delivered. I would not have had the slightest idea where to go, had I been alone. But Emily led me to a money-changing counter, then towed me through the streets to the very hotel where she had stayed with her mother, and expressing herself very prettily in French, inquired for a large room with two beds, and even asked if it would be possible to add a child's cot. She bade me upstairs as though playing the hostess in her own home, and we washed and freshened up, "to give ourselves courage," as she said.

Then we went to send a telegram to her mother. I wrote it out myself, my hand trembling with the unthinkableness of what I was doing. I was afraid of being accused of running off with the child, and sought the wording anxiously, as she bent over my shoulder.

Emily safe. Had to travel to Continent urgently found Emily followed me onto boat. Cannot return nor send Emily alone so taking her with me. Hope return within week. Duncan.

I left the telegraph office filled with the fear that I would be followed, arrested, and accused of terrible misdeeds, at this critical time. I felt as though I had stolen one child and was about to steal a second. Full of misgivings, and yet deeply convinced that my fears were only for myself, whereas Emily truly walked in the Biblical ways of righteousness, I followed her through winding streets which she remembered perfectly, with the natural talent of a geometer, until we came to a miserable tenement house with peeling walls and cracked panes. There, we climbed to the very top of a horrible and rickety staircase smelling of onions, and knocked at the door. It was soon opened by a thin and undeniably evil-looking woman with a kerchief tied around her lank hair. She recognised Emily at once.

"Ah, vous êtes revenue?" she snarled unpleasantly.

"Oui," said Emily with charming politeness, "voici ma gouvernante. Nous sommes venues emmener Robert."

"En effet, votre mère m'a ecrit qu'elle enverrait bientôt quelqu'un," said the unpleasant personage. Emily turned to me eagerly.

"You see, Mother wrote that someone would soon come to take him, and she believes it is us!" she whispered. Meanwhile, the lady had retired into the depths of her dingy flat, and was calling "Robert! Robert! Allez, viens vite!"

The little boy who then appeared was like another copy of poor little Edmund. He was extremely thin and fragile, his eyes were enormous and frightened, and he looked so abandoned and miserable that I understood all of Emily's panic on his behalf. He looked from the woman to us as though wondering what was to befall him now, but when his eyes lit on Emily, he sprang towards her passionately and clutched her dress.

"Oh, have you come to take me?" he cried out in English.

"Yes, yes, we have, come Robert, come with us now, darling! Come away — we shall leave, and you shall never come back here again!" she answered, clasping him in her arms. "Pouvons-nous avoir ses vêtements?" she added in her prim, studious French, turning to the woman.

The woman turned away, and soon came back with a canvas sack into which she had stuffed various ill-assorted rags.

"Votre mère me doit de l'argent, mademoiselle," she began aggressively.

Emily took out her little purse, extracted a wad of notes, and handed them to the woman with a coolness worthy of a princess, then turned away, taking Robert by the hand, without even waiting to see if she would count the money, or complain. We heard vociferations and imprecations behind us as we descended, but she must have been too pleased to get rid of the undesirable little boy to insist further. Ten minutes after having arrived, we were on our way, with one little blond boy in tow and one canvas sack of useless items. Emily poked into it with distaste.

"Tomorrow we shall shop for him first thing," she began. Then, seeing my face, she suddenly clapped her hand to her forehead. "No, we shall *not* — we shall do what *you* need to do, dear Miss Duncan. I promise total obedience. Please tell

214

me whatever it is, and we shall do it."

I could not help laughing. "I need to travel to Brussels tomorrow, and see a lady who lives in a village near the city," I told her. "You shall help me with the tickets and the rooms, and if we are lucky, we shall find time to shop for little Robert tomorrow. For tonight, let us be contented if he is washed and well fed."

"Oh, yes!" she said joyfully. "We shall have dinner at the hotel, all three of us together. Come — let us go there now!" And we did dine modestly on fish and green beans, served by a harassed waiter who expressed himself habitually in a peculiar mixture of French and English, which language he had personally developed to deal with the great numbers of English tourists who occupy the hotel daily. We then betook ourselves upstairs to our room, where we are at this very moment. Emily is washing Robert as best she can in front of the cracked washbasin behind the tattered screen, as I write to you.

Oh, Dora — I feel as though you are near me, as though if I looked up I could see your sweet face in the candlelight. Surrounded by the peaceful domestic atmosphere, the gentle sounds of splashing, the scratching pen, the extraordinarily still and timeless moment in this quiet room — I feel we are all three protected, for a moment, within a magic circle, as though we have been allowed a brief rest in our struggle against the whirlpool of dreadful events which threaten us.

I feared this moment of being able to do nothing but wait. But it is not so — writing to you, and feeling Emily's great release from anguish and little Robert's incredulous wonderment at finding himself surrounded by love and care again, after so much misery and abandonment, make me realise that this moment is as full as all the others. I feel renewed courage; the map of Europe lies open before me — tomorrow to Belgium!

I will post this letter tomorrow, and write again at the very next one of these secret moments which seem to lie at the heart of the storm.

Your fearful, weary but courageous

Vanessa

Brussels, Tuesday, May 29th, 1888

My dearest Dora,

Today was so endlessly long, so filled with travel, with valises and stations and trains, carriages, horses, seeking addresses and hotels, that I feel as though I have been travelling for weeks!

And yet, we have been only from Calais to Brussels, and from Brussels to Wavre, or rather, to a farm in the nearby countryside, inhabited by a certain Madame Walters, formerly Miss Akers, sister to Mr. Akers and his next of kin.

We arose early this morning; how sweet it was to see Robert's flushed face asleep upon his tumbled pillow, and to see him awaken giggling from Emily's sly tickles. Emily loves him with a fierce passion which mingles protectiveness for the abandoned and threatened waif, and (perhaps unconsciously) all her adoration for the father she twice lost, and whom Robert and Edmund closely resemble.

The little boy is really adorable; sweet, desperately eager to please, full of good-will. He is bright-eyed, and I would guess that he must be a very lively and active little boy; I would naturally expect him to make a rumpus as little Violet and Mary do in class, and would love to see his cheeks flushed with some of their rosy colour. But he does not behave so; he is subdued and quiet, and seems to repress his natural energy. It cannot be easy for him, to have been twice snatched from familiar surroundings and flung into the unknown; the first experience must have taught him an unchildlike fear, which the second shall try its best to undo.

His father always spoke to him in English, so that although he may have forgotten a little during the last month, spent in the dreadful household we briefly saw, he still speaks charmingly. He is too young to have yet learned to distinguish between tender, childish language, and ordinary speech. Today, taking Emily's hand lovingly, he called her "my little birdie in a nest", and she looked at him with amazement, then realised that she must be hearing, as though from the grave, the echo of her own father's tender words to his child. Tender and loving the little boy's parents obviously were, however at fault they may have been to be parents at all.

After breakfast in the crowded hotel dining room — I could swallow only tea, such was my haste to depart, we paid our bill, and hastened on foot through the streets to the railway station, whence we were soon on our way to Brussels. I could not take my eyes from the scenery outside; countryside, just as in England and not so very far, yet so different! The distance was not too long, and after a reasonable time, we found ourselves descending in the Belgian metropolis, which turned out to be hardly more than a delightful village with a lovely central square, in comparison with the bustling capharnaum of London. I felt quite at home there, in spite of the fact that many less English people were to be heard than at Calais; the streets are small, charming and reassuring, and many useful words such as Hotel and Restaurant are identical to the English, so that one does not feel unlettered as one walks through them; then, also, I am presently accompanied by an accomplished little Frenchman, who in spite of his tender years, comes gravely to our aid whenever we are missing the necessary words to express ourselves.

My first care was to send a telegram to poor Mrs. Burke-Jones. I felt that I must not only reassure as to Emily's wellbeing, but immediately break the news that we had taken little Robert, so that she could reflect upon her future decision concerning him (and also, perhaps, to avoid the fearful scene of breaking the news to her directly!) I spent some precious time over the wording, trying to explain all without undue waste of words, and finally wrote: *Emily insisted take Robert from Calais. Both children well travelling Germany tomorrow. Duncan.* I then set about the task of feeding my little brood, in spite of my burning impatience to hire a cab and ride at a gallop towards Wavre, and my tormenting fear that Madame Walters may be out for the day, or even away altogether, and that I might be obliged to wait, or to continue my journey without the knowledge I felt so certain she detained.

Thank Heaven, my fears proved groundless. After a modest meal, we proceeded to hire a hansom — the man was peculiar and leered, and I felt nervous, and began to feel that the presence of Emily and little Robert protects me greatly from many vexations — and he drove us several leagues, to a tiny village on the outskirts of Wavre. There, we were compelled to ask him to wait, as Emily and Robert descended and asked an old farmer passing down the lane with a load of hay, if he knew where Madame Walters resided. The man knew, of course, as the village is entirely visible from one end to other when standing at a single spot, and he showed us her farmhouse, standing at the edge of the fields some way off. Our cab driver took us as near as he could, but the way became muddy, and he began to become angry, and demanded his fare. I dared not demur, and paid him the rather exorbitant sum he required — thank goodness dear Emily had once again reminded me of the necessity to obtain something of the local currency at the railway station — after which we descended and he went cantering off to Brussels, although we had asked him to await our return.

"It doesn't matter," cried Emily gamely, "we shall walk back, if need be; I do not think it was over a few miles! Or perhaps we shall find a farmer's wagon to take us back."

Lifting our skirts, we stepped along the muddy lane, seeking as best we could to place our feet upon the various rocks and stones, until we came to the path leading to the farmhouse. My hopes rose as I saw the thread of smoke rising from the chimney, and the light which glowed within the cheerful windows against the dark, grey day.

We knocked at the door, which was soon opened by a woman no older than Mrs. Burke-Jones, with brown hair pulled away from her face tightly, and an enormous apron — her face was wary, but not unfriendly. The sound of our English voices appeared to hearten her.

"We are so terribly sorry to disturb you," I said, "but we have come a long way to see Madame Walters on urgent business."

"I am she," she said, speaking her native tongue almost as though it were rusty with disuse. "You are lucky to find me in today; I should be working out in the fields, but I am unwell."

She led us inside; the door gave directly onto a spacious farmhouse kitchen, with an enormous fireplace and a large wooden table, surrounded by benches. We sat down, and she set a kettle directly over the fire on a hook, set mugs of milk and biscuits in front of the children, and inquired of us whence we came, and for what purpose.

"It is about the murder of your brother, Madame," I told her. Her eyes flashed. "I was told that the murderer had been arrested, and will be condemned!" she snapped.

Before I could reply, Emily leaped to her feet. "Oh no, dear Madame Walters," she cried urgently, leaning forward, clinging to the table in her urgency. "It is a mistake, a dreadful mistake! Mr. Weatherburn never killed your brother. He could not possibly have done it! Please, please believe us!"

The face of the lady changed several times at Emily's words — first she seemed affected by Emily's desperate tones, but then it flashed across her mind that we must, then, be friends or family of he who she had been assured was the murderer. She stared at us with hostility.

"I am sure I can do nothing for you," she said quite coldly.

I feared that we had begun badly, and became alarmed at the prospect of being summarily ejected. I decided to adopt a different tactic, and speak only of manuscripts, and not of murderers. I glanced at Emily, hoping she could read my thoughts.

"I want to tell Madame Walters about her brother's mathematical idea," I said.

"Oh — look at the lovely cat!" suddenly interjected Robert, as a very large, grey animal entered the kitchen with a distinguished step, its extremely furry tail erect, and stopped enquiringly in front of him. He immediately slipped off the settle, and began to play with the creature under the table. Madame Walters smiled, looking slightly mollified.

"Her name is Reine," she told him, leaning down to watch for a moment, and reaching under the table to pass her hand through the cat's thick, soft fur.

"We only ask you for one small thing," I said to her, taking advantage of this momentary softening; "only a few moments. Please do let me explain." I placed my valise upon the floor, opened it and extracted Mr. Beddoes' manuscript, which I had flattened out neatly at the very bottom, together with Mr. Morrison's translation of the announcement of King Oscar's Birthday Competition.

"I believe that the gentleman who wrote this manuscript of mathematics stole something from your brother," I began carefully.

"Who is he? What did he steal? And how can I know anything of it?" she answered suspiciously.

"He stole an idea," I began, "a mathematical formula."

"I know nothing of such things," she said again, and I saw that she clung to the idea that her brother's murderer had been discovered, and that we were his friends, and therefore she must regard us as enemies, with mistrust.

"Oh, please — do let *me* tell you," cried Emily eagerly. "There was a great mathematical competition — why, it's still going on, and your brother had a wonderful idea to solve the problem that was set! Perhaps he would have won the prize. But he died, and nobody found anything he wrote down, except that he wrote down one formula for Mr. — for — for a friend of his, but then he put it back in his pocket, and then he was killed, so he could never send in his manuscript to the King of Sweden. And we don't want his solution to be lost forever! He put it in his pocket, so my uncle said it must have been sent to you when he died. Oh, that is what you are looking for — that is why you are here, isn't it, Miss Duncan? My uncle says it is ever so important!"

I thought that Madame Walters would be entirely taken aback and confused by this whirlwind of competitions, uncles, Kings and formulae. Instead, unexpectedly, she became very pale, and sank onto the bench across, leaning heavily upon the table.

"You are right, you are right," she gasped. "The competition, the King of Sweden — Geoffrey wrote to me about it! He wrote that he believed he had a chance to win the grand prize, the golden medal, and he was keeping it all the deepest secret. How could you possibly know about it? "

"We found it out little by little," I told her. "And now we have found something which may allow us to rediscover your brother's lost idea. I have here a manuscript which may possibly hold the key to it."

I held Mr. Beddoes' manuscript out to her, and she looked at the strange sentences and formulae in confusion.

"How can we know if you are right?" she said.

"As Emily said, on the evening of his death, Mr. Akers told a — another friend about his idea," I told her. "Your brother was a suspicious man, but like all men, he needed friends, he needed to talk. He was wonderfully proud of his formula, and could not resist the desire to show it to his friend, but then he quickly folded up the scrap of paper and thrust it into his breast pocket. We need to know if it is still there, Madame Walters. If the formula it contains is the same as this one — " and I showed her the central formula of Beddoes' manuscript, heavily underlined, "then we shall be practically certain that this manuscript here contains the essence of your brother's work! And it may yet be saved, for the greater honour of his memory."

"I don't understand," she told us, her face grey with distress. "That manuscript you are holding is not in my brother's handwriting. Yet you say it may contain his ideas. What does it mean? Did the author of this one steal my brother's manuscript and copy it?"

Emily looked at me in surprise. "That's a funny idea," she said, "my uncle told me that the manuscript is odd, as though Mr. Beddoes wrote down things and then questioned them afterwords. Perhaps Madame Walters is right. He might have just copied Mr. Akers' manuscript directly! Maybe he thought Mr. Akers' handwriting was too messy, or else he wanted to take it home and study it there, and Mr. Akers didn't want to let his own manuscript out of his sight. It would make sense, look! When Mr. Beddoes tried to read through what he had copied, he found he didn't understand some of it, and that's why he wrote the questions in the margin!"

"I should tell you that a man already came here from England, weeks ago, near Easter. He told me much the same story as you have, about my brother's secret work, and like you, he said that he was trying to discover it and save it from oblivion. He said he knew the police had sent me all of my brother's personal affairs, and he needed them in order to solve the mystery. I brought them out to show him, and stood at this very table with my husband and he looked eagerly at everything, above all at the many different scraps of paper my brother had in his pockets, all full of writing such as this," and she indicated Mr. Beddoes' manuscript.

"There was one paper which excited him particularly, as well as my brother's pocket diary," she went on. "He tried hard to convince me to let him take them away with him, telling me they were essential for his research. My husband would have let him, but I could not do it. Oh, Miss, these are my only, last memories of poor Geoffrey. I told the man to copy the papers down for himself if he wanted them; what difference could it have made to him? But he did not care to,

222

and went away, quite angrily, I thought."

Emily and I glanced at each other.

"That is very interesting. What was his name? What did he look like?" I asked quickly.

"He said his name was Mr. Davis," she replied. "As to his looks, it is difficult to say, really; he was very ordinary. He seemed distinguished and quiet, not young, but he wore a dark overcoat and hat, so it is difficult to describe him better."

"Would you know him again?" asked Emily breathlessly.

"I believe I would."

"Who could it have been?" Emily wondered aloud. "It's funny that he should have been angry about not being allowed to take the paper. Why should he have cared? It's just a formula! He could have copied it out."

"I didn't like that man," said Madame Walters, her brow furrowed. "Something seemed wrong with him — I felt very suspicious. Oh God, oh God — what does it all mean? Let me show you everything." And she arose, and went into the inner rooms. After a moment she returned, carrying a soft cloth bag, whose contents she poured out upon the table. It contained the entire contents of Mr. Akers' pockets at his death. Just as Mr. Morrison had told us, we saw keys and coins, a handkerchief, the pocket diary and quite a large number of bits and pieces of paper scribbled over with notes and computations.

I opened Mr. Beddoes' manuscript to the page containing the central formula, and then began to take up the papers one by one, and compare their contents to that of the page before me, to see if the formulae were identical. Several were unfamiliar and unintelligible to me, but at length I came upon one which immediately appeared to me to be the right one. One side was covered with Mr. Akers' usual illegible scribbling, that he used in writing for himself, but on the other side, which had been blank, he had written out the entire central formula in a clear, bold hand, and underneath, "the series converges!"

I felt absolutely certain that I was holding in my hand the very paper that Mr. Akers had written in the Irish pub for Arthur, on the last evening of his life. Madame Walters and Emily compared the two formulae, laboriously, Greek symbol for mathematical symbol, and agreed with me that they were identical.

I then took up Mr. Akers' pocket diary, and began turning the pages. I started by looking at the very date of his death, the 14th of February, and saw two brief entries: first "ABC 2 p.m.", then "dinner W."

"This is the day on which your brother died," I said, showing the page to Madame Walters.

"That must be Mr. Weatherburn, then!" cried Emily, and Madame Walters flinched, for she identified this name with the hated murderer of her only brother.

"What is ABC?" asked Emily.

"I know!" I answered, as this piece of information worked its way perfectly into the puzzle I had been fitting together. "I believe that it is the name used for a little secret society, which met to work together on the n-body problem! A must be for Mr. Akers, B for Mr. Beddoes and C for Mr. Crawford. Let us see if they met at other times."

I turned backwards through the pages, looking curiously through the brief, austere record of the poor man's life. Certain events could be identified — "Morrison lecture" I saw on October 11th — but for the most part, it was difficult to guess much from the single initials Mr. Akers habitually employed. On December 13th, I located another entry "ABC 2 p.m.", and again on October 18th.

"They always met on a Tuesday," remarked Emily.

"You are right! October, December, February — they met every two months, on the same day of the week, at the same time. It was probably convenient for their teaching hours. I wonder where they met?"

"*I* wonder if they meant to meet again in April," mused Emily.

"That is a good question. Let us look. Why, yes, they did! April 17th — "ABC 2 p.m.". There is no entry for June, though."

"Perhaps, at each meeting, they fixed the date of the next one," said Madame Walters.

"Oh, no! Surely it was because they were working for the competition. They would have to be finished by June 1st!" cried Emily.

"You may be right," I answered, my mind churning and full of thoughts. "Madame Walters, I must tell you the truth. I have come, not only to save your brother's lost work, but also because as Emily told you before, I am convinced that the man who has been arrested for his murder is not the true murderer. Mr. Akers was killed for his idea, and I believe I know who killed him, and I need this evidence to prove it. I beg you to lend me this pocket diary and this paper written by your brother. I swear on my honour, on the Bible if you prefer, that I will keep them absolutely safe and return them to you as soon as everything has been made clear."

"Is it the man who came here?" she asked, gathering up the paper and diary with trembling hands.

"I believe it is," I told her.

"I believe it too," she said suddenly, and thrust the bundle into my hands. "I knew it, I knew it! I felt it — there was something wrong with him. *He was afraid* — I could feel it, and his eyes were shifty, and he wanted the papers too much. Not just to see them, but to have them. It was for that that I did not give them to him. I felt that he wanted to destroy them!"

"I am sure that that is what he wanted," I answered.

"Do you not think, if you know who he is, that I should travel to England and identify him?"

"Not yet," I said. "I still do not have enough proof; his visit here alone would do nothing to prove his guilt. I myself am not returning to England immediately, for I believe that evidence of major importance, concerning your brother in the deepest possible way, lies in Stockholm, and I am travelling there with the children before returning home. Still, it may be necessary for you to come to England later, if I succeed in gathering enough evidence that the Judge wishes to confirm it all."

"I do not know why, but I believe you; I believe you are honest and sincere," she said. "I thank you for what you are doing, and wish you luck and Godspeed. How are you returning to Brussels? Did you come by cab? Has he waited for you?"

I had completely forgotten about the impetuous departure of our sour-faced cab driver. Seeing our discomfited faces, Madame Walters went outside, and in stentorian tones, called a young man who was working in a field some distance away.

"He will drive you to the city in the wagon," she told us. "I pray that what you are doing is right, and that if truly the man accused of my brother's murder is innocent, God save him."

And we took our leave, and trotted back to Brussels in a farm wagon drawn by an old and very solid cart horse, Robert chattering gaily with the farmer youth the entire way. What a happy little boy he seemed to be, his own miseries briefly forgotten, unaware of the clouds of fear and danger which hovered vaguely about us. He was delighted with his ride in the fresh countryside, and more delighted still, when, in order to cheat the remaining hours of the day of their frightening emptiness, I took the children shopping, and we purchased a sturdy little sailor suit for him and various other necessaries to replace the contents of his dingy canvas bag. Emily insisted we also visit a toy store.

"Oh, Emily," I remonstrated, thinking of murderers and lawyers and ruthless, hard-faced juries. "It seems so frivolous in the midst of questions of life or death!"

"A child's happiness is also a question of life or death," she said firmly. "It's like your charade, Miss Duncan — do you remember it?

My second with "you" forms a phrase of great joy
To a child who's offered a gaily wrapped toy.

It was 'for you' — and you called it great joy! It isn't at all frivolous. If you don't believe me, just imagine what Mr. Weatherburn would say."

The little imp! In immediate reaction to her words, my imagination produced an image of Arthur, standing next to me, considering little Robert with a grave twinkle, quietly approving of the deep and simple bond of love which so instantly unites a child and a toy. Little Robert's cheeks were all flushed with delight, as he clutched to his chest the locomotive that he and Emily picked out together. Emily insisted on paying for it with her very own money, and we left the shop a happier trio than we had entered. Now we have settled for the night in a small pension whose address was given to us by Madame Walters, and tomorrow at dawn, we arise and depart for Stockholm.

I retire in the comforting knowledge that your loving thoughts are with me, as mine are with you,

Vanessa

Malmö, Thursday, May 31st, 1888

My dearest Dora,

Two strange days have passed since last I wrote to you — two days of travel, nothing but travel, trains, cabs, walking, dingy hotels and dingier railway stations. Wiring to Mrs. Burke-Jones from Calais and Brussels was easy enough, but from Germany difficult and from Denmark and Sweden a task rendered alarming by our ignorance of the language and customs. Yesterday, early in the morning, we left Brussels by train for Germany, and by nightfall, weary, dirty and under-fed, we found ourselves in the northern city of Hamburg. How grey and sordid it seemed, with its tall, dirty chimneys

227

against the dusky sky. How difficult it was to seek for an hotel, and how depressing when the first three we tried had no rooms available. Emily's German is far more limited than her French, since she does not converse with Annabel in that language, but merely studies the rules of grammar; she soon taught me "Wir möchten ein Zimmer für drei, bitte", and in the end we found refuge in a small dark room at the very top of a twisting staircase, and were all three too afraid of the maze of streets to descend and seek for dinner. We had bought bread and fruit at the railway station, and made do with them for the evening, promising ourselves to make up for it at breakfast the next morning, when the sunlight would surely cheer us.

It was a relief just to be in a room with a bed, and to be able to wash, and stretch, and even to laugh, for children will always laugh, and Emily caused such startling adventures to befall the little locomotive that both children's ringing voices soon filled the room and spilled down the stairs, lightening my dark mood. Emily has sworn to help me in every way, and indeed, even if she did nothing else, her constant proximity, her steadfast strength, and her youthful lightheartedness are already better than a tonic for me. What a treasure! I hardly dare imagine the sufferings and anxiety of her poor mother, in spite of my reassuring telegrams *Emily and Robert well and happy, travelling northwards together*. I cannot deny that I am fearful of the days ahead, and venturing as far afield as Denmark and Sweden appears to me rather like wandering in the wilderness.

So far, thank goodness, my fears have not really been justified. Today's trip through Denmark was long and weary, but the country is charming, the people kind, and many of them speak some words of English, so that to our surprise, our Danish day turned out oddly pleasant in spite of the fact that the greatest part of it was spent seated in various vehicles, and all the food came from baskets. I have now discovered that, assuming Robert to be a typical specimen, little boys adore trains big and small, and that tumbling them about in a swaying, rattling conveyance, with the ever-changing landscape sailing continually past, is apparently a sufficiently delightful activity to occupy all their natural energy and playfulness for hours on end.

With the instinct of a budding physicist, Emily set about to study the effects of the big train on the tiny one, and set it upon the floor to see how its movement would be affected. Quite naturally, it took to rolling along in the opposite direction to ours, towards the back of the carriage, and (it must be admitted) rather frequently into the feet of the people sharing our compartment. They did not really mind, as the inhabitants of third-class carriages are used to such behaviour; children and food were everywhere, and the atmosphere was one of general rumpus. In any case, I found myself quite unable to remonstrate with any real intensity, as the sound of their joyful laughter was so sweet, and I was so relieved that they were not quite simply rendered bored and peevish (as I was, rather) by the endless riding.

We reached Copenhagen in the late afternoon, and it was not too late to sail across to the port of Malmö. Ah, these northern countries are orderly and beautiful. I felt a wave of triumph as I set foot on the ground (in spite of the peculiar manner in which it tilted beneath my feet). Sweden at last! Tomorrow — on to Stockholm, and to the final proof!

Ever your own

Vanessa

Stockholm, Friday, June 1st, 1888

My dearest Dora,

We have spent the whole of this endless day journeying northwards, ever northwards to Stockholm. We arrived here late, worn out and (for myself) weary with the ever renewed fear of failure. The moment we reached the city, I gave way to my increasing sense of urgency, and bundled the children into a cab without giving them a moment, poor dears, to rest or look about them. Only one thought was in my mind: *today is the very day of the opening of the submissions to the King's Birthday Competition.* They will be opened — perhaps have already been opened — by the Director of the Competition, Professor Gösta Mittag-Leffler.

Mr. Mittag-Leffler is very famous here, and I soon was able to discover that he resides in a villa in Djursholm, a pretty town on the outskirts of Stockholm. Although a professor at the University of Stockholm, his offices lie, and his main work is done in his lovely home where he has already collected one of the greatest mathematical libraries in the world. All his work as an editor of the journal *Acta Mathematica* is done from his home where the manuscripts were to be sent. I wrote down the address carefully: Auravägen 17, Djursholm, and I showed the paper to the driver, who set out on a brisk trot through the gracious streets of the city.

A city? It is an archipelago, truly; they call it the city of twenty-four thousand islands. It seemed that we constantly crossed water, and the sun was on the horizon by the time we drew up in front of Mr. Mittag-Leffler's imposing villa. The large building is dominated by a round tower in one corner, stretching nobly upwards, which very nearly gives it the aspect of a small castle.

I paid the man and alighted from the cab, and taking the children by the hand, I began to walk up the wide path leading to the stately entrance. My knees trembled beneath me, and Emily and Robert were silent with wonderment, knowing or feeling that I was reaching my heart's destination. We stood long in front of the heavy main door, as I tried to control the dreadful knocking in my chest. The sun had now sunk altogether below the horizon, and the entire sky was drowned in deepest blue, though no stars were yet visible. I raised my hand to the large bell, and rang.

After a short wait, the door was opened by a kindly lady. Her surprise was extreme upon perceiving us; truly we must have had the aspect of three waifs, having travelled so long, eaten so little, and — worst of all — having had so very little time to make ourselves presentable. This morning, I had put on my nice grey dress for the first time, having desired all these last days to keep it fresh and clean for this very moment, but the endless day of travel had somewhat removed its bloom; as for Emily, her lovely white dress with its many flounces was desperately crumpled and wilted, as she had not thought to bring another on her impetuous departure. Poor little Robert looked weary and disordered. We all three straightened up, however, in front of the plump servant, and put on our very best airs of distinction and pride. I addressed her in English.

"We come from England, and must see Professor Gösta Mittag-Leffler," I began.

I do not believe she spoke a single word of English, for only the last words produced some reaction in her rounded features. She looked extremely doubtful, but clearly she was not in the habit of turning away any visitors of the illustrious professor, no matter how unimpressive. She ushered us into a small waiting room near the door, beckoned a maid who stood in the hallway to keep an eye upon us, and bustled away, arousing in my breast the fierce hope that I may, after all, find the professor at home and disposed at least to speak with me.

It was not long, indeed, before Professor Mittag-Leffler himself descended, and entered the modest waiting room to greet us. He was a hale, energetic gentleman in his forties, imposing and yet extremely kind. I saw immediately that he would be forthright and courageous in his views, and that in spite of his strict and ceremonious appearance, he was quite prepared to listen to whatever I chose to tell him. Perhaps there was even a twinkle of amusement in his eyes, at the

231

sight of the motley crew we represented, with Robert as inseparable as ever from his cherished locomotive.

He addressed me in nearly impeccable English. "Please tell me in what way I may be of use to you?"

I was moved by his kind reception, but too overwhelmed by a sense of desperate urgency to answer with the ceremony he clearly deserved and expected. I had risen upon his entrance, and now, as he advanced towards me, extending his hand politely, I seized it impulsively in mine.

"I am here to beg you for an immense, an unheard-of favour," I began immediately. "It is a question of life, death and murder!"

His face blanched somewhat, and I perceived he thought me mad. I continued as hastily as I could.

"I come from Cambridge, England, sir," I told him. "Three mathematicians have been murdered there within the last months."

"Ah, yes," he murmured, his brow clearing. "I have heard of the dreadful spate of deaths at the University of Cambridge. It is truly terrible, and I regret that a young lady like yourself should be in any way concerned with such events. Yet I fail to see how I can possibly be of service to you."

"I have come to you directly from England," I told him, "because a man has been accused, wrongly accused of the murders, and I believe you and you alone hold the key to the truth."

"I?" He was utterly taken aback, most completely amazed by my words. "But I cannot possibly have the slightest idea, Miss ..."

"Duncan ..."

"Miss Duncan, about the identity of the author of the terrible Cambridge murders!"

"Professor Mittag-Leffler," I said to him, with all the earnestness I could muster, "you do not know, you cannot possibly know, how great a role was played by the n-body

232

problem, and King Oscar's Birthday Competition, in motivating the murders."

I saw that he became more and more amazed; he remained silent for a long time, and when he spoke, he seemed genuinely shocked and saddened by my words.

"Who could have believed such a thing?" he said softly. "If your words are true, I will regret having participated in organising the competition for the remainder of my life."

"No, please do not say that!" I said. "No evil can be attributed to the existence of the competition. I have come to you, because as I said, I believe you may well have something which will provide the final proof against the murderer."

I saw that now, he began to understand.

"Are you referring to the manuscripts submitted to the competition?" he enquired directly. "Are you suggesting that one of them may contain the clue to which you refer?"

"Precisely," I told him.

He reflected for a moment. "The manuscripts are secret and anonymous," he observed.

"Anonymous!" This came as a startling surprise to me. "Anonymous! you mean you do not know the authors?"

"No, I do not know the authors," he replied. "The rules stated that each manuscript should be accompanied only by an epigraph."

"Of course. I saw that in the announcement of the Competition. But there were also the names in sealed envelopes marked with the epigraphs. I thought you would open them! Otherwise, how can you attribute a prize?"

"The manuscripts will be read anonymously and judged on their merits," he said. "When the winning manuscript is selected, the envelope with the corresponding epigraph, and only that one, is to be opened by King Oscar himself, and the name of the author published."

"And the other names will never be revealed or known?"

"Never. That would be against the rules decided on and approved by His Majesty."

My mind leapt and twisted, seeking some opening, some way of avoiding the obstacle which thus arose before me. I decided that he could come to no decision about the extent to which he must transgress the rules in the cause of justice, unless he knew something more of the situation.

"It is my belief that a mathematician from Cambridge submitted a memoir to the competition, containing a complete solution to the n-body problem," I told him. His eyes flashed with a purely mathematical interest.

"Really!" he exclaimed. "This is a marvellous and unexpected development!" But his face then darkened somewhat. "Yet something is wrong. I opened each and every one of the submitted memoirs today, in the presence of my colleague Edvard Phragmén, who is staying here, and I did not perceive any manuscript at all coming from England."

It was my turn to be taken aback. "But you must have!" I said pleadingly. "I do not know where it was actually posted from, but I cannot believe it doesn't exist. Are you sure it cannot have escaped your notice, buried within the large pile of manuscripts you examined today?"

"I have not examined such a very large pile," he replied, "there were but twelve in all. And not a single one in English."

"What languages are they written in?" I enquired faintly, engulfed by a wave of dismay.

"French, or German, or both," he answered.

"Both?"

"Yes, a couple of manuscripts arrived in a double version, in the two languages, written out in different hands."

A light began to shine within me.

"Could not an English mathematician have had his manuscript translated into French and German and copied out by others, so as to hide his identity forever in the event of not winning the prize?" I said.

"Well, it is not impossible, of course," he answered thoughtfully.

234

"I believe we may be able to tell, only from looking at the manuscripts, if they correspond to the memoir I mean," I told him. Feverishly, I set my valise flat upon the floor, unbuckled it and extracted the now much-fingered manuscript of Mr. Beddoes, and from within its pages, the famous paper written by Mr. Akers.

"Please look at these," I told him. "They are rough forms of the complete solution of the n-body problem which I believe must be given in one of the memoirs you opened today. Surely, by examining each of the twelve submissions, you will be able to tell whether one of them contains the mathematics corresponding to what is written here."

He grasped the papers I held out to him, sat down abruptly in a comfortable armchair, and bent over them, concentrating intently, pushing up his small round spectacles, turning the pages, murmuring to himself. Mr. Akers had been a disorderly man, but Mr. Beddoes' neat, regular handwriting was easy to follow, and I saw that the Professor was fascinated by what he read, and that the ideas expressed there rang a bell within him, like the echos of thoughts which he might have had but never did.

We waited for some time in complete silence. Even Robert hardly moved, simply rolling his little train back and forth silently over the cloth-covered table, and lifting his large eyes occasionally to the illustrious Professor's face. After ten or fifteen minutes, Professor Mittag-Leffler looked up from his reading, a surprised and confused expression on his face.

"What I read here is truly remarkable," he said. "The manuscript contains the germs of at least two excellent ideas. I do not perceive any actual error in the reasoning lightly sketched here. And yet, my intuition tells me that such methods cannot, should not be able to provide the result. It seems incredible to me. But a mathematician's intuition, while a splendid guide, should not be trusted absolutely; I have been surprised before. If this is a new example of such a surprise, it is a truly marvellous one, and will almost unquestionably win the competition."

235

"But, Professor, what I have shown you here is not a memoir submitted to the competition," I reminded him gently. "It is merely a brief sketch. It remains to see if the work was completed and submitted with full details."

"You are right," he said, "and we can examine the manuscripts and determine if that is the case quite quickly. Please allow me to invite you and your children to accompany me to my study." He looked at me briefly, and added "Although these cannot possibly be your children, my dear young lady. But I do not presume to ask why they have accompanied you here. Let us go."

We moved down a long and admirably decorated hallway, and encountering a maidservant, he spoke to her in Swedish.

"I have asked her to call for Phragmén to come and join us," he told me. "I strongly wish to have his opinion on the manuscript which interests you." We arrived at the room which the Professor called his office, although many more, if not most, of the rooms in this splendid villa were obviously devoted to the pursuit of mathematics. There, on his desk, neatly piled, lay the twelve memoirs he had opened on that day. Next to them lay a sheet on which he had carefully inscribed the title of each manuscript and the epigraph with which it was signed in lieu of a name.

"I will tell you, in secret," he said with a slight smile, "that one of our candidates has, probably unwittingly, broken the rule, and sent a signed letter together with his epigraphed manuscript. However, had he not done so, I would have known him by his handwriting. It is number nine, the extraordinary Henri Poincaré," and he slipped one of the manuscripts out of the pile with a tender, caressing movement. "I do not need to have read it to know that it is bursting with the ideas of a genius," he said, his voice soft and vibrant with respect. He replaced the manuscript in its place, and extracted another from some way above it. "I believe there is some chance that the bilingual manuscript numbered seven may have a relation to the papers you have just shown me."

He took both the French and the German versions of the manuscript from the pile, and laid them before me. The titles were as follows:

Über die Integration der Differentialgleichungen, welche die Bewegungen eines Systems von Punkten bestimmen,

Sur l'intégration des équations différentielles qui déterminent les mouvements d'un système de points matériels,

and the epigraphs read

Nur schrittweise gelangt man zum Ziel.

Pour parvenir au sommet, il faut marcher pas à pas.

The Professor took them up in his hands. "On the integration of the differential equations which determine the movements of a system of material points," he translated; "to rise to the top, one must advance step by step." He set Mr. Beddoes' notes upon the desk, open to the page which appeared to contain the central result, and laying the French manuscript upon the table next to it, he began to turn the pages slowly, looking over the statements and formulae and comparing the two manuscripts.

"This is the one," he said, his voice vibrating somewhat with excitement and tension. "If you look here, you will see the key formula, and around it, the rest of the argument contained here. It is unmistakable."

I looked where he pointed, and immediately recognised the very formula, now so familiar, which appeared on the paper scribbled by Mr. Akers at his very last dinner. The Professor continued to compare the two manuscripts, nodding his head and indicating to me the similarities.

"The French manuscript is much longer, and contains many details and computations," he said. "Indeed, it hardly corresponds to the opinion expressed in the original announcement of the competition, that Mr. Lejeune-Dirichlet's proof, at least, was not based on long and complex calculations. Yet at the root of these calculations, there lies a stroke of genius, if the result is true."

Something in his tone caught my attention. "Do you doubt its validity?" I asked him.

"I ... don't ... know," he answered, slowly. "I myself have thought long and hard about this very problem. As I told you before, I was absolutely convinced that such methods as those used here could have no chance of solving it. And yet, I desire only to be pleasantly surprised. The manuscript must be read and checked carefully in every detail. I myself will work on it, and my associates also."

In his deep passion and interest for the work at hand, Professor Mittag-Leffler had entirely forgotten that I myself was driven onwards by a very different question. I hardly dared to ask him something he had already told me was expressly forbidden, but one thought of Arthur, and the extreme danger he was running at that very moment, persuaded me.

"Professor Mittag-Leffler," I began humbly, "I must ask you, I must beg you to open the sealed envelope which accompanied this manuscript. It is imperative to discover the author. "

"It is impossible," he answered. "The King's wishes cannot be lightly disdained. The sealed envelopes are to be handed to him personally for safe-keeping until his birthday, next January."

"January!" I cried horrified. "It is far too late! A man's life is at stake, Professor. He who has been accused of the Cambridge murders stands to lose his life—and he is innocent!"

"And you believe that you know the author of this manuscript?"

"I believe it is one of two people," I told him. "I must know if I am right, and if so, which of them it is. The guilt or innocence of not one, but two people depend upon it."

"Can you not tell it by the handwriting, then?" he asked

"I wish I could. But if he had his manuscript translated, and posted from Europe, then they would not be in his handwriting, would they?"

"If he had them translated professionally," replied the Professor, "then, although the languages themselves would be written correctly, the mathematics would probably be expressed in a somewhat peculiar manner, as the typical idiom is foreign to any but a mathematician."

He took up the two manuscripts, and began perusing them more closely.

"It is hard to tell," he said, "for these two languages are not my own. But I do seem to detect some peculiar expressions in both languages. It is not absolutely impossible that they were translated from the English by someone with a perfect knowledge of the languages, but an imperfect one of the mathematical discourse. I cannot be absolutely sure."

At that moment, there came a discreet knock on the door, and a young man entered, wearing the selfsame earnest but ardent expression on his face that I was becoming used to seeing on those of my various mathematical acquaintances. The Professor welcomed him, and introduced us to each other briefly. But the young Dr. Phragmén had eyes only for the mathematics.

"Are you looking at the manuscripts, Professor?" he asked, his voice quite vibrating with eagerness. "Have you come across something particular?"

"Indeed yes," cried the Professor, thrusting the anonymous manuscript number seven in front of the face of his surprised associate. "Miss Duncan has called the central result of this paper to my attention, and I must say that at first sight it appears so astonishing as to be nearly unbelievable! Have a look at the main theorem. Why, this author claims to show a closed formula for the series in the case of the perturbative three-body problem, and deduces that the series describing the movements of the bodies must then converge!"

"What?" responded the clearly astounded Doctor. "A complete solution to the perturbative three-body problem? But this is more than we dared hope for in the best of cases!"

His amazement and rejoicing were such that I could not

remain quiet, although it would certainly have been more seemly to do so.

"Is it so very important, then? What has he proven?" I asked.

"Oh, yes, it is of capital importance!" cried the enthusiastic young Doctor, stabbing at the famous formula with his finger. "He has given a formula for the mysterious series in terms of known analytic functions, and deduced from this that the classical series describing the motion of the bodies converges, that is, has a real value at any given time, rather than a meaningless, infinite value. That means that in this case, what we call the perturbative three-body problem, that is where one of the bodies is very large compared to the other two, like a star and two planets — our own Earth and Jupiter, as it may be — one is able to predict the orbits of the planets, instead of having no idea whether they will not end up by drifting away through space."

"Good heavens," I exclaimed. "I thought it was well-known that the Earth orbits regularly about the sun. You don't mean that without the solution given here, we might have to fear its departing at any moment?"

"Well, no, the nature of the series does tell us that the Earth will certainly continue its orbit for many years yet — but not so very many! We have no guarantee that in a million years it will still be doing the same!"

"Oh," I said with a tinge of disappointment. It is perhaps natural for citizens of a country as stable and peaceful as Sweden to feel threatened by the prospect of turmoil a million years from now, but I myself was concerned with far more immediate circumstances. I still wished nothing but to know the name of the author of the fated manuscript. Yet I feared to insist upon seeing it, for I was afraid to hear a reiteration of the Professor's previous refusal. My mind was seared by the image of Arthur, waiting in the dock, silent and withdrawn, scarcely interested in the battle over his destiny waged around him by lawyers, judge and jury — the outcome of which could — would, probably, send him to his death — and the Professor was thinking about planets! I tried to speak, to tell him what was in my mind, but tears collected in my eyes, and spilled over. Perceiving them, Professor Mittag-Leffler immediately became distressed. He took several rapid steps about the room, thinking intensely.

"I know what worries you, Miss Duncan," he said. "And yet — I cannot do what you wish. But wait! Do not give way to despair. There may be a solution."

"Please tell me what it is," I begged him, trying in vain to control my voice which wavered desperately, while Emily and Robert approached me and wrapped their arms around me tightly, looking at the Professor with their large eyes full of severity and distrust, like little wild cubs in a lair, suspecting the creature creeping about outside of being a threatening predator.

"I see only one thing to do," he said in measured tones. "We cannot open the envelopes because the King has forbidden it. The only one who can go against these orders is the King himself. We must petition him with our request."

"Shall we see the King?" asked Emily with breathless respect. For myself, I felt as though my very heart was pressed in from all directions with fear. I imagined that the King would certainly refuse a request so puny, as compared with his royal concerns. Even more, I feared that we would have to endure a great delay, while our petition was made with all the proper ceremony.

"The matter is desperately urgent," I told the Professor. "The trial has been going on for two weeks already, and the judgement may be pronounced at any moment, any moment at all. It may even have happened today, for aught I know. There is no time to lose."

"My relations with the King are close," he said. "I will send a messenger to the Palace now, with a message to be delivered as soon as he rises tomorrow. I will express the urgency of the situation, and we will go to the Palace immediately tomorrow morning, so as to be already present, should he send for us. If all goes as you wish it, and as I wish it also, I do not hesitate to say, I myself will provide you with conveyance to the station, and with the tickets you need to travel home again. This seems but a minor service which I can render to justice, in the name of mathematics. Let me now have you shown to bedrooms for the night. I beg you will repose yourself as much as possible; I will have you called at six o'clock, that we may be ready for every eventuality."

I saw that he understood my feelings, and that there was no need for me to attempt to express them; I saw, also, that he was doing everything that he possibly could to aid me, and that going against the express wishes of the King, in however trivial a matter, appeared absolutely impossible to him — even now, even when it concerned a question of life or death! I pressed my teeth together, not to allow my anguished impatience to burst out (oh, the idea that the very envelope I so desired to open lay within the very house, and we could have seen inside it in a moment! How I longed, but did not dare, to suggest steaming it secretly open over the kettle and then sealing it up again ...) and thanked him with as much calmness as I could muster. He led us ceremoniously and kindly to the hall, and summoned the buxom lady who had bade us enter earlier on, and spoke to her in Swedish; she showed us to the beautifully furnished adjacent guest rooms where we are now. Taking charge of the children, she swept them away, pausing only to say "bad, bad" to me with a motherly smile, from which I concluded, not that the children were misbehaving, but that they were to be washed. She took charge of my valise, also, and I undressed and fell into bed. But thoughts whirled too strongly in my brain, and I finally admitted to myself, Dora dear, that I should not find sleep before I had committed everything to paper, for it has become such a habit with me, during these long, dreadful weeks, that I can no longer do without it, and it somehow relieves my anguish and momentarily restores hope to me. Now that I have given you a complete account of the events of this crucial day, I shall return to bed, and try to sleep, and not to think too much about the fact that perhaps, tomorrow morning, I shall find myself pleading for Arthur, no longer with charwomen, children, policemen, lawyers and mathematicians, but with a King!

Please pray for me, as always

Vanessa

Malmö, Saturday, June 2nd, 1888

Oh, my dear Dora,

What a day this has been! I have learned much, and reality has superseded my foolish imaginings about Royalty.

As Professor Mittag-Leffler had promised, we were called at six o'clock. I was brought tea in bed, and then shown to a large bathroom wherein a steaming bath had been placed, together with large towels and every luxury. I made a detailed toilette, for I detected more than mere politeness in such gracious treatment; I understood that it also contained a component of careful planning in view of our Royal reception, in which I admit I could still hardly believe.

When I took up my grey dress, I saw that it had been steamed and pressed during the night. Once I had put it on, however, I still hesitated to descend, for my hair was wet and I could not do it up. But the kind housekeeper soon reappeared, and towelled my hair kindly, and fluffed it with her fingers, and brushed it with a brush, and bade me with gestures come down to breakfast, and that she would take care of my hair later. It was already beginning to dry and wave thickly over my shoulders, and I felt a little ashamed, as though I were descending in negligee, but I must needs go, so I went.

I was delighted to see Emily and Robert already installed at the well-laden table before me, happily eating toast with jam, large aprons wrapped around them, laughing together, although their eyes were still small and their cheeks rosy with sleep. The Professor was conversing with them most cheerfully, and he bade me join the meal, and in his kindness and understanding, which I shall never forget, immediately addressed my deepest concerns.

"It is now seven o'clock," he told me, looking at a beautiful silver watch he extracted from his pocket, "the King will receive the message in one hour. By then, we shall already be in the Palace, and his response will be conveyed to us immediately."

He paused to pass me the various crystal pots and covered dishes and to see that I took a sufficient quantity of each, and then continued.

"I have made the acquaintance of these two delightful children, and am now much more familiar with the full circumstances of your journey and your double quest. I am filled with admiration, and wish to support you in every possible way, for I perceive that you are moved to very daring acts by the simple perception of injustice."

I remembered something.

"We are twin souls, then, sir, for I have heard that you insisted on naming, here in Stockholm, the only woman University professor in the whole of Europe, when no other country would have countenanced such a thing, not even Germany, where at least women are allowed to study."

He smiled. "So you have heard of the famous Sonya Kovalevskaya," he said. "She is one of the greatest mathematicians alive today, and what may have seemed like a disgrace to others appears a great honour and good fortune to me. I wish you could meet her. I do not ask you anything about the details of your quest, for I perceive that you must keep your suspicions secret until you are certain of their truth, and in any case I know almost nothing of the protagonists, dead or alive. But should all pass as you hope and believe that justice would require, I pray that there may be some future day, when your life is full of peace and pleasantness, and you have sufficient strength and time to undertake the long journey hither once again. I would welcome you here with the greatest pleasure, and introduce you to my dear Sonya who would appreciate you very much, I think. Now, we must prepare our departure."

We arose, and the maid removed the large aprons which protected the children's clothing from the various drops of jam and honey which naturally fell about them. I was amazed and delighted to see that not only had they been bathed and scrubbed to perfection, but somehow, their clothes had been washed and — more surprisingly — dried during the night. They must have kept a great fire burning to accomplish it so quickly, for clothing is generally most reluctant to dry in the darkness. Emily's dress had been ironed and starched, and her soft, dark hair drawn back with a band, and her shoes polished; the gracious princess I was used to seeing at lessons had returned to replace the laughing gypsy of the past week. Robert also had been washed and brushed and pressed and polished, and looked for all the world like a much-beloved little boy of good family; I perceived more strongly than ever his delicate charm and strong resemblance to Edmund.

I was led upstairs, where the personal maid of the Professor's wife — who was still asleep — took charge of my hair and wound it with easy precision into an elegant chignon. She perched my hat on top of it, pinned it carefully, and guided me downstairs to where the Professor and the children were waiting in the hall, already wrapped up in their outdoor things. The Professor's handsome carriage was at the door, and we mounted and set off through the wide, lovely streets to the capital, the Professor bearing a leather case containing the full set of manuscripts and sealed envelopes submitted to the King's Competition.

The distance to the centre of Stockholm was not far, and

before eight o'clock had struck, we drew up before the Royal Palace. The palace is an extremely regular building, absolutely square and similar on all sides, four stories high, with a grand courtyard in the centre, and four symmetric wings extending from the corners, two from the front and two from the back, enclosing grand esplanades between them. The facades are sculpted in niches in which stand statues. The Swedes call their king's palace *Kungliga Slottet*, which sounds quite strange to our British ears, except for the echo it contains of something "Kingly".

We drew up at the front esplanade and descended, whereupon we were immediately surrounded by uniformed guards, who questioned us closely and kept us waiting while they sent for information, before finally ushering us within the precincts of the Palace itself. There, we were shown up and down long and noble halls, to a large antechamber where quite a large number of people were already waiting.

"This is the antechamber to the King's offices," the Professor told us. "He works here, and receives visits and petitions. We must now wait for an answer to our message, which should have already been delivered. The King has no time to waste, so the message was a brief one; I represented the extreme urgency of the situation and begged him to spare us only a very few minutes. My relationship with the King is a close and trusting one, and I hope that he will be able to send us at least a brief message in answer at any moment.

Indeed, we had not waited for longer than half-an-hour (during which time I was on tenterhooks, not only for fear of a negative answer, but lest Emily or Robert behave in some way incompatible with our Royal surroundings) before a uniformed guard entered the room and called for Professor Mittag-Leffler. They spoke for a moment, and the Professor turned to us.

"The King will make a short space of a few minutes in his schedule, to receive, at ten o'clock, upon the departure of the Danish Ambassador," he said. "I would have preferred to prepare the King by speaking to him myself, but as we have so short a time, we shall enter all together. I shall speak to him first, and you, Miss Duncan, will answer any questions he may put to you. Please remember to conclude each sentence with the words 'Your Majesty'."

"Of course!" I assured him, rather taken aback at the idea that my lack of experience in dealing with kings might somehow jeopardise the outcome of my quest. I tried to imagine myself speaking to the King, and it was not easy — I felt I must look like nothing so much as Alice respectfully addressing the Cheshire cat! The wait was long; I dearly wished that I had something to read. These many long moments of enforced inactivity, when all inside me is burning to act, have truly proved the most tormenting aspect of my entire journey. However, the time passed; the many waiters and petitioners in the room talked in low voices, so that Emily and Robert felt it was not forbidden to do as much themselves, and I began to catch occasional snatches of the tale of Sleeping Beauty, recounted with great attention to detail. Finally, ten o'clock struck; I wondered greatly what form our summons would take. The large double doors at one end of the antechamber — not that from which we had entered — opened, and one of the uniformed guards appeared in the opening, and called out in stentorian tones:

"The King will receive Professor Mittag-Leffler and his suite!"

We arose, much to the annoyance of all those in the room who had arrived long before us, and would probably have to wait much longer, and were ushered through the small room beyond, whose main purpose appeared to be to house the guard and separate the King from the noise of the antechamber, into his very Office, where I had my first glimpse of the Royal Personage.

The King is near on sixty years old. His bearing is noble and haughty, his hair white and scant, his beard grizzled and firm, and his moustache so very long that its two ends extend

247

down into the beard and then outwards in two well-waxed points as long as fingers. He was seated behind a large desk. We remained standing. Although I could not understand a word that passed between them, it was clear that the King was inviting the Professor to state his business as rapidly as possible, for he spoke only very briefly. The Professor began by showing him the pile of papers and sealed envelopes which he had collected. The King nodded briefly and said something, and the piles were handed over to him. The Professor then spoke some more, and I heard the urgency in his tones, and knew that he was coming to the heart of the matter. The King said a few words to the Professor, and rang a small bell. My heart nearly stopped, as I saw the door opened from the outside by the guard, for I thought we were being summarily dismissed. But the Professor shook the hand of the King — one short, sharp shake, as though no time could be lost even for such a brief ceremony, and then saying to me "The King will see you alone," he allowed himself to be ushered out by the guard. The door closed firmly, and the king addressed himself to me in English.

"Professor Mittag-Leffler has told me that you are Miss Duncan, that you come from Cambridge, that you have interested yourself in the murder of three mathematicians there, that you believe the person now on trial, himself a mathematician, is innocent and yet runs a great risk of condemnation, that you believe you know the true course of events, and that one of these envelopes here contains an important proof of your theory."

I saw how such a man could be a King. If the country was run as efficiently as this, then it was well run indeed.

"Miss Duncan, I am willing to open and look at the name contained in the envelope whose number you indicate to me, for I know nothing of the contents of the associated manuscript. But I am reluctant to communicate the name which I will see there to you, for I would not somehow suggest the name of the murderer to you by this procedure. However, if it is true that you believe yourself to be informed of his identity, then you need only write down the name on this piece of paper, and the number of the envelope you wish me to open, and I will let you know whether you are right or wrong."

I was in a quandary. I was not absolutely sure of the author of the critical memoir — it could be one of two people. I thought of Mr. Akers and his medicine. I closed my eyes briefly, sent up a prayer, wrote a name upon the paper, and then the number seven.

He took the paper, read it, slipped out the envelope numbered seven, slit it open with a silver paper-knife, extracted the paper within, and looked at it. Each of his gestures was as sharp and precise as his speech. He looked directly into my eyes with a nod, and spoke.

"Yes, Miss Duncan. You are correct. I congratulate you on your insight and wish you success in your endeavour."

My heart leapt with triumph and relief. Now I knew! I truly knew! I had only to rush back to England, as though on wings, and confront the Judge with my discoveries!

The King reached towards his little bell. I felt Emily tug at my dress, and turned to her. She wished urgently to speak, but felt too nervous.

"What do you wish, my child?" said the King, addressing an unexpected smile at the children, of whom he had not taken any notice hitherto.

"Your Majesty, Miss Duncan will need proof to bring back to England and show the judge, in order to save Mr. Weatherburn, please, Your Majesty!" she burst out, all pink.

He reflected for an instant.

"You are right, child," he said. "Yet I am reluctant to render this thing public. Hold — I will write and seal a letter, to be opened and read uniquely by the Judge, which you will transmit to him for me. What is his name?"

"Mr. Justice Penrose, my Lord — no, Your Majesty!" I stammered.

The King dipped his pen in the ink, took a beautifully

embossed sheet of paper, and wrote a few sentences on it, while Emily, Robert and I tried to look elsewhere, and prevent our eyes from straying irresistibly towards the page. When he had finished, he said, "I have written that you came to see me with the belief that the person you named was the author of the manuscript received by Professor Mittag-Leffler, and that I personally confirm the correctness of your guess."

He folded the paper, slipped it into an envelope also embossed with his crest, and sealed it with a large and impressive seal in red wax. He addressed the envelope in his large, noble handwriting to "Mr. Justice Penrose, Cambridge, England" and handed it to me. He then shook each of our hands, saying to Emily, "You have been very helpful, my child."

"Oh, thank you, Your Majesty, thank you for everything!" she gasped.

The King took up his silver paper-knife, and held it out to her, smiling.

"You may have this," he said, "and keep it as a gift. So, you will always remember your friend, the King of Sweden. I wish you 'Bon voyage'."

He pressed his bell, while we still sought to express our stammering thanks!

The guard appeared, and we passed out, myself feeling weak in the knees and clutching the envelope tightly, Emily clinging to her paper-knife. We were taken to yet another antechamber, where the Professor was waiting for us.

"Your interview went well?" he asked immediately.

"Yes!" I told him. "The King opened the envelope; he would not tell me what was in it, but bade me tell him, and then confirmed my guess. He wrote a letter to the Judge," and I showed him the envelope.

"You are very lucky," he told me. "Keep it carefully. I will now accompany you to send you on your return to England. I would like to purchase a small strong-box for you to carry this important letter back with you, for the risk of your losing it or having it stolen from you is too great."

I tried to remonstrate, but the Professor had the situation well in hand. His carriage was brought, and we mounted; he told one of the footmen to descend, purchase the strong-box, and to meet us at the railway station. Thither we then drove, and the Professor himself accompanied us to the counter, and — oh, Dora — he bought and paid for our first-class tickets all the way to London, and wrote down on a piece of paper for me the name of the small "pension" in Malmö where we are at this very moment! The footman arrived with the small, flat strong-box meant for holding papers, and the Professor enclosed the King's letter within it almost religiously, as well as Emily's paper-knife, locked it up and gave me the key, enjoining me to hide it as well as humanly possible.

"If only I had Rose's petticoats!" exclaimed Emily, as I tried to find a place to conceal the strong-box as well as the key.

"Is there any other service I can render you before your departure?" asked the Professor.

"Oh — we should send a telegram to my mother!" said Emily. "We really ought to do it every day, poor Mother."

"I shall send it the moment you depart," he assured her with a smile. "Let us write the text of it out now, shall we?" And taking out a bit of paper from his pocket — mathematicians seem never to be without these infinitely useful scraps — he penned a few words.

"How does this sound? *June 2nd, 1888: Emily and Robert met the King of Sweden this morning, they leave Stockholm for Malmö today, on their way to London.*"

"Noooo," said Emily, "why, she'll never believe it — she'll think we've gone mad on the way!"

"Leave it," I said. "It is the simple truth! Oh, do let us rush. We must go as fast as we can; I think we can be there in three days."

"In three days — you will kill yourselves travelling so fast! It is hardly possible!"

"We it must do it — every day is fundamental! The Jury may be deliberating at any moment. We must pray that Mr. Haversham has enough witnesses, whoever they may be. We cannot delay at all!"

"You are right," he said. "Your courage is admirable. I wish you the very best of luck and success. Depart at once; I will telegraph immediately."

"Please — telegraph also the Judge — Mr Justice Penrose, Courts of Justice, Cambridge! Tell him that I am coming with new evidence," I cried as we climbed on the train.

How admirable are the Swedish people. One feels, in their calm and beautiful country, that miscarriages of justice could hardly exist, and that each and every person has the leisure and the wherewithal to smooth away every difficulty. But it cannot really be so. It must seem so only because I hobnob with a social class which includes Kings, and travel in luxurious first-class carriages which look more like small sitting rooms than trains.

My dear, I am so filled with renewed hope, which bubbles up inside me like rising yeast, that I sometimes nearly forget that Arthur is still in grave danger, and that I may even now be too late. I pray constantly, and feel that your prayers are joined to mine.

Good night,

Your loving Vanessa

Ostend, Tuesday, June 5th, 1888

Oh, Dora, help!

I am writing to you from Brussels — we arrived here last night. If only we could have travelled faster! I would have willingly travelled all night, but the trains do not run in the nighttime. Still, I believed that all was not lost, that we were arriving as hastily as humanly possible, and that at this very moment — it is early in the morning yet — we would be on a boat sailing to Dover, and thence to London, and to Cambridge before the afternoon! All my plans are dashed, and we are prisoners here in the port of Ostend, for a great storm lashed up in the Channel overnight, and the boats cannot sail. Oh, what does it all mean? Can it be a judgement upon us? No, I must not give way to despair. The boats are ready, and we must only wait for the storm to subside.

It stormed wildly all night, with rolling thunder and cracking lightning, so that Robert could not sleep, and huddled shivering in my arms. I held his fragile little body close, and we comforted each other. The morning seemed endless in coming, although we did eventually sleep a little. I wish I had awoken to a fresh, rain-washed sky, but such was not the case, for it is still raining extremely violently, although the thunder has stopped, but the waves are crashing onto the shore, and I can imagine that crossing would be desperately dangerous and frightening. There is nothing to do but wait, and pray. I have taken the children to a café, where we are trying to beguile the dreadful hours with coffee and chocolate, cream and croissants. The children are as impatient as I am; Robert is very tired, and Emily very anxious to return to her mother and, above all, afraid of her mother's reaction to the newcomer.

"I shall tell her that if she tries to send him away, even to boarding school, I shall run away again," she began firmly.

"No, Emily, do not say that," I quickly interposed. "You must use your close and tender relations with your mother to persuade her, not threats."

"Maybe you are right," she mused. "Mother often listens to me. But not always. She refused to send for Robert for nearly two whole months. Oh, what shall I do if she refuses now! I can't understand why she should. How, how can anyone want to send away a darling little orphan boy?"

I tried to imagine how Mrs. Burke-Jones might feel about

the little boy who was the fruit of her husband's disastrous and forbidden relations with the mistress whom he loved more tenderly than his wife, and to concoct some explanation of these things which could touch Emily without blackening her bright vision of the world. She listened carefully, but still insisted that the little boy was not to blame, and should not be punished.

"Feelings are very strong, and not always just," I told her. But as her eyes began to fill with tears, I hastened to add, "I do not want to make you believe that your mother will do what you most fear. Please be patient until you see her, and even when you are talking it over with her, remain patient, not passionate."

"Then you must remain patient as well," she smiled. "And perhaps you will not have to for too long, as I believe that the rain is lightening up somewhat."

It is lightening a little, though still coming down hard, so I shall seal up this short letter, and we shall all hasten back to the port to see when the boats may leave. The day at court begins at nine o'clock and closes at five; if the boat does not leave until midday, then I may arrive too late!

God help me,

Vanessa

Cambridge, Wednesday, June 6th, 1888

My dear, dear Dora,

For the first time in weeks, I write to you with peaceful feelings — even though I do feel somewhat numbed and scarred by all that has happened!

Yesterday, the weather finally becalmed itself, and the boats were able to leave towards midday. How long the journey to Cambridge appeared, how dreadfully, painfully endless, as the excruciatingly slow boat trip was followed by the wait for a train to London and then another to Cambridge. I would have sent a telegram saying that I was on my way, but I did not know whom to send it to, for I doubted that anyone would be at home.

One point of light — who should be waiting for us when we descended from the boat, but Mrs. Burke-Jones! She swarmed towards us with uncontrolled emotion and gathered us all three in her arms; tears rolled down her face as she kissed her daughter and told her in confused snatches how desperately worried she had been. She had been waiting for the boats from the mainland since early this morning, and had spent hours of agony as the storm continued, and then of worry as several boats arrived at nearly the same time and she feared to miss us. The dear lady — I saw that she had gone through her inward struggle during our absence, and that she had determined to behave to little Robert quite exactly as though his arrival was an arranged and expected event; she hugged and kissed him, and swung him up into the railway carriage with the practiced gesture of long years of motherhood. She was remarkable — she treated him quite exactly as though he were her own little boy, not a precious, newly found one, but one whom she saw every day and whose presence was a simple, natural, necessary, tender fact. She did not go out of her way to make his acquaintance by asking questions, but got to the point immediately, admired his locomotive, produced a basket of delicious things to eat, and — oh joy in the midst of my fears — produced first class tickets to Cambridge for us all!

Thus, though the trip seemed long and weary, it at least passed in comfort and the joy of reunion. Although I was not sure if Mrs. Burke-Jones had been following Arthur's trial, I hastened to ask her if she had any news of it, and if Mr. Morrison had received my telegram and been able to act on it.

"For you know that I have been to Belgium and Stockholm to collect evidence to defend him, and I must rush to the

Court immediately, to present it to the Judge," I explained.

She stared at me, and then looked at her watch. "My dear child," she said in dismay, "in my fear for the children, I had completely forgotten. Look at the time — I am afraid you are in danger of finding the trial over and the prisoner condemned!"

"Wha-at?" I cried, my worst fears realised.

"Charles has told me that the last witnesses were questioned yesterday, and that when the Judge received your telegram, he read it, and then announced to the Court that the closing statements of the Counsels should begin this morning, and that if no further evidence had come to light by five o'clock in the afternoon, the Jury would be sent to deliberate. I do not know how long their statements will be, but if they conclude and the Jury is sent out, everybody believes that they will not remain over a few minutes. Mr. Haversham has tried hard, but his line of defence collapsed completely with the evidence of the two ladies from London, and since then, he has not really rallied, although he has produced a great many witnesses to all kinds of complicated details which do not prove anything. I believe he is simply trying to gain time in the hopes of your return. At any rate, you can count on him to spin out his closing speech as long as is humanly possible!"

I felt faint with dismay, and leaning back in my seat, I closed my eyes, trying to recapture my spirits. Emily, meantime, longed to talk to her mother, but hesitated, for lack of privacy and for fear perhaps of what she might hear. As I fell silent, she began to chat of this and that, as though seeking for a port of entry. Finally, she asked, "How is Edmund, Mother? Is he better?"

"He is better now, dear," her mother replied softly. "But when you were away, he was terribly ill. He was feverish and delirious. Even the doctor was afraid. He could not give Edmund anything that would soothe him, and finally, he came to me, and told me that Edmund's illness was a nervous one, and that it stemmed from fear. He asked me what it was that Edmund feared so strongly that in order to avoid it, he would make himself ill for weeks on end."

"Oh, Mother — you know what it is," began Emily.

"Yes, I know now. I knew it before, dear, because you told me time and again. But you never told me all that Edmund told you. And perhaps if you had, I should have been unable to believe it. I remained in his room for days, Emily, and I know now that he cries in his sleep, and talks of his school in his delirium."

'So you will not send him back? Have you told him?"

"Naturally, as soon as the doctor asked me the question, I realised what he meant, and told him that I believed Edmund feared being sent back to school. He told me that if I wished him to become well again, I should begin, at that very instant, to assure him again and again that he would never be sent to another boarding school. 'And mind that it is true, Madam,' he told me, 'for another relapse of this kind, which may be due to the absence of the sister on whose protection he relied, may well be fatal'."

'So you told him, and he is better?"

"Yes, he is better, though still pale and weak, and eagerly waiting for your return, Emily, and for the arrival of Robert. And in fact, I thought ... I had an idea, Miss Duncan, about these two little boys, which I hardly dare submit to you."

"Whatever can it be?" I enquired, surprised to be addressed in the midst of this private family discussion.

"You are a daring and audacious young woman, Miss Duncan, and thanks to people like you, times will change, and received ideas will be modified," she said thoughtfully. "I wonder if you have ever asked yourself why little girls and boys must be educated separately and differently?"

"No, I have not asked myself the question exactly," I admitted, "I simply contented myself with finding the idea foolish and rather a pity."

"Do you?" she asked eagerly. "And what would you think of completing your class with the addition of two small boys?"

I laughed.

"For myself, I would be simply delighted," I told her. "I am quite ready to undertake it. I only hope I will not lose all my other students because of it."

"I will talk with the other mothers myself," she said. "If I find any that are set against the idea, we will see what course to follow. But I am quite ready to believe that a certain number of them will be eager to follow my example, and enroll the brothers of their daughters in the school, at least those below a certain age."

I must admit, Dora, that the prospect enchanted me. A whole class of little boys and girls together — it appeared to me so natural, yet so modern, as to suit my tastes entirely. I teased little Robert.

"You shall come to me for lessons in the afternoon, then, Robert, perhaps, shall you? You know, I do not teach French in my class, because I do not speak it. But now you can replace me, and teach the other children, and I can offer French lessons. I shall become rich!"

"Before you become too enthusiastic," Mrs. Burke-Jones told me, "I would like to make you aware that even if some of the mothers of your present pupils agree to the arrangement, there is still a risk that you find yourself considered as engaged in a scandalous project by the community at large. You must reflect carefully what your position in such a situation would be. It might even be — I am envisaging the worst possible situation — that your landlady would refuse to keep such a school within her rooms. In that case, I would gladly offer you to open it in my house."

"Oh, yes, oh, yes, that would be wonderful!" shouted Emily.

"Now, Emily," said her mother, "it is not for us to decide. We must see how things turn out."

I felt more and more inclined to follow my heart, and be daring, and risk scandal.

"I can hardly provoke more scandal than by what I am about to do at this very moment," I mused, trying to envision my arrival at Court.

It was not far short of five o'clock already. But we were in the train to Cambridge, and it was rolling along swiftly through the green countryside. I looked at my watch for the thousandth time.

"It may not be too late," I said.

"It depends on the closing statements," she said. "If, as I imagine, Mr. Haversham draws out his closing statement until the utmost limit of five o'clock, then that is when the Jury will be sent to deliberate. It is very close to five o'clock now. There is nothing to do but be patient; we shall get a cab to take you to the Court the very moment we set foot in Cambridge."

By this time, the train was drawing into Cambridge, and I put all exciting thoughts of becoming the new scandal of the town by introducing unheard-of modern schooling methods out of my thoughts, and concentrated myself on what I should say as I arrived in the court, and how I could impress upon the judge that he must listen to me, no matter what point the trial had reached, and even if Arthur had already been condemned, or for that matter, already hung.

I opened my valise and extracted the whole bundle of papers comprising the evidence I had put together.

"Good," said Mrs. Burke-Jones, "now, I shall take your valise home with me — and here, you shall take this leather bag for your papers ..." she tipped her own things out of it, and placed them in the picnic basket, with gestures that for all their haste never ceased to be charmingly precise and lady-like, "... and my dear, let me look at you. Here, perhaps this comb — no, let me do it, you have no mirror."

She unpinned and removed my hat, and combed my hair carefully, replacing a pin or two. Then she sat back and looked at me critically.

"Here, my dear," she said, "you shall wear my hat." And

before I could say a word, she had removed it from her hair and balanced it carefully on mine.

It was truly a lovely hat, the kind which is very expensive and very simple, and belong only to ladies who can afford a great many hats. It was in black velvet. I felt it was really too beautiful for my dress.

"Not at all," she said, "quite the contrary. Your lovely figure and your way of walking, together with the hat, lend a great deal of elegant simplicity to the dress. I cannot help you much, in this difficult and crucial moment, but I can do this small thing: make sure that your appearance will help you impress the judge properly. Now, we have arrived. I will get you a hansom."

Out we rushed, and although everyone in the train wanted to flag a hansom, Mrs. Burke-Jones' simple, distinguished gesture was the first to succeed. The top-hatted driver stopped in front of her with eager respect, tipped his hat and opened his door. She ushered me in, and gave him a bill and the address of the Courthouse.

"Thank you, thank you so much," I called as he whipped up his horses.

"I wish you courage," she called back.

"Mother, please can we not go to the Courthouse too?" cried Emily as I drove away.

"Certainly not! It is not a place for children!" replied her mother, and swept her little brood down the street, as my coachman and I turned the corner.

"You in a hurry, Ma'am?" he called smartly down to me.

"Oh, *yes*, the biggest possible one!" I told him.

Suddenly, all my fear and apprehension seemed to melt away. I felt as though time had stopped, and could not resume its steady march until I reached the Courthouse and released it. We trotted along sharply enough, my driver taking care to pass others along the streets, abusing them vigorously the while, until finally, he drew up in front of the imposing entrance, hopped down and opened the door for me. It was just after six o'clock.

"Here you are, Miss," he said, "it's all paid for, hurry along now."

I added his gentlemanliness, and his kind eagerness to help me, to all the other generous and beautiful gestures I had encountered in my long quest, to be remembered and treasured later. Storing it in my heart, I jumped out and ran up the steps to the stately entrance, calling back, "I hope I meet you again someday!"

I pushed the doors, and entering the hall, addressed myself hastily to the clerk at the desk.

"Can you tell me, please, about the trial of R. vs. Weatherburn? Is it over yet?"

"No, Miss, the Jury's out, been out this quarter of an hour. A painful long speech Counsel for the Defence give. Most people was sleeping. The Jury's not expected to take long. The Judge held the trial up a bit today over midday — some say he was waiting for another witness — but finally he called for the Closing Statements."

"I am the witness he was waiting for, and I have only just arrived," I told him. "Can you take an urgent message to the Judge, immediately, and show me the way to the public gallery?"

"Oh, Miss — it may be too late now," he said, looking very doubtful. But he pushed paper and pen toward me, and indicated a door behind him with his thumb. As fast as I was able, I penned a few words to the Judge, blotted them, handed them to the clerk and dashed into the public gallery.

I waited there for a few dreadful minutes. The Jury was still out, and the members of the public were murmuring to each other. They appeared to think that the outcome of the trial was a foregone conclusion, and that the Jury would be returning at any moment. I looked over at Arthur, and felt my heart gripped with agonising tenderness. He looked like a man who has quietly abandoned the turmoil of living; he did not see me, did not lift his eyes even a single time, nor feel my

261

burning gaze, but remained as still as a man who has already quietly accepted death and defeat. It was easy to see that, like the smirking public in the gallery, he was in no doubt at all of his conviction, and that he had not conserved even the slightest vestige of hope; his was not a fighting nature, and his reaction to the blows of Fate was one of withdrawal and silent despair. My heart seemed to stop, watching him.

Quite suddenly, at the very back of the Courtroom, two doors opened simultaneously. From the left-hand one issued a Bailiff, who proceeded to hold the door and usher in the twelve members of the Jury. One by one, they took their seats in the jury box. From the other issued a very young, smartly dressed messenger boy, carrying my message. He brought it respectfully to the Judge and handed it to him with a bow and some murmured words.

I held my breath. The Judge read my message. He looked up. He looked over at the Jury. He looked at the public. He appeared to reflect. The foreman of the Jury watched him patiently, waiting to be called upon to give the verdict. The Judge finally turned to him.

"Members of the Jury," he said, "have you reached a verdict?"

"Yes, my Lord," replied the foreman.

Every person in the Courtroom knew what the Judge's next sentence should be, and the foreman's answer. I found I could not breathe. I restrained the impulse to leap to my feet, to call out, and concentrated myself upon the Judge, willing him to say something different. He opened his mouth.

"Members of the Jury," he said, "you have worked hard and long on this case. Now you have finally finished that work, and I am going to make a very unusual request. I am going to ask that you hold back the decision you have reached, and that we listen to the statement of one final witness. This witness has only just arrived from abroad. I would like to tell you that I had decided to exclude the testimony of this witness if she did not arrive by five o'clock today, as every other witness had been heard, and the closure of the trial could not be indefinitely postponed. However, she is now here, and it appears that she carries such evidence as may help to avert a very grave miscarriage of justice. I therefore propose to Counsel for the Prosecution and the Defence, and to you, members of the Jury, to hear this witness. She is a witness who has already been called to testify during this trial. After hearing her complete testimony, we may either adjourn the trial until tomorrow, if the Prosecution would like to seek answers to the newly arisen testimony, or else, Prosecution and Defence may *briefly* renew their closing statements, and you, Members of the Jury, may deliberate once again. I would like to know if MISS VANESSA DUNCAN is presently in the court?"

"Yes, I am," I said ringingly, standing up in the middle of the public gallery.

"Then, in spite of your extremely unorthodox proceedings, Miss Duncan, I would like to invite you to step into the witness box," said Mr. Justice Penrose, quite benevolently.

I left the public gallery through the same door by which I had entered it, and asked the clerk to guide me into the Courtroom proper, as a witness. He did so, and I walked down the alley and stepped into the box, encouraged by the consciousness of the documents I held in their leather bag, and of the quiet elegance of Mrs. Burke-Jones' hat.

"Miss Duncan," said the Judge, "you have already been questioned and cross-questioned in this court. However, you say here that the information you bring is entirely new. The situation we find ourselves in at this moment is an extremely unusual one, and therefore I am willing to follow an unusual proceeding. I invite you to simply tell your tale in your own words, subject to the objections of Counsel if you rely too heavily on suppositions or hearsay in any part of your testimony."

"Thank you, my Lord," I said, trying to control my voice, which wavered somewhat with sudden nervousness. And I began to speak.

"I would like to tell the members of the Jury, and everyone else in this Courtroom, a great many facts about the murders of the three professors of mathematics, Mr. Akers, Mr. Beddoes, and Mr. Crawford. I believe that I have been able to retrace the full sequence of events leading to their deaths, and I have done my very best to substantiate each of my statements with concrete evidence. I would like, if I may, to recount all the events leading up to the murders, although this may take some extra time."

"Please do," nodded the Judge.

"I will begin, then, with King Oscar II of Sweden, and the announcement of his Birthday Competition. This announcement appeared in volume 7 of the mathematical journal *Acta Mathematica*, published in 1885-1886. I have an English translation of it here."

I opened Mrs. Burke-Jones' leather bag and extracted the translation of the announcement that Mr. Morrison had made for me at a gay tea-party which seemed long ago. I handed it to the Judge, who looked it over, and handed it down to the lawyers, who then handed it to the Jury.

"As you may see, the closing date for submission of entries to the Competition was June 1st, 1888; just four days ago," I said, "and the prize, an award of money and a golden medal, to say nothing of the great honour involved, is considerable. The main subject of the competition is known as the n-body problem, where n is any number of bodies or particles subject to the laws of physics known as Newton's laws. Newton himself solved the problem of the behaviour of such bodies when there are only two of them, but the problem of three or more bodies has not, until now, been completely solved.

"Now, the world's foremost experts on this problem, and on the other problems posed in the announcement of the Competition, are not British, but French and German mathematicians. I have often heard the name of a certain Henri Poincaré as being one of the candidates in the Competition most expected to obtain astonishing new results. However, the Competition was, as you may see from the announcement, open to every mathematician, everywhere. And here in Cambridge, a group of three mathematicians, all more or less specialists in subjects related to these, decided to join forces and work together, in complete secrecy, to see if they could not pool their different capacities to produce a solution. These three mathematicians were Mr. Akers, Mr. Beddoes and Mr. Crawford.

"At this point, I would like to produce a second piece of evidence: Mr. Akers' personal agenda. I collected this agenda from Mr. Akers' sister, presently living in Belgium, to whom the police had transmitted her brother's personal effects. In this agenda, on the dates of October 18th, December 13th and February 14th, we find the following notation: *ABC* 2 *p.m.* Similar notation appears for a date occurring after Mr. Akers' death, the 17th of April. Note that the group called ABC met regularly every two months, on a Tuesday afternoon.

"Clearly ABC stands for Akers, Beddoes and Crawford, and the purpose of these regular meetings was to collaborate and combine efforts in the direction of solving at least part of the n-body problem in time for King Oscar's Birthday Competition. Recall that Mrs. Wiggins testified that a few people occasionally met in Mr. Crawford's rooms; she specifically remembered clearing away traces of a whisky-drinking party of three in Mr. Crawford's rooms around mid-February. These were certainly the traces of the ABC meeting of February 14th. As for the choice of Tuesday afternoon, it can easily be checked that this must have been the best choice of day and hour in the week, in order for their separate teaching and tutoring schedules to combine to allow each of them a free portion of the afternoon.

"Having established the link between these three mathematicians, I would like to add that they decided to keep their efforts a secret, perhaps in order to avoid any public disappointment should the outcome appear unsatisfactory.

265

However, they were but human, and it was difficult for them to keep their activities entirely secret. It is natural for a mathematician to wish to share his triumph when he produces a particularly good idea, and at least some mathematicians of my acquaintance were vaguely aware that both Mr. Akers and Mr. Crawford were working on the n-body problem. Mr. Beddoes, however, was extremely discreet. In my presence, having been told that Mr. Akers had talked about the n-body problem to Mr. Weatherburn, and that Mr. Crawford appeared to be secretly working on the question, he reacted with shocked annoyance, which he then hastily explained away by making the ridiculous observation that those two mathematicians were quite incompetent to deal with such a problem. I remember the scene very clearly, although at the time, I was not aware that his annoyance was a natural reaction to the realisation that his two colleagues were each, separately, throwing out vague hints which contradicted the promise of secrecy they had made to each other. I do not know of anyone who was actually explicitly told about the joint effort, or the regular collaboration meetings, but it seems clear that they occurred.

"Let me now address the events of February 14th, and the murder of Mr. Akers. An ABC meeting took place on that day at 2 p.m., and according to Mrs. Wiggins' testimony, it took place in Mr. Crawford's rooms.

"We shall never know exactly what happened during the meeting, as the only three witnesses are now dead. However, judging by subsequent events, the meeting must have run more or less as follows. At some preceding meeting, Mr. Crawford, who had the reputation of being a brilliant and inventive mathematician, although lacking in rigour, must have put forth the germ of an excellent idea towards the solution of the n-body problem. All three mathematicians would have spent the next two months working on this idea or ideas of their own, hoping to find some new element to be submitted to the subsequent meeting. What actually happened is

266

that some time before the February 14th meeting, a most extraordinary idea occurred to Mr. Akers; an idea of an essentially computational nature, with explicit formulae, which could complete Mr. Crawford's idea and bring it to fruition. Explicitly, he believed that he could adapt Mr. Crawford's idea to obtain a complete solution of the *three-body problem*, the first fundamentally unknown case of the general problem with n bodies for any number n. Before the meeting, Mr. Akers had verified and developed his idea to a certain extent, and sketched it in a carelessly written manuscript of several pages. Then, fired by the enthusiasm of his own discovery, he came to underestimate the importance of Mr. Crawford's contribution, and to consider that he had solved the problem by himself. I believe that he attended the ABC meeting with the intention of announcing to his colleagues that he had solved the three-body problem, and that he intended to pursue his own researches to their conclusion and submit a manuscript independently to the Competition.

"Mr. Beddoes and Mr. Crawford must have been very angry, and argued with him. Mathematicians tend to be extremely prickly about the possession of ideas, and it is quite probable that if Mr. Beddoes and Mr. Crawford had been entirely convinced that Mr. Akers' idea was absolutely independent and original, they would have been ready to congratulate him. However, from whatever he let fall, they must have perceived that his idea was not so much a new direction, as a brilliant way of making Mr. Crawford's idea work. Then I believe a serious quarrel occurred, during which Mr. Crawford downed an entire half-bottle of whisky, as he tended to do in moments of extreme stress or excitement, observed by both Mr. Akers and Mr. Beddoes.

"Mr. Akers left Mr. Crawford's rooms, and went to the library, his mind filled with his discovery to the exclusion of moral considerations. Mr. Crawford remained in his rooms and began to reflect hard on his own idea, no doubt feeling that if Mr. Akers had been able to make it work, he might

267

have a chance at arriving at the same result, although his talents lay in a different direction. For his part, Mr. Beddoes must have considered Mr. Akers' behaviour quite simply unacceptable, and he must have determined within himself to prevent him from continuing his work alone, and to compel him to share it. At any rate, he betook himself to the mathematics library of the University, and there, he saw his colleague Mr. Akers, talking quietly among the bookshelves to Mr. Weatherburn. Mr. Beddoes heard how he was unable to keep the triumph of his discovery to himself, and he heard him invite Mr. Weatherburn to dinner at the Irish pub, no doubt, as Mr. Beddoes thought, to gloat. He determined to slip into Mr. Akers' rooms in College during the dinner, and search them to find any trace of written work expressing the idea which he felt that Mr. Akers had no right to keep to himself.

"It must have been rather difficult for him to locate the manuscript, of whose existence he may not even have been completely certain; Mr. Akers' papers were always in a great state of disarray, and his handwriting was difficult. Mr. Beddoes must have searched among them at some length, finding it necessary to decipher several papers before reaching the conclusion that they concerned mathematics irrelevant to the n-body problem.

"While Mr. Beddoes was searching Mr. Akers' rooms, the latter was having dinner with Mr. Weatherburn. During dinner, unable to contain his pride and delight in his original and brilliant discovery, he began once again to refer to it to his dinner companion, even going so far as to pull a scrap of paper from his pocket, and write down the most important formula upon it. He then, however, thought better of revealing so much to a third party, and pressed the paper back into his waistcoat pocket. I have it here, and submit it to you as my third piece of evidence. I obtained it from Mr. Akers' next of kin, his sister living in Belgium, to whom it was sent together with the rest of his personal effects.

"Let me remind you of one other point raised in Mr. Weatherburn's testimony: that of Mr. Akers' medicine. Mr. Akers' doctor testified that Mr. Akers suffered from arhythmia of the heart, and took steady doses of digitalin to control it, at a rate of ten drops, three times a day. During the dinner with Mr. Weatherburn, Mr. Akers asked for a pitcher of water, poured some into a glass, and took a medicine bottle from his pocket. Mr. Weatherburn testified that he poured a drop or two into the glass and then said 'What am I doing' or words to that effect, stopped up the bottle, and thrust it back into his pocket. No explanation has been offered for this peculiar behaviour, although it does not seem that Mr. Weatherburn would have any motivation whatsoever to have invented it. The bottle of digitalin was not found on Mr. Akers' dead body. I propose to explain these facts shortly.

"It took Mr. Beddoes quite some time before finally, in some dusty corner, he lit upon the manuscript he was looking for, and recognised it for what it was. He took it up, perhaps with some idea of looking through it sufficiently to grasp its import, or perhaps carrying it off altogether. At that precise moment, the entrance door to Mr. Akers' rooms opened, and the resident entered, the dinner at the Irish pub not having been unduly prolonged. If he had merely seen Mr. Beddoes waiting for him in his rooms, he would perhaps not have been particularly surprised, but seeing him standing in the doorway of the study with the fatal manuscript in his hands, he became enraged and quite probably launched an accusation if not a threat, or possibly even a threatening gesture. Mr. Beddoes reacted by seizing the poker and striking out with it at the man who was ready to attack him professionally and perhaps even physically. Mr. Akers fell to the ground, and Mr. Beddoes dropped the poker, slipped out of the tower and returned quietly home, clutching the manuscript. He may have verified immediately that Mr. Akers was dead, or else he must have spent a very dreadful night, wondering about the effects of his desperate blow. But the following day brought him the official news of Mr. Akers' death. He came under no suspicion whatsoever, and as days followed days, he perhaps came to feel that Mr. Akers had deserved what came to him, and that no untoward effects would follow from his act.

"Now, Mr. Beddoes was a passionate mathematician, if less creative than his colleagues. He was afraid to keep the stolen manuscript, so he copied the entire thing out in his own neat handwriting, got rid of the original, and hid his copy in a special place known only to himself. He studied the manuscript with great care and attention, as witnessed by the many questions and annotations he added in the margins. I submit this copy to you as my fourth piece of evidence. It was found quite by accident after Mr. Beddoes' death, in the secret hiding place where Mr. Beddoes kept it, namely under the mattress of one of the cat baskets in the cat house at the bottom of his garden. One might be tempted to ask at first what makes me believe that this paper is not a mathematical manuscript due to Mr. Beddoes himself, but closer examination shows that the formulae and results are often annotated with question marks and even explicit questions, and it would certainly be strange if Mr. Beddoes did not understand his own theorems!

"Mr. Beddoes probably conceived of the possibility of understanding Mr. Akers' idea completely by himself. Whether he then would have made himself the master of these ideas, and submitted an independent manuscript to the Competition, will never be known, but it is very likely that such thoughts were in his mind; at any rate, it is clear that he hesitated to mention his find to Mr. Crawford, not wishing to awaken any suspicion.

"I was present at a certain dinner party, a few days after Mr. Akers' murder, and heard several people asking Mr. Weatherburn to describe his last dinner with Mr. Akers. Mr. Beddoes was also present, and it was there that he first became aware that Mr. Akers had told Mr. Weatherburn something about his discovery, and worse still, that he had written down the main formula on a paper which he had then thrust into his pocket. This paper, and Mr. Weatherburn's knowledge of it, became a threat to Mr. Beddoes' desire to claim the result for himself, and he determined to get hold of it. He attempted to have it shown to him at the Police Station, but was told that it had already been sent away to Mr. Akers' next of kin, his sister living in Belgium. Mr. Beddoes then discovered the name and address of the sister, and near Easter, he travelled to visit her, and representing himself as a mathematician who wished to save the lost but brilliant ideas of her murdered brother from oblivion, he tried to obtain from her not only the fatal paper but also Mr. Akers' pocket diary, containing the dates of the ABC meetings. She suspected him, however, and refused to deliver them, offering him to copy them down instead. He refused, and left quite angry, foiled in his intentions. If necessary, this lady, Madame Walters, has accepted to travel to England and identify her visitor, at least from a photograph.

"Mr. Beddoes must soon have found that alone, he was not able to come to a satisfactory understanding of Mr. Akers' computations, and finally resolved to obtain Mr. Crawford's help by hook or by crook. An ABC meeting had already been planned for April 17th, and even though Mr. Akers was dead, Mr. Beddoes went to Mr. Crawford's rooms on that day, at 2 o'clock. Recall from Mrs. Wiggins' testimony that in mid-April, Mr. Crawford had an afternoon visitor, and both took a glass of red wine. There, showing him only his own handwritten version of the manuscript, he attempted to obtain explanations of the difficult points from Mr. Crawford, while simultaneously attempting to claim the ideas for himself. It was an awkward procedure, and such an experienced mathematician as Mr. Crawford is unlikely to have been taken in by it. He must have understood that Mr. Beddoes had obtained access to Mr. Akers' idea by some method or another. By this time, Mr. Crawford had worked steadily and ceaselessly on his own idea without a break for two entire months, wearing

271

himself out with trying every possibility that occurred to him, but all in vain. He must have been extremely frustrated, and all of a sudden, in the most unexpected manner, the key to solving all his difficulties appeared in Mr. Beddoes' hands — and Mr. Beddoes himself did not really understand it! During their discussion of Mr. Beddoes' questions, Mr. Crawford must have obtained at least a certain amount of information as to what lay in the manuscript. Still, I can well imagine that Mr. Crawford wanted to look over the whole manuscript carefully himself, and was highly suspicious of Mr. Beddoes' refusal to allow him to do so; this is probably what engendered the quarrel between the two of them described by Mrs. Beddoes in her testimony.

"However, as Mr. Crawford had thought long and hard about every aspect of the problem, he was able to seize the key idea hidden in the central formula even from the small amount of information that he could glean from Mr. Beddoes' questions, and then his only desire was to lock himself up alone once again in his ivory tower and work it out until he reached a final, complete version of what he considered to be a blossoming out of his own original idea. The moment the door closed behind Mr. Beddoes, Mr. Crawford went back to work, and after a lapse of a week or so spent in working out details, he believed himself to be in possession of a full and complete solution of the so-called perturbative three-body problem.

"Now, his fevered brain began to envision himself as the winner of the King's Birthday Competition, internationally famous, honoured and considered on a par with the famous Henri Poincaré. This vision soon became an obsession, and day after day, he convinced himself that only Beddoes, with all his knowledge of the true provenance of the ideas contained in the manuscript, stood between himself and glory. Moreover, the ideas which Beddoes claimed as his own were very unlikely to really be his own, and indeed, the fact that he had them in his possession at all was extremely suspicious;

Mr. Crawford probably, at least half-consciously, identified Mr. Beddoes as the murderer of Mr. Akers.

"For a week or so, Mr. Crawford was so busy writing and thinking that he kept these ideas at bay, but then came the day on which the manuscript was complete, and only the danger due to Mr. Beddoes' knowledge of the true situation prevented him from sending it off. This brings us to around the day of the garden party, the 23rd of April. Mr. Crawford decided to lay his plans very carefully. To begin with, he knew that a manuscript submitted in English to the Competition would attract attention, as no English specialists in the subject were expected to submit. Naturally, he wished his manuscript to attract attention *if it were to win the prize*, but if that were not the case, then he surely felt that it would be a very dangerous thing that anyone should make even a superficial connection between a manuscript from England and murder in Cambridge. Therefore, he sent his manuscript to be translated into both French and German, so as to make it virtually impossible to guess where it came from. The rules of the Competition stipulated that the manuscripts were to be submitted anonymously, with only an epigraph in lieu of signature, and that the true names of the authors were to be supplied in sealed envelopes marked with the epigraphs. Only the envelopes corresponding to the winning entries were to be opened. Therefore, by submitting French and German versions of his manuscript, Mr. Crawford thought to protect himself from identification forever, in the case of his manuscript not being considered a winning entry (for example, if M. Poincaré of France had provided an even more astonishing solution). In case his manuscript would be the winner of the Competition, Mr. Crawford's desire for the fame and honour which would ensue was so great that he was ready to take any risk.

"He also took advantage of naturally running into Mr. Beddoes at the garden party to show him that he held no grudge over their quarrel, and let him know that he wished to dine with him. I saw this myself; Mr. Beddoes appeared very surprised when Mr. Crawford spoke to him. At the time, I merely thought that he was taken aback by Mr. Crawford's brusque manner, but now I realise that his surprise was due to the fact that the last time the two men had met, a week earlier, they had quarrelled bitterly.

"He then proceeded to an extraordinarily evil action. On April 30th, he invited Mr. Beddoes and Mr. Weatherburn to dine together with him at the Irish pub, and at the last minute, he excused himself, alleging ill-health. The inclusion of Mr. Weatherburn in this invitation was obviously intended to throw suspicion on him, as he had already dined with the victim of the previous murder, and the manoeuver succeeded only too well."

I paused here in my speech, and looked directly at Arthur, as did everyone else in the Courtroom. For the very first time since the beginning of this painful trial, I saw his eyes fixed, burningly, upon me. It strengthened me.

"Mr. Crawford then installed himself just within the front gate of Mr. Beddoes' garden, in the shadow of some large lilac bushes, and waited in the darkness with a large rock gathered from the garden in his hand. Eventually, he heard Mr. Weatherburn and Mr. Beddoes return from their dinner, and bid each other goodnight at the gate. Mr. Weatherburn turned away, and Mr. Beddoes closed the gate and turned towards the house. He received the blow suddenly, silently and powerfully on the back of his head. Mr. Crawford was a very large, strong man. The blow fell instantaneously, Mr. Beddoes uttered no cry, and no one was aware of anything. Mr. Crawford let fall the rock and returned home; Mrs. Beddoes discovered her husband's body only later in the evening, as she was leaning out of the front door in the hopes of spotting his arrival.

"Mr. Crawford must have obtained his translations very soon after this. The main judge of the Competition, Professor Mittag-Leffler of Sweden, looked at them, and told me that they appear to have been translated by native speakers, but not by mathematicians. I guess, therefore, that he sent them to an ordinary translating agency; if proof is needed, I have no doubt that this agency can be located and identified.

"Hearing of the arrest of Mr. Weatherburn, Mr. Crawford soon was assured that he was under no suspicion, and on the 4th of May, he took his two manuscripts, sealed them into an envelope, addressed it, and went to post it, probably to someone on the mainland who forwarded it to Stockholm. I visited Stockholm, met with the organiser of the Competition, Professor Gösta Mittag-Leffler, and saw the envelope and manuscripts there with my own eyes. However, as the manuscripts were anonymous, and the handwriting, language and envelope did not indicate Mr. Crawford explicitly, I was forced to make a special request to open the sealed envelope mailed together with the suspicious manuscript, marked with the epigraph of the author, and containing his name. Professor Mittag-Leffler had not the authority to open the envelope himself, and insisted that such authority could come only from the King of Sweden, patron of the Competition. Thus I had to meet and present my petition to the King himself. He opened the envelope, and confirmed that the author of the manuscript was Mr. Crawford. He has written this letter to you, my Lord, to inform you of it."

An agreeable gasp went round the Courtroom, as I extracted the King's gloriously embossed and sealed letter from my leather bag, and handed it to the Judge. There was a breathless silence as he broke the seal and read the brief message aloud.

"I pray you continue, Miss Duncan," he said, turning to me. "I remain with bated breath waiting to understand how Mr. Crawford met his death."

"That was mysterious to me, too, at first," I told him. "Recall that on the occasion of the quarrel within the ABC group on the 14th of February, Mr. Crawford had drunk a full half-a-bottle of whisky in his excitement. Such an act was most infrequent with him, as a matter of fact, and accompanied only moments of tremendous stress and excitement. The mailing of his manuscript to Sweden was such a moment, especially as he could not share it with a single person. He returned home, alight with secret triumph, took down his whisky bottle, still half-full as he had not touched it since the day of the ABC meeting on February 14th, and drank it down in two large tumblerfuls. As it contained a large dose of digitalin, he fell dead of cardiac arrest within a few minutes.

"But who had placed the digitalin in the whisky? At first, I believed that it was Mr. Beddoes, who had extracted the flask from Mr. Akers' pocket after murdering him. But this explanation did not satisfy me completely. For one thing, I could not see why Mr. Beddoes should have taken the flask, for surely he could not have conceived of killing Mr. Crawford already at that moment — they had not yet quarrelled and were still the best of friends. I thought he might have somehow predicted their future disagreement, but that seemed unlikely and really too diabolical. Furthermore, it gave no explanation of Mr. Akers' peculiar behaviour with his medicine in the Irish pub during the last dinner of his life. It took me some little time to realise that I had been led astray by the Prosecution's insistence that Mr. Akers' bottle of digitalin was stolen from his pocket by his murderer.

"In fact, what happened was much simpler. During the fatal ABC meeting of February 14th, Mr. Akers must have understood perfectly that Mr. Crawford had no intention of allowing him to proceed with his intentions, submit his paper, and savour his triumph alone. A bitter, impulsive and asocial man, he suddenly decided to eliminate Mr. Crawford, probably having almost no thoughts for the consequences. Seeing Mr. Crawford, not for the first time, down a full half-bottle of whisky at a single sitting, he must have imagined, not incorrectly, that this was a habitual practice with him, and in a quiet moment, he contrived to empty his bottle of digitalin into the half-bottle of whisky which still remained. He could easily have arranged to visit a doctor in London within the next days to obtain a renewal of his medicine without arousing the suspicions of his regular doctor. If he had done so, he might well have never come under suspicion for the crime, for no one but his doctor knew of his reliance on digitalin, and no one but Mr. Beddoes knew of his special and secret association with Mr. Crawford. However, he made a serious slip at his dinner with Mr. Weatherburn. Automatically following his usual habit, without thinking, he ordered water, poured out a glass and attempted to put his usual ten drops of digitalin into it. However, no more than a drop or two remained in the bottle, as he had emptied it within the afternoon. He must have immediately realised the foolishness of his gesture, as he had now a witness both to the fact that he was in possession of some medication, which might be associated with the death of Mr. Crawford, and that the flask was empty. However, there was nothing to do about it. On an impulse, he threw the telltale bottle of digitalin away, probably in the restaurant when he went to wash his hands. He was quite agitated during the dinner, and indeed, so he should have been, as he must have felt that it was yet time for him to prevent the grisly murder he had undertaken. I hope, I wish to believe, that he would surely have done so that same evening, had his own death not so unexpectedly overtaken him. I hope so, but we will never know.

"My Lord, Gentlemen of the Jury, that is all that I have to say. I sincerely hope I have been able to explain all of these events to your satisfaction."

I stopped speaking, and remained standing shakily in the witness box. A strange noise, like a wave, began at the back of the public gallery and swelled about the Courtroom, and I realised after what seemed a long time that it was applause. The Judge banged his gavel upon his desk and said "Silence in the Courtroom!"

He then turned to the barristers. "Would the Prosecution like to adjourn until tomorrow to prepare its response to Miss

Duncan's evidence?" he said politely.

The Prosecutor stood up.

"I will make my closing statement now, my Lord, if you please," he replied firmly.

He turned to the Jury and spoke very briefly.

"Members of the Jury, you have now heard two very different explanations of how three mathematicians were murdered, and two very different explanations of the same body of evidence, that concerning the disappearance of the bottle of digitalin, the presence of the accused with each of the first two victims just before their deaths, and so on. The witness we have just heard has added new evidence. It is up to you, now, to compare the two possible explanations of the evidence, and to determine, beyond a reasonable doubt, which is the true one. I rest my case."

Automatically, Counsel for the Defence arose, and his speech was even shorter than the Prosecutor's.

"Members of the Jury, I explained to you before how the accused could be perfectly innocent of the horrendous crimes imputed to him, and guilty of nothing more than being in the wrong place at the wrong time on two separate occasions. The additional information brought to you by this new witness completes my presentation of the case. I have nothing more to add."

Mr. Justice Penrose bowed his head apologetically towards the Jury. "Members of the Jury, please deliberate once again, and return when your verdict is ready."

No trial can ever have closed more speedily. The Jury returned in less than two minutes. They sat down, and the Judge asked them: "Members of the Jury, have you reached a conclusion?"

"Yes, my Lord."

"What is your verdict?"

"We have changed from our previous conclusion, my Lord. We now unanimously believe that the prisoner is not guilty. We wish to say that we feel we have very narrowly escaped being led into grave injustice."

The Courtroom erupted in cries of all kinds and the Judge banged his gavel again.

"The prisoner is hereby acquitted and released without a stain on his character!" he shouted over the noise in stentorian tones.

All of a sudden I could not bear the noise and the crowd and the hundreds of eyes for a single second longer. I rushed from the Courtroom and stepped into the quiet darkness of the streets, where I wandered about for a long time before returning home. It has been too much and too long and too hard, and I feel too numb to triumph tonight.

Tomorrow, however, I shall begin a new adventure!

Vanessa

Cambridge, Sunday, June 11th, 1888

My dearest sister,

The whole of this past week has been full of sunshine and roses, outdoors, indoors, and within my very heart. Each morning, I awake, and recall afresh that Arthur's trial is over, and with it the very trial of my soul; my entire life feels renewed and joyful. And each day has brought its own unexpected, delightful surprise.

The first one came the very day after the end of the trial. Naturally, the unexpected and dramatic ending was reported in our local newspaper. I was so tired after my performance in the witness box, that I tumbled into bed and slept like the dead until *astonishingly* late the next morning, and was awoken by Mrs. Fitzwilliam entering with a tea-tray in her hands, upon which lay a newspaper.

"Well, my dear," she said to me, as she drew the curtains kindly and let in a wave of brilliant sunshine, "you must be tired enough to sleep so long! I know you've had a hard time of it all, and I thought I'd bring your breakfast in this morning, so you may have some much-deserved relaxation. And do have a look at this, dear — you're on the very front page of the newspaper! Just think!"

Oh dear, it was perfectly true. There was a picture of me, taken as I left the Courthouse, framed within the doorway, almost a silhouette against the lighted background. It was followed by a very foolish article. I did not like to read it at all; it presented things in a very silly way, not at all properly. No one, reading it, would imagine that I was simply driven to search for the truth and avert a dreadful injustice — they all seemed to foolishly impute some deeper reason for it all! Such motivations as mine must lie below the visual field of ordinary journalists.

The very next afternoon, I received visits from the mothers of nearly all the little girls in my class. With amazing speed and efficiency, Mrs. Burke-Jones had been to call on each and every one of them, and had presented her proposition of widening the class to contain boys as well as girls, and welcoming it, if necessary, in her home.

My class contains several pairs of sisters (and even one collection of three), so that in fact, my twelve little students possess only seven mothers between them; Mrs. Burke-Jones aside, I was called upon by the other six. Rose's mother was the first to call. She praised me with enthusiasm for my role at the trial, and told me that she would have been delighted to send any brothers of Rose to join my class, if only she had had any, but alas, Rose was an only child. To cut a long story of discussions and negotiations short, three mothers, one of whom has two daughters, said that they could not agree to continue to send their daughters to a class as daring and scandalous as what I, or rather, Mrs. Burke-Jones, was proposing. I had been afraid of this reaction, and had half made up my mind to say that I had not taken any decision on the subject yet. But that is not how it went, for I found myself stubbornly upholding the project, and in the end found my little class to be reduced from twelve to eight.

And yet, it is at the same time most interestingly increased, for not only are Emily's two brothers to attend, but — good heavens — I had no idea, but the mother of the three little girls followed them up directly by a series of three little boys, none of whom have begun lessons yet. I am to take the oldest one immediately, and the following two in subsequent years. And two other little brothers are to join us, making a total of five boys in all, beginning immediately. They are all very little boys, with the exception of Edmund, as all the older ones are in school already. It will be most awfully sweet!

The calls and visits were followed by a lengthy discussion with Emily, her mother, and Miss Forsyth. I am to continue residing in Mrs. Fitzwilliam's rooms, but the schoolroom will now be located in Mrs. Burke-Jones' large nursery, and Miss Forsyth will be my assistant for part of the afternoon; she will teach French, and help me with the smallest children if they become overexcited, as seems more than likely. There is to be a break in the middle of the afternoon, during which the children may run about in Mrs. Burke-Jones' lovely garden. She is overjoyed at the whole idea, and appears to have recovered a purpose for her life in it; I quite believe that she sees herself as a kind of honourary headmistress, and who knows, perhaps she will end up as the headmistress of an excellent and reputable and very modern school!

The next morning, I received *your* letter. Oh, Dora, how exciting! All the changes in my life, which seemed so great to me, and the varied experiences I have had during these last weeks, pale before those which await you now that you have accepted Mr. Edwards' proposal. How beautifully he expresses the feeling that at such a distance, one's true needs and desires become clear and sharply outlined, whereas in the confusion of daily presence, they become blurred and confused. Poor Mr. Edwards — so many people would burn to confront the long and mysterious journey to vast, hot and unfamiliar regions, filled with natives and strange illnesses, which awaits him, and he yearns only to return home to the English countryside and live amongst the fresh green fields. Still, Dora, in your quiet way, you have always been more stubborn than I; simply reserving yourself for the great moment. I know you; now that you know what you are waiting for, you will be able to reserve yourself as long as necessary, with an infinity of obstinate patience, while Mr. Edwards works until the government permits him to return. Surely it cannot be more than a small number of years! And after all, we are only twenty, you and I.

By the same post, I also received a letter from Professor Mittag-Leffler. He had heard all about the final results of my efforts, and wrote to congratulate me and once again encourage me to return to visit him in Stockholm. One paragraph of his letter has left a profound and striking impression upon me.

Because of the amazing nature of its contents, the manuscript number seven was immediately and intensively studied by myself and my associate Dr. Phragmén. I regret to say that quite soon, we came to realise that the computations, although brilliantly virtuoso in style, contain a deep flaw in one particular place. It seems to me that I remember, in the partial manuscript you showed me written in very legible handwriting, that the author had written a question in the margin next to this very point. He may have believed himself simply unable to understand it, but he was more perspicacious than he thought, and the author of the manuscript submitted to the Competition desired success too keenly to exercise his critical judgement. I am sorry to say that the entire conclusion of the manuscript is invalidated by this error. In any case, the paper submitted by M. Henri Poincaré has shown that such a classical solution to the three-body problem (and in fact to the n-body problem in general) is in fact an impossibility, and that the problem must be approached in an entirely different way. He begins this radically new study in his article, which is a work of genius that will unquestionably mark the whole of the century to come.

So it turns out that all three of them murdered and were murdered for nothing. This fact leaves me with a most remarkable impression of the inanity of the things of this world.

I longed to share this letter, and all of my experiences, with Arthur, but I had not seen him since the end of the trial; nobody appeared to know where he had gone. I tried to occupy myself with a thousand things, but my thoughts were always upon him, and I jumped at every sound, every knock on the door. He appeared, finally, towards the end of the afternoon.

I heard his step in the hallway, and his gentle knock, and opened the door at once. We stood in the doorway for a moment; he took my two hands in his, looking down at me. I looked up at him, and we remained there in silence — silence will ever be our most intense mode of communication, I think. I felt his touch, and found no words. He seemed to wish to speak and change his mind a dozen times. Time stopped; I would have waited forever. Finally, he said, "Will you marry me?"

I said yes. There was another silence.

"I'm afraid it won't be easy for you," he said slowly. "You know, I have never been very strong on the business of living, and though I have tried in these last days to forget and recover, something, somewhere inside me, feels broken forever. I could not find any interest in anything at all — except the thought of you."

"I'll mend it — I can mend anything!" I said stoutly.

He took me in his arms.

Fellows of the University are not allowed to marry, and a Fellowship lasts for several years. But what of it! We are young, and the future is long, and my class needs me, and the days stretch before me filled with loveliness, and poetry and wild flowers growing in the hedgerows. Beyond that, it grows misty, and I prefer it that way.

How wonderful to think that I will be home so soon. I can

hardly wait to see our darling old house. I have been away for so long — I have become used to town houses, all square and stone and straight. How I miss the crooked rafters and low ceilings, and tiny diamond-paned windows half-covered with leafy vines. To think I will see it all again in just a few days, and the cats, and our solid little ponies — and you! I long to ramble in the fields for hours with you, Dora, as only twins can. Just walking, and talking — about all the things which cannot be fitted into, or even between, the lines of letters.

Your loving sister

Vanessa

The End

Mathematical History in *The Three-Body Problem*

The mathematical framework of the Three-Body Problem is absolutely historical. The Birthday Competition[1] occurred exactly as described, down to the unsigned manuscripts identified by epigraphs; several of the authors, in fact, have never been identified even to this day. The manuscript concerned in this story has borrowed its title from one of those.

The Competition was organised by Gösta Mittag-Leffler (1846-1927)[2] under the auspices of King Oscar II of Sweden; Mittag-Leffler's villa still exists and is now a famous mathematical institute. The announcement of the Competition in the mathematical journal *Acta Mathematica* is accurately reproduced, and the end result of the Competition was historically just as described in the book. There was in fact a further development; Poincaré discovered that his prize-winning paper contained an error, which he rectified after all the copies of *Acta Mathematica* had already been printed; he insisted on paying himself for them all to be reprinted, which cost him all of his prize money. The events concerning the supposed solution of Lejeune-Dirichlet (1805-1859) to the n-body problem and his deathbed confidences to Leopold Kronecker (1823-1891) also occurred as told.

Arthur Cayley (1821-1895) and Grace Chisholm (1868-1944) were really members of the Cambridge Mathematics Department during the period described; Cayley's defense of teaching Euclid and Chisholm's departure to Germany in order to write a thesis are factual. Karl Weierstrass (1815-1897) and his famous student Sonya Kovalevskaya (1850-1891) were real people, and Kovalevskaya was as described

1 The book *Poincaré and the Discovery of Chaos* by June Barrow-Green contains a great deal of interesting scientific information as well as a historical chapter.

2 A Website containing brief biographies of a great number of mathematicians can be found at *http://www-gap.dcs.st-and.ac.uk/~history/BiogIndex.html*

the first woman professor of mathematics in Europe. Henri Poincaré (1854-1912) was of course one of the greatest mathematicians of his time. The n-body problem was a burning subject of research in the 1880s, and Poincaré's work on it was seminal; it is still a most popular research subject today. As Poincaré showed, there can be no general solution in closed form; however, many astonishing special solutions have been found in recent years[3]

The Victorian girls' magazine *The Monthly Packet* really existed; it contained many mathematical tales and problems by Lewis Carroll (1832-1898), including the *Tangled Tale* reproduced in the book. For that matter, Oscar Wilde really did undertake to edit the magazine *Woman's World*, and evinced a great interest in women's clothing, being strongly against corsets and all other fashionably constrictions: "It is from the shoulders, and from the shoulders only," he wrote, "that all garments should be hung".

A final remark: the answers to the tea-party charades are Vanes-sa (as in "weathervanes" and "sa majesté") Dun-can, Weather-burn, Miss-For-Scythe.

3 Moving versions of some of these special solutions can be charmingly visualised on the internet at *http://cse.uscc.edu/~charlie/3body/*